RED PILL

RED PILL

Hari Kunzru

Alfred A. Knopf   New York   2020

THIS IS A BORZOI BOOK
PUBLISHED BY ALFRED A. KNOPF

Copyright © 2020 by Hari Kunzru

www.aaknopf.com

Knopf, Borzoi Books, and the colophon are registered
trademarks of Penguin Random House LLC.

Library of Congress Cataloging-in-Publication Data
Names: Kunzru, Hari, [date] author.
Title: Red pill : a novel / Hari Kunzru.
Description: First edition. | New York : Alfred A. Knopf, 2020.
Identifiers: LCCN 2019053311 | ISBN 9780451493712 (hardcover) |
ISBN 9780451493729 (ebook)
Subjects: LCSH: Psychological fiction.
Classification: LCC PR6111.U68 R43 2020 | DDC 823/.92—dc23
LC record available at https://lccn.loc.gov/2019053311

Jacket image: *The Wanderer above the Sea of Fog* (detail)
by Caspar David Friedrich. Hamburger Kunsthalle,
Hamburg, Germany. Bridgeman Images.
Jacket design by John Gall

Manufactured in Canada
First Edition

For Katie, Ryu and Mila

My only, my highest goal has been brought
low. . . . No truth is discoverable here on earth.

—HEINRICH VON KLEIST,
letter to Wilhelmine von Zenge,
22 March 1801

RED PILL

WANNSEE

I THINK IT IS POSSIBLE to track the onset of middle age exactly. It is the moment when you examine your life and instead of a field of possibility opening out, an increase in scope, you have a sense of waking from sleep or being washed up onshore, newly conscious of your surroundings. So this is where I am, you say to yourself. This is what I have become. It is when you first understand that your condition—physically, intellectually, socially, financially—is not absolutely mutable, that what has already happened will, to a great extent, determine the rest of the story. What you have done cannot be undone, and much of what you have been putting off for "later" will never get done at all. In short, your time is a finite and dwindling resource. From this moment on, whatever you are doing, whatever joy or intensity or whirl of pleasure you may experience, you will never shake the almost-imperceptible sensation that you are traveling on a gentle downward slope into darkness.

For me this realization of mortality took place, conventionally enough, beside my sleeping wife at home in our apartment in Brooklyn. As I lay awake, listening to her breathing, I knew that my strength and ingenuity had their limits. I could foresee a time when I would need to rest. How I'd got there was a source of amazement to me, the chain of events that had led me to that slightly overheated bedroom, to a woman who, had things turned out differently, I might never have met, or recognized as the person I wanted to spend my life with. After five years of marriage I was still in love with Rei and she was still in love with me. All that was settled, a happy fact. Our three-year-old daughter was asleep in the next room.

Our very happiness made me uneasy. It was a perverse reaction, I knew. I was like a miser, fretting about his emotional hoard. Yet the mental rats running round my bedroom, round my child's bedroom, had something real behind them. It was a time when the media was full of images of children hurt and displaced by war. I frequently found myself hunched over my laptop, my eyes welling with tears. I was distressed by what I saw, but also haunted by a more selfish question: If the world changed, would I be able to protect my family? Could I scale the fence with my little girl on my shoulders? Would I be able to keep hold of my wife's hand as the rubber boat overturned? Our life together was fragile. One day something would break. One of us would have an accident, one of us would fall sick, or

else the world would slide further into war and chaos, engulf-
ing us, as it had so many other families.

In most respects, I had little to complain about. I lived in
one of the great cities of the world. Save for a few minor ail-
ments I was physically healthy. And I was loved, which protected me from some of the more destructive consequences of
a so-called midlife crisis. I had friends who, without warning,
embarked on absurd sexual affairs, or in one case developed a
ruinous crack habit that he kept hidden from everyone until
he was arrested at 3 a.m. in Elizabeth, New Jersey, smoking
behind the wheel of his parked car. I was not about to fuck
the nanny or gamble away our savings, but at the same time,
I knew there was something profoundly but subtly wrong,
some urgent question I had to answer, that concerned me in
isolation and couldn't be solved by waking Rei or going on the
internet or padding barefoot into the bathroom and swallowing
a sleeping pill. It concerned the foundation for things, beliefs
I had spent much of my life writing and thinking about, the
various claims I made for myself in the world. And coinciden-
tally or not, it arrived at a time when I was about to go away.
One reason I was awake, worrying about money and climate
change and Macedonian border guards, was that an airport
transfer was booked for five in the morning. I never sleep well
on the night before I have to travel. I'm always nervous that I'll
oversleep and miss my plane.

TIRED AND PREOCCUPIED, I arrived in Berlin the next day to begin a three-month residency at the Deuter Center, out in the far western suburb of Wannsee. It was just after New Year, and the wheels of the taxi crunched down the driveway over a thin crust of snow. As I caught my first glimpse of the villa, emerging from behind a curtain of white-frosted pines, it seemed like the precise objective correlative of my emotional state, a house that I recognized from some deep and melancholy place inside myself. It was large but unremarkable, a sober construction with a sharply pitched gray-tiled roof and a pale façade pierced by rows of tall windows. Its only peculiarity was a modern annex that extended out from one side, a glass cube that seemed to function as an office.

I paid the driver and staggered up the front steps with my bags. Before I could ring the bell, there was a buzzing sound, and the door opened onto a large, echoing hallway. I stepped through it, feeling like a fairytale prince entering the ogre's castle, but instead of a sleeping princess, I was greeted by a jovial porter in English country tweeds. His manner seemed at odds with the somber surroundings. He positively twinkled with warmth, his eyes wide and his chest puffed out, apparently with the pleasure induced by my arrival. Had my journey been smooth? Would I like some coffee? A folder had been prepared with a keycard and various documents requiring my signature. The director and the rest of the staff were looking forward to meeting me. In the meantime, I would find mineral water and towels in my room. If I needed anything, anything at all, I had only to ask. I assured him that the only thing I wanted was to change and take a look at my study.

Of course, he said. Please allow me to help you with your cases.

We took an elevator to the third floor, where he showed me into a sort of luxurious garret. The space was clean and bright and modern, with pine furniture and crisp white sheets on a bed tucked under the sloping beams of the roof. The heaters were sleek rectangular grids, the windows double-glazed. In one corner was a little kitchenette, with a hot plate and a fridge. A door led through to a well-appointed bathroom. Despite these conveniences, the room had an austere quality that I found pleasing. It was a place to work, to contemplate.

When the Deuter Center wrote to offer me the fellowship, I immediately pictured myself as the "poor poet" in a nineteenth-century painting I'd once seen on a visit to Munich. The poet sits up in bed wearing a nightcap edged in gold thread, with gold-rimmed spectacles perched on his nose and a quill clamped between his jaws like a pirate's cutlass. His attic room has holes in the windows and is obviously cold, since he's bundled up in an old dressing gown, patched at one elbow. He's been using pages from his own work to light the fire, which has now gone out. His possessions are meager, a hat, a coat and a stick, a candle stub in a bottle, a wash basin, a threadbare towel, a torn umbrella hanging from the ceiling. Around him books are piled upon books. Flat against his raised knees he holds a manuscript and with his free hand he makes a strange "OK" gesture, pressing thumb against forefinger. Is he scanning a verse? Crushing a bedbug? Or is he making a hole? Could he possibly be contemplating absence, the meaninglessness of existence, nothingness, the void? The poet doesn't care about his physical surroundings, or if he does, he's making the best of things. He is absorbed in his artistic labor. That was how I wanted to be, who I wanted to be, at least for a while.

The Center's full name was the Deuter Center for Social and Cultural Research. Its founder, an industrialist with a utopian streak, had endowed it with some minor part of a fortune made during the years of the postwar economic miracle, with the aim of fostering what he airily called "the full potential of the individual human spirit." In practical terms, this meant that throughout the year a floating population of writers and scholars was in residence at the Deuter family's old lakeside villa, catered to by a staff of librarians, cleaners, cooks and computer technicians, all dedicated to promoting an atmosphere in which the fellows could achieve as much work as possible, without being burdened by the practical aspects of daily existence.

I was what they call an "independent scholar." I had an adjunct gig at a university, but it was in a Creative Writing department, and I tried not to think about it except when it was actually happening to me, when I was sitting in a seminar room, pinned by the hollow stares of a dozen debt-ridden graduate students awaiting instruction. What I wrote was published by magazines and commercial publishers, not peer-reviewed journals. Academics found me vaguely disreputable, and I suppose I was. I've never been much for disciplinary boundaries. I'm interested in what I'm interested in. Five years before my invitation to Berlin I had published a book about taste, in which I'd argued (not very insistently) that it was intrinsic to human identity. This was barely a thesis, more a sort of bright shiny thing that kept the reader meandering along as I strung together some thoughts on literature, music, cinema and politics. It wasn't the book I was supposed to be writing, an ambitious work in which I intended to make a definitive case for the revolutionary potential of the arts. The taste book sort of drifted out of me, first as a distraction from the notebooks I was filling with quotations and ideas for my definitive case for the revolutionary potential of the arts, then as a distraction from the creeping realization that I really had no definitive case to make at all, or even a provisional one. I had no clue why anyone should care about the arts, let alone be spurred by them to revolution. I cared about art, but I was essentially a waster, and throughout my life other people had never liked the things I did. The only political slogan that had ever really moved me was *Ne travaillez jamais* and the attempt to live that out had run into the predictable obstacles. The trouble is there's no outside, nowhere for the disaffected to go. Refusal is meaningful if conducted *en masse,* but most people seem to want to cozy up to anyone with the slightest bit of power, and nothing is more scary than being left at the front when a crowd melts away behind you. Why, after all this time was the "general reader" suddenly going to find me persuasive? Why would I even want to persuade him or her? What would starting an argument achieve? If I wanted a fight, all I had to do was look at my phone. So I kept my head down and wrote my distracted essays.

I'd been a freelance writer since I was twenty-three. It is a ridiculous thing to do. It's time-consuming and poorly paid. You live on your nerves. Sure, you can lie on the couch if you want, but eventually you will starve. I was in despair because I'd wasted so much time on the revolution book, and I'd just got together with Rei and needed money to make things happen for us, and suddenly I couldn't summon the energy for the pretensions of a system, so I just wrote about some things I liked, things that made me happy, and my exhaustion must have transmitted itself in some positive manner onto the page—I am the first to admit that I'm usually a hectoring and difficult writer, given to obscurity and tortuous sentences— because a publisher offered me a contract and along with it a way out, a plausible excuse for shelving the impossible revolutionary art project, smothering the damn thing with a pillow. A mercy killing would otherwise have been embarrassing, since I'd been talking about the book for years, doing panel discussions and think-pieces and sounding off at parties. I finished the little taste book fairly quickly, and unlike my previous work, it sold. You see, said my agent, all you had to do was stop battering people over the head.

I did the things you do when you have a successful book. I gave interviews. I accepted invitations to festivals and conferences. Translations were sold. People bought me dinner. Then, gradually, my editor began to inquire about what I was doing next. Mostly what I was doing was getting married and moving apartments and having a baby and not sleeping and realizing that a successful book is not the same thing, financially, as a successful film or a successful song, and writing a couple of prestigious but underpaid magazine essays and agreeing to teach another class and still not sleeping much, but more than before, though still not enough to find it easy to write without self-medicating. I knew I needed to publish again, as soon as possible, but somehow the prospect of completing (or even seriously beginning) a manuscript seemed to recede in front of me. Just when things were getting really tricky, I came to the attention of whatever board or jury awarded the Deuter fellowships. I received a letter from Berlin on pleasingly heavy stationery, inviting me to apply and strongly hinting that I would receive preferential treatment if I did. And so it turned out. I begged for references from the most prestigious writers I knew, and some months later a second letter arrived, informing me that I'd been successful. Three months. Three months of peace.

I ushered the porter out of the room, trying not to make too much eye-contact, noticing the glassy military shine of his shoes as I closed the door. I'd pictured—if I'm honest, possibly only because of the word *center* in the title—the Deuter Center for Social and Cultural Research as being somewhat like a meditation retreat: a "Center," as opposed to an "Institute" or an "Academy" or, God forbid, a "Community." The word implied focus but also a certain hands-off quality: not too many rules or too much unwanted social contact. I was beginning to feel that I might have misunderstood. It was immediately apparent that the culture of the institution was formal and old-fashioned. The porter's good humor was underpinned by a parade-ground stiffness. As he had emerged to greet me, I'd caught a glimpse of some kind of lodge or control room with a desk and a row of monitors, tiled with surveillance images of the house and grounds.

I unpacked my cases and put my toiletries in the bathroom. As I moved around, I could feel my spirits lifting. The view from my window was starkly beautiful. A snow-covered lawn led down to the shore of the lake, where a wrought-iron fence marked the boundary of the property. Beyond it, a few small boats, their decks sheathed in plastic covers, were tied up at a little pier. The surface of the water was gray and gelatinous, close to freezing, undulating rather than rippling in the wind. When I opened the window, I could hear an eerie clinking, incongruously like alpine cow bells. After a moment of confusion, I realized it must be the sound of the aluminum rails and ladders of the boats as they knocked against their moorings.

I thought about some lines from Hölderlin:

> *Die Mauern stehn*
> *Sprachlos und kalt, im Winde*
> *Klirren die Fahnen*

The walls stand speechless and cold, the weathervanes clatter in the wind. I was pleased, even a little smug, that these words had sprung so easily to mind. Their presence in my consciousness, so available to be applied to the view from my window, suggested that even before I'd formally begun it, my new project was already under way.

My proposal to the Deuter Center had been titled "The Lyric I." I had decided to write about the construction of the self in lyric poetry. The topic was a departure for me—I was no poetry scholar—but for some reason it felt like the key to large and urgent questions in my life. I wrote about the lyric as "a textual technology for the organization of affective experience, and a container in which modern selfhood has come to be formulated." This sounded important and good. I quoted Madame de Staël on the difference between the self in lyric poetry and fiction. "Lyric poetry is expressed in the name of the author himself; no longer is it borne by a character. . . . Lyric poetry recounts nothing, is not confined by the succession of time, nor by the limits of place. It spreads its wings over countries and over ages. It gives duration to that sublime moment in which man raises himself above the pleasures and pains of life." I noted along with Adorno, that "lyric expression, having escaped from the weight of material existence, should evoke images of a life free from the coercion of reigning practices, of utility, of the relentless pressures of self-preservation." I agreed with Hegel that "the content is not the object but the subject, the inner world, the mind that considers and feels, that instead of proceeding to action, remains alone with itself as inwardness and that therefore can take as its sole form and final aim the self-expression of subjective life."

I have a friend whose relationship advice I used to take until I realized that he was a solipsist. If, for example, he told me that I ought not to have an affair, because it would be very destructive to my marriage, it was because just then he wanted to hear someone say that to him. Instead of addressing whatever issue I'd raised (which could have been something completely different) he was conducting an argument with himself, against some current impulse to cheat on his wife. When the Deuter Center accepted my proposal, and I was forced to reread it and consider it as a piece of work that might actually have to be executed, I realized that it had precisely this character. Deep down I had no real desire to understand how lyric poets had historically experienced their subjectivity. I wasn't that interested. It was a piece of wishfulness, an expression of my own desire to be raised above the pleasures and pains of my life, to be free from the reigning coercions of a toddler, the relentless financial pressure of living in New York. I wanted to remain alone with myself as inwardness. I wanted, in short, to take a break.

Rei had a demanding job, as a lawyer for a non-profit that worked on immigration and civil liberties. She'd not been thrilled at the idea of me spending so long away, in sublime contemplation of my expressive self, but she'd seen how hard it was for me to work. We lived in a small apartment, and since Nina came along, we'd been trying to save money, so I'd given up the office in Williamsburg, the little room with the skylight which I'd had as my own space since before we were married. I'd been trying to write at a table in the spare room, and the only quiet time I got was late at night. Mornings with a three-year-old always started punishingly early, so I spent my days surrounded by toys, trying to focus through a haze of tiredness. The less sleep I got, the worse the troubles of the world appeared. One evening Rei had come back from the office and found me crying over war videos on my laptop while Nina, unsupervised, decorated the kitchen with a bag of flour she'd found in the pantry.

There are times when you know you're being a pig, and you carry on anyway. Something compels you, a sort of self-destructive pettiness. I'd convinced myself that I was hero-ically trying not to impose my mood of panic on my family, but really I was doing the exact opposite. No one was ever allowed to forget it. We were all on edge. Me, Rei, Nina, Paulette the sitter. I needed to remove myself—from the domestic field of battle, from the world. So Rei set about making arrange-ments. The stipend would pay for some additional childcare, and Paulette said she was happy to work some weekends. Rei and I agreed that I owed her, and at some point in the future she would be free to take off and do something similar while I looked after the family. We both knew my book stood for something more than itself, some wider problem that I was having, and I was aware that I'd come to Berlin with the tacit agreement that I would return changed, that I would deal with it, whatever it was, and not drag it back home with me.

I showered and changed, and took the elevator down to the lobby. I knocked on the door of the lodge and asked to be shown to my study. The porter had told me his name, but I'd failed to register it, and this was preoccupying me (Otto, Ulli, Uwe?) as he walked me through a large reception room hung with abstract paintings, descendants of the kind of work that used to be exhibited in West Berlin as evidence of American vigor and creative liberty. We passed a dining room with French windows giving out onto a snow-covered terrace. Beyond the dining room was a glass door which led to the annex I'd seen from the taxi, a large open space with desks and filing cabinets arranged in little irregular clusters, atolls of wood and metal on a sea of blue carpet tile. I assumed this was where the administrative staff worked, so I was surprised when the porter tapped his keycard on the door and gestured for me to step inside. The room was a glass box supported by a metal frame, an unornamented yet somehow fussy space designed by some suburban devotee of the International Style. The porter consulted a little chart and showed me to one of the desks.

"Here," he said. "You'll find everything you need."

I told him I didn't understand.

"Your workstation. You have a high-speed internet connection. The password is in your welcome pack. If you need the use of a computer, it will be the pleasure of the IT department to supply one. The small key gives you access to a storeroom where you will find office supplies. Pens and files and paper and so."

He demonstrated the task light, which switched on and off with a wave of the hand. I looked around at the other desks, some of them clean and bare, others with the telltale signs of regular occupation—books and papers, family photos, coffee cups. A line of small plastic soldiers marched along the top of one monitor. A stack of wire in-trays was decorated with a sort of bunting made of colored paper. I don't know what I'd expected—an oak-paneled carrel, an airy biomorphic pod— but the one constant to all my fantasies about my working life at the Deuter Center had been privacy. Seclusion and a lockable door. The porter must have noticed my stricken look, but he misread it.

"Most of your colleagues are away right now. And of course it is the weekend. The place is much more friendly when everyone is here."

"Friendly."

"Also the chair can be altered to your preferences. Some people have problems at first, but it is very easy."

He bent down and began to show me how to raise and lower the seat, how to make the back recline, how to prevent it from doing so, how to adjust the armrests.

"I'm sorry," I said. "I can't work here. It's just not possible. I need to be alone."

He looked blank.

"I couldn't concentrate, for one thing."

His blank expression crumbled into one of intense sympathy, as if I'd just announced that I'd been bereaved, or diagnosed with a serious illness.

"Please don't worry. It is always one hundred percent silent. The rules are very clear. It is strictly forbidden to talk. The atmosphere is of a library. If people must make phone calls or meetings, there is another space."

"But it's . . ."

I realized I was embarrassed by what I was trying to say. When I was younger, I'd worked in many public places, university libraries, coffee shops, even bars. The question of noise wasn't at the heart of the creeping horror I felt at the idea of an open-plan office. The desk I'd been assigned was in the middle of the room. As I wrote, people would be moving around behind me, out of my view. Other "workstations" (the porter's chilling word was already sticking to my mind like chewing gum to the sole of a shoe) were located nearby, in positions where I'd be able to see their occupants' screens. My own screen would be visible to others, perhaps not close enough to read a piece of text, but certainly enough to judge whether it displayed a document or a video playing on a social media site. I would be visible from every angle. My body, my posture. I have developed a visceral dislike of being watched while I write, not just because the content might be private, but because all the things one does while writing that are not actually writing—stretching, looking out into space, browsing the internet—seem somehow shameful if they're monitored by others. The feeling of being watched induces an intolerable self-consciousness.

Somewhere in Sartre's *Being and Nothingness,* the writer imagines himself as a peeping Tom in a darkened corridor, terrified by the sudden possibility that he'll be caught, that The Other (that important Existential personage) will shine a flashlight on him and reveal his shame. As long as he feels he's unobserved, his entire being is focused on what he's doing. He is a pure consciousness, existentially free. As soon as there's even the possibility of observation—a rustling sound, a footstep or the slight movement of a curtain—all his freedom vanishes. "Shame," he writes, "is shame of *self*. It is the recognition that I am indeed that object which the Other is looking at and judging. I can be ashamed only as my freedom escapes me in order to become a given object. . . . I am in a world which the Other has made alien to me."

Most people have working lives that include this kind of alienating surveillance as a matter of course. The police function of the open-plan office is not news to anyone who's ever worked in one. In a call center or at a shipping warehouse, bathroom breaks are monitored, your work rate is rigorously quantified and penalties are imposed on those who fall behind. But surely none of this applied to me. I was a writer who had won a prestigious fellowship. An uncommon level of self-motivation could surely be taken for granted. I certainly didn't need to be surveilled by The Other in order to ensure my productivity. The workstation was a kind of insult, an assault on my status. It was entirely unacceptable.

I told the porter that I was sorry I'd forgotten his name but under no circumstances would I ever write a word in that space. I would speak to the program manager when she came in on Monday. There was no real problem. My room was very comfortable. I would be perfectly happy to work in there.

"Of course you must do as you wish, but . . ."

He trailed off unhappily.

"Perhaps I can refer you to the statement of principle in the handbook, which you will find in your welcome pack. Herr Deuter's philosophy is made clear."

Something about the phrase made me angry. I didn't give a damn about "Herr Deuter's philosophy." I needed my privacy. I controlled my temper and assured him, with exaggerated formality, that I'd be sure to consult the welcome pack once I'd eaten. At the mention of food, he became solicitous again, and mentioned that a light supper had been prepared for me in the dining room.

Somewhat mollified, I sat down in stately isolation at the head of one of the long tables, and ate salad and cold cuts under the eye of the founder, whose faintly expressionist portrait hung high on the end wall. He was a lean, clean-shaven man with a prominent forehead and dark hair with streaks of gray at the temples, his arms folded over the wide lapels of a double-breasted jacket. The picture had none of the macho colossus-bestriding-the-globe quality that most executives require when commissioning representations of themselves. His expression was pensive, even slightly uncertain. He looked sideways out of the frame, instead of meeting the viewer's eye.

Somehow the picture made the idea of its subject possessing a "philosophy" less pompous and absurd.

Later, in my room, I lay on my bed and looked at the handbook. There were color pictures of the house and grounds, and portraits of a few distinguished past fellows—a middle-brow novelist, a famous painter whose work, I now realized, hung in the reception room. The brochure was illustrated with a lot of boilerplate about Deuter's commitment to the values and ideals of openness, free markets and the sacredness of individual choice. Deuter's hagiography took up several pages: the Wehrmacht officer who became a stalwart Christian Democrat, the young industrial chemist who had climbed through the rubble of his family home to retrieve a few things to sell for food, but within five years found investors to back him in a major project, repairing and recommissioning a plant to refine Titanium Dioxide, the ubiquitous white pigment that brought light into the darkness of Germany's postwar domestic spaces. There were pictures of Deuter examining gleaming white bathroom tiles, white painted walls, white plastics, toothpaste, Deuter chatting to young women working at conveyor belts strewn with white tablets, conferring with technicians beside giant fractionating columns.

He was picked out by the fledgling BRD government as a talent worth supporting, a necessary man, one of the conjurers of the *Wirtschaftswunder,* the national economic miracle. TiO_2 white is prized for its optical brightness, I read. It is prized for its opacity.

By 1960 Deuter had built a huge conglomerate, with divisions specializing in food, agriculture, pharmaceuticals and paint. From a standing start in 1946, it was an incredible feat. In 1962 he was pictured with Chancellor Adenauer, at the opening of a shipping terminal in Hamburg. In 1975 he addressed a meeting of the Confederation of German Industries, quoting Cicero: *We are not born for ourselves alone, but our country claims a share of our being, and our friends a share; and since, as the Stoics hold, everything that the earth produces is created for man's use; and as men, too, are born for the sake of men, that they may be able mutually to help one another; in this direction we ought to follow Nature as our guide, to contribute to the general good by an interchange of acts of kindness, by giving and receiving, and thus by our skill, our industry, and our talents to cement human society more closely together, man to man.*

In this period, Deuter gave many interviews and occasionally even wrote editorials expressing his belief in "cementing human society" through industry. He was photographed with liberal intellectuals, and was frequently quoted as saying that the royal road to the future lay in confronting the darkness of the past. The values of openness and transparency were the foundation of Deuter AG's contributions to the "general good."

In 1977, during the so-called German Autumn, Deuter was sitting on the terrace of the villa reading a newspaper, when a young Red Army Faction terrorist, who gained entry by pretending to be delivering flowers, forced her way past the housekeeper and shot him three times with a handgun. The class enemy was hit in the leg and stomach, and spent several months in hospital. According to the handbook, he never fully recovered his health, and his death in 1985 was hastened by the injuries.

The anonymous author of the handbook wrote that Herr Deuter's encounter with terror reinforced his belief in the values of openness and transparency. "The Deuter Center was conceived," according to the copywriter, "as a microcosm of the wider public sphere. Scholars at the Center contribute to the development of their own communal space, providing open access to their decision-making and research processes, sharing time and resources, negotiating among themselves and pooling their thoughts in the public labor of scholarship. The Center is thus an experimental community as well as a world-class center of excellence."

I assume that at some point in the application process I must have read this paragraph, but, focused as I had been on the offer of free accommodation and a stipend, I had failed to register the radical nature of the Center's ambitions. All the same, I did not understand why my participation in the public sphere, microcosmic or otherwise, had to take place in that awful open-plan office. I skyped Rei to tell her that I'd arrived safely. How was it, she asked. Fine, I said. A little weird.

THE FOLLOWING MORNING I breakfasted alone in the dining room, looking out at the frozen lake and feeling like an off-season guest at a grand hotel. Would I care for eggs? The waiter introduced himself, a man in his thirties with the ripped-open smile of a nurse or a home help, someone whose personality had been formed by long hours of affective labor. We engaged in a short conversation, appropriate to two people who would be seeing each other every day for several months. He turned out to be a local history enthusiast, pointing out houses on the other side of the water that had once belonged to artists and actors, part of a summer colony that had made Wannsee into a fashionable resort in the years before the First World War. "And of course," he said, lowering his voice as if someone were there to overhear us in that big empty dining room, "the gray villa next to the tall white building, the one half-hidden by trees, is the venue of the Wannsee Conference." I nodded and said I had heard of it, but he felt the need to complete his explanation. "Where the final solution to the Jewish Question was planned in 1942." Politely I looked in the direction he indicated. The house was too far away to see clearly.

After breakfast, I went back to my room, which I found thoroughly clean and tidy. My three pairs of shoes stood in a row in front of the cupboard. Dirty clothes had been folded and put in a pile on the chair. I experienced the odd combination of shame and excitement that hotel housekeeping services always induces, the feeling that one's privacy has been violated, but with such obsequiousness that it constitutes an invitation to discount the particular human existence of the violator, the one who has done the wiping and folding and lining up in rows.

I locked the door on my neat room and went to meet the director of hospitality, who was in charge of my orientation. Frau Janowitz turned out to be a woman in her fifties with a tight ponytail and a ponderously hostile manner. After a few pleasantries I explained "my situation," and she said I should, of course, do what was best for my work. That "of course" contained more than a hint of its opposite and it was clear that she intended me to understand that my objections were both absurd and inconvenient. Unfortunately, the process of orientation had several stages, and we were obliged to spend the morning together. We made pained small talk (she liked sailing

and had previously worked for a hotel) and she took me to see
various staff members who would be assisting me during my
stay. I signed paperwork for the librarian and the accountant
who was going to issue my per diem. Two shifty-looking men
from the IT department issued me with a keycard and a fancy
biometric ID. I felt uncomfortable sitting and staring into their
iris scanner, distracted by the sleepy-eyed cartoon frog on the
technician's tee shirt as he adjusted the equipment. I considered objecting ("why is this necessary?") but I couldn't articulate my reasons and it seemed simplest to comply. They said
some more stuff about openness and transparency and I nodded along while they droned on about logs and data retention.
Finally, exhausted, I stood with Frau Janowitz as she knocked
on the door of the executive director, Herr Doktor Weber. He
was, she informed me, a very cultured man, a former career
diplomat.

Dr. Weber occupied what must have once been a reception
room on the house's second floor, a high-ceilinged space with
French doors that led out onto an expansive balcony with a
view over the lake. We found him reading the feuilleton of
the *Frankfurter Allgemeine Zeitung* behind a large and meticulously tidy desk, dramatically framed against an antique Chinese screen with pictures of ladies crossing a bridge. He stood
up to greet me and said several effusive things about honor and
pleasure and I managed to stumble through a sentence about
the Center's scenic location and my gratitude at being chosen as a fellow. As we executed our conversational duties, my
attention was drawn to a gnarled hunk of stone about the size
of an upended shoebox, sitting on an ornate rosewood plinth
on the mantel. Dr. Weber followed my eyeline, and informed

me, with a collector's relish, that it was a "scholar's rock," a piece of limestone from Guangdong, naturally sculpted by erosion. For centuries, he said, such rocks had been prized as objects of contemplation. Aficionados cultivated the ability to perform a sort of mental or spiritual wandering, imagining the complex surfaces as fully realized landscapes that they could pass through and explore.

"Of course I am too old to travel now."

I was surprised by this melancholy remark, for Dr. Weber was lean and tan and exuded the offensive good health of a competitive cyclist. I didn't know how best to respond. Ought I to assure him that, really, he was a man in peak condition, or instead nod sympathetically?

"They say it looks like a certain mountain shrouded in mist. I'm afraid I can never remember which mountain."

I still had no response. Finding himself at a social impasse, the old diplomat deftly retraced his steps and drew my attention to a little brush painting, placed on an easel by his desk. I had the feeling that, if he thought he could get away with it, he would show me his entire collection, piece by piece. There were a number of figurines and small jade pieces on a coffee table near the window. A tall vase guarded the door. Directing the Deuter Center was, I imagined, a prestigious but untaxing job, a reward for something or other, maintaining or defending some part of the establishment. What did Dr. Weber do, now he'd finished doing whatever it was he'd done before? Maybe he just spent his days at his desk, wandering through imaginary landscapes.

I had lived much of my life in London, was that correct? Yes I had.

"But your parents were from India."

"My father's Indian. My mother's English. I moved to New York to do a doctorate at Columbia."

"What in?"

"Comp. Lit.—comparative literature."

"You didn't mention this on your application."

"Well, I didn't actually complete it. I kind of went off on my own."

"I see, but you are going back now. I'm surprised you aren't writing about Indian poetry."

"Why?"

"Because it's your culture."

His face was completely bland. I didn't think he meant it as an insult, or a way to question my credentials. It was impossible to tell. I said something about not believing in the idea of national literature. He nodded.

"I understand, and personally I am a great supporter of German poetry. But, well, we have so many scholars of German poetry."

"I wanted to talk about the, uh, Workspace."

"Yes, Frau Janowitz mentioned this. However I am unable to help you. The terms of the fellowship are strict. We cannot deviate from our founder's instructions."

After that our meeting petered out. He told me that he hoped I'd be comfortable for the rest of my stay, and would make full use of the facilities, perceptibly weighting the phrase "full use," so it sounded like a reprimand, a reminder of a standard that I had not met.

I spent the rest of the morning in my room, arranging books and papers and answering email, preparing myself to go down to the Communal Workspace. After a while, I realized I was staring at a table that was bare but for an open laptop, a small pile of books and a fresh cup of coffee. Everything was in order. I had made it ready for writing, but I wasn't supposed to write there, on that perfectly good pine table, sitting on that perfectly comfortable chair. I was not supposed to drink that coffee. It seemed like a waste.

I decided to go for a walk.

I set off down the villa's long driveway and out into the street, crunching along an icy path past iron gates and high fences, behind which I caught glimpses of imposing houses in various styles: a white modernist villa, a fantastical gothic castle, just as tasteless as it must have been when it was built, the pride of some Wilhelmine brewer or mill owner. Security cameras poked over hedges, watching me as I loitered. Many of these old family summer houses were now institutions (a security consultancy, a think tank) or belonged to diplomatic missions. Here were the Saudis, there the Colombians. On the side of the street facing the water, the buildings were immense. On the other, denied the lake view, they were more modest. In some cases, you could tell that grounds and gardens had been sold to developers, so that low-rise apartment blocks adjoined older, larger structures. This denser housing seemed like a relic of a vanishing democratic era, litters of suburban middle-class piglets importunately nuzzling oligarchic sows. Two decades into the twenty-first century and we were back in the time of the big houses. Soon the apartment blocks would be bought up and scraped away, the popular incursion brought to an end.

The border of the old summer colony was marked by a wide road, running parallel to a railway: weathered brick walls and wire fencing. The station platforms, visible through the chain link, were marked by signs lettered in Gothic *Fraktur*. A café was the only unshuttered shop in a dismal parade. *Berlin-Wannsee,* on the main line heading east, towards Poland. A characterless bust of Bismarck, many times life-size, was planted on a plinth behind the bus stop. Executed in some kind of pale friable stone, the old chancellor's worn face was now completely without expression, hanging above the commuters like a blank Prussian moon. Slippery steps led down beside him to a wide concrete promenade that faced commercial piers with barred gates. Ferries hibernated alongside them, waiting for the season to start in May. Large boards advertised summer routes round the lake and through various waterways into the city center. It was hard to imagine that pleasure trips could ever start from such a bleak place. The devastation of winter was absolute, as if the lake were enchanted. The ticket office was shuttered, the water half-frozen, a gray jelly lapping trash at the jetties.

I walked down a path by a neck of water that led me into the relative warmth of a space under a road bridge. On the far side were several crude shelters, presumably built by homeless people. As I watched, a figure crawled out of a tent and squatted to empty a plastic bottle of liquid into the water. The figure—a man, I was fairly certain—stood up, as if watching me. It was too far away to see a face, but I felt the force of the attention directed towards me, the uncomfortable sensation of contact with a stranger.

My face was beginning to feel numb, and though my feet were dry, they were uncomfortably cold. I thought about turning back, but I have an aversion to reversing direction on a walk. When you're going back somewhere, it is hard to think of anything but the destination. You fall out of the present, into a strange state that is a blend of anticipation and recollection, a blend of the future and the past. You see for a second time the landmarks on the route you're retracing, and drift to thinking of the routine you'll follow when you get back home. Onwards is always better. And so I went on, emerging from under the bridge, passing a boatyard and another bus stop into a little interstitial space on the far side of the road, a not-quite park that contained a few trees and some municipally tamed brambles. On the other side I found a cobbled street running next to the railway. I followed it and found myself in another part of the old summer colony, passing again through its distinctive streetscape of villas, bathed in the stealthy aura of money.

Kleistgrab, said a sign. The Kleist grave. The site was a wedge of land between an ugly white stucco mansion and a rowing club's boathouse. From the street you could see an undulating path, and a sort of hump or small hill topped by a stone marker. It seemed like good fortune to stumble upon a famous writer, so close to where I'd come to work, but I couldn't help wishing it were someone else. I didn't care for the work of Heinrich von Kleist, and what I knew about his life didn't inspire sympathy. If the shade of a writer was going to hang over my time in Berlin, it ought to have been one of the great calming Germans: Rilke, walking inside his own vast solitude and meeting no one for hours; Hölderlin, whose very madness was stately and canonical, the gold standard of Romantic insanity. Goethe would have been ideal. Kleist, on the other hand, was a hysteric, a writer of jarring plays and fragmented stories full of hectic action, battles and earthquakes and psychic shocks. And now I had run into him, only a short walk away from my desk. When it comes to my work, I have certain—what to call them? Not quite superstitions, something more than habits. I cannot, for example, ignore chance encounters. It is a sort of method. It is the way my mind has always worked.

I walked down towards the grave. Somehow, it came as no surprise to find that the inscription on the stone ended in an exclamation mark:

Nun o Unsterblichkeit bist du ganz mein!

Now, O immortality, you are all mine! The scream of someone who has grasped for something and achieved it, who has made a grand gesture—that being, in Kleist's case, suicide, or more precisely a suicide pact with a woman named Henriette Vogel. Picking my way carefully over the icy path, I wandered back towards the road to read the text on a board placed at the site by the tourist authority. It seemed that Kleist chose as his death partner not a lover, as I'd always assumed, but someone described as "a social acquaintance," and "the wife of a friend," phrases that captured precisely nothing about what it takes for two people in their thirties to go to an inn by a lake, then walk out to the shore and shoot themselves dead.

Or rather he shot her, and then himself. Her name was on the grave, but it was the *Kleistgrab*. Her death was merely an ornament to his. Is that how the two of them understood it? The magician and his assistant? They did it in November. It must have been very cold. I certainly felt cold. An insidious mist rose up off the lake, seeping through my jacket into the fibers of my sweater. Enough of Kleist. I turned and walked back along the main road, gradually upping my pace. Fast, to get warm. Faster. Kleist! It would have to be Kleist. He'd proposed it to others, before Henriette. She was just the one who said yes.

That evening, after a long hot shower, I walked down to the

water, crossing the wide sloping lawn and passing through a gate that led onto the dock. Next to the villa was a little boat-house, the property of a local boat club, and a slipway that led back up to the road. The vessels moored there were all small sailing yachts, most shrouded in canvas for the winter, the largest no longer than twenty feet or so. There wasn't much to see. A few lights on the other side of the lake, near the Wann-see Conference house.

I ate another solitary dinner at the table by the window. The waiter greeted me cordially, and warned me that I should be careful on the dock, as it was icy and badly lit. I thanked him, slightly surprised that I'd been observed. As he served me soup, I stared absentmindedly around the room, think-ing of nothing in particular but the food. I noticed a camera, mounted high on the wall near Herr Deuter's portrait. There was also a motion sensor, which blinked red each time the waiter crossed the room back to the kitchen. Despite myself I became slightly self-conscious about the way I was eating. I dabbed at my lips with a napkin. I found myself sweeping away breadcrumbs from the table cloth, making sure my soup spoon was aligned correctly in the empty bowl.

Pleasantly tired, I climbed the stairs to my room. It was a relief to close the door behind me. The little garret felt wel-coming, even cozy, and at last I managed to do some work. I've always liked to stay up late, writing by lamplight. It is good to be in a quiet place, to have a cone of illumination that I can fill with my thoughts. I could hear the usual small noises of a big house, and the tiny metallic clink of the boats at anchor, a ghostly rattle of chains that made the lake half-present in the room, its cold gray water lapping round the legs of my chair.

I wanted to start my book with an essay on the Goethe lyric known as "Wanderer's Nightsong II." Eight simple lines, some of the most celebrated and perfect in German, written by the poet on the wall of a mountain hut in Thuringia and copied down by his friends. There is a "you" in the poem, who feels a profound calm descend over the peaks. The birds fall silent in the trees. Everything is *Ruh,* a deep and ancient word, rooted in the Iron Age. It is the word for the absence of sound, but also for spiritual rest. The poem ends:

> *Warte nur, balde*
> *Ruhest du auch.*

Just wait, soon you too will grow *Ruh.* And suddenly the poem is not about the weather, or the time of day, or some chance atmospheric phenomenon of the mountains, but about death.

There is a speaker in Goethe's poem, someone who tells the reader about the mountains and the treetops and the birds. What interested me was the person the poem was talking to, the "you" who would soon be at peace. If I were a poet who went for a walk and was reminded of my mortality, the obvious thing would be to write "I." "I heard the birds fall silent, it made me think of death . . ." But instead there was this "you." Who was addressed? Was it Goethe talking to himself? To a lover? Some hill-walking poet friend? Eventually I stopped scratching at my pad, no longer thinking about "the turning away of lyric utterance from the world," "the subject contemplating itself," or any of the other important-sounding literary-critical phrases whose significance was just then escaping me. For the first time in however many readings of the poem, I understood it, or perhaps I should say I felt it, physically experienced its meaning as a small cold pebble in my stomach. The "you" was me. Me in particular. I too would fall into silence. I would die.

AT BREAKFAST, I saw signs that other people had eaten before me. The empty cups and cereal bowls triggered all my most misanthropic impulses. Furtively, I looked around for a tray. When I couldn't find one, I filled my pockets with fruit and bread rolls and carried a precariously piled plate and a mug of coffee out of the dining room. As I was climbing the stairs, the friendly porter, Otto or Ulli, emerged from his lodge. He frowned at the plate of food I was carrying, as if he wanted to say something.

"You are going back to your room to eat?"

"Yes. Why?"

"No reason. Please, go ahead."

Upstairs I pushed back the books and papers on my desk to make room for my breakfast. As I ate, I looked at the notes I'd made on "Wanderer's Nightsong II." They did not seem useful. By day, the poem might as well have been a shopping list. I sat for a long time with my coffee, looking out of the window at the lake. Not sure how to proceed, I listened to an old radio play by the French writer Georges Perec, called *The Machine*. It had been broadcast in 1968, when the new discipline of cybernetics, which promised to regulate and mechanize all sorts of messy human activities, seemed to be ushering in a sinister and rather antiseptic future. The play imagined a computer that had been programmed to perform endless algorithmic operations on the words of "Wanderer's Nightsong II." Recorded in German, the actors enunciated with robotic formality. The machine's "controller" had a female voice, and the three "processors" sounded male. They recited the poem at various speeds, omitting, shuffling, doubling and negating lines, adding and removing syllables and eventually rewriting the text in various styles (epic, comic) and adding extra material to explode it into "encyclopedic diversification." Despite the computer's fancy voice interface, it also seemed to be necessary to press buttons and feed punch cards into a slot, like operating a nineteen-sixties mainframe. As drama the play was a failure, but all the same I listened intently. Perec's wit disguised a deep anxiety. He was performing a sort of autopsy of the poem, hunting for something among its entrails. Logically, if you're afraid of death, you must feel you have something to lose. Perec was frantically shuffling the words of the poem, looking for this special something. By night I thought I'd found it. Now I could have taken a scalpel to my deepest feelings, and cut and cut until I was left with nothing but scraps.

That night I went down to dinner and found that my table by the window had been pushed together with another table and covered in a white cloth. A candle had been lit. Four place settings were laid around a small floral arrangement. Staring at those four place settings, I felt a twinge of panic. I had, in some way, fundamentally misunderstood the nature of the Deuter Center. There would be no meditative solitude. If I wanted to eat, I would have regular and unavoidable company at the end of every day. I was, admittedly, "on a fellowship," and there is no getting round the incontrovertibly social meaning of that word. I'd even been sent some kind of list, though of course I hadn't read it. Suddenly, the thought of human interaction was horrifying.

As if summoned from the pit, my three companions entered the room. I had the completely unfounded suspicion that they'd been watching me from the library, an oak-paneled den on the other side of the hall. I backed towards the row of windows that looked out onto the lake, baring my teeth in a fake smile. It was a terrible, brittle situation. It was like a scene from a violent computer game.

We made introductions and sat down. Finlay, the young black American art critic, shot his cuffs and offered me his smooth dry hand. He was a formally dressed bird, pecking at the table, arranging his feathers and fixing his beady eye. He said almost nothing during the meal, surreptitiously checking his phone. He'd been at the Deuter Center for two months, and I formed the impression of a man in the trenches, a survivor of some heavy bombardment. He seemed on good terms with Laetitia, the elderly scholar of Chinese, who had the same shell-shocked fragility. A tiny Frenchwoman, possibly Eur-asian, with an evident weakness for silver jewelry, she fussed agitatedly, almost knocking over a glass of water with a trem-bling bangled hand. The big guns belonged to Edgar the Neu-rophilosopher, an Endowed Chair in his sixties with the air of a prosperous pirate. He sported—that would be the word—a spade-like salt-and-pepper beard and had a physical bulk that somehow factored itself into the intellectual reckoning, as if his immense body were some kind of sign or metaphor for his mind. His every word and movement conveyed an overbear-ing practicality: a man like a hammer looking for a nail. He took an arch and combative tone with me, firing off questions, playfully letting on that he suspected there was more to me than met the eye.

"I haven't seen you in the Communal Workspace," he said.

"No."

"Your station is untenanted, the bookshelves bare."

He made an unlikely fluttering motion with his stubby fin-gers, as if the books had flown away like little birdies. The effect was horrific. I told him I preferred to write in my room.

"Protecting the sacred mysteries?"

I didn't know what to say to that, so I nodded thoughtfully, as if acknowledging a cogent point. He tried again.

"Not wanting to show the class your workings?"

Laetitia summoned a wan smile. Beneath the lacy collar of her blouse, a tiny vein throbbed in her neck.

"You're very daring," she said to me.

Daring didn't sound so good. Daring meant I'd made myself the object of gossip. Finding no suitable reply, I performed a sort of conversational lunge.

"What do you work on, Laetitia?"

Dutifully she began, in a quiet and rather circumspect way, to tell me. As she spoke, Edgar affected wolfish interest, dabbing his beard with his napkin and shifting in his chair, movements that made her flinch. Though nominally an archaeologist, she was essentially a textual scholar. Other people dug, she "merely interpreted the findings." I couldn't decide whether this modesty was genuine, or a plea to be allowed to slip back into silence, to remove herself from Edgar's line of sight. The ancient Chinese aristocracy used ritual objects when making offerings to ancestral spirits. She was studying the inscriptions on these objects, mostly bronze vessels and bells. She was, she said, particularly interested in a group of artifacts that seemed to have come from the household of a royal functionary of the Western Zhou period.

"Which is?"

"Roughly the ninth century BC, Edgar."

I see, he said, in the tone of a rich uncle bestowing a shiny penny on a young relative. The starter arrived, a little arrangement of smoked fish on a bed of salad. For a few blessed moments everyone concentrated on the food, but Edgar dispatched his portion in a few ruthless bites and resumed his interrogation.

"You say a royal functionary of—what was it?—the Western Zhou. You've never told me what function."

"You've never asked. He was a *shanfu*. He transmitted the king's commands."

"I see."

I couldn't decide. Did Edgar not realize that Laetitia saw how transparently uninterested he was in her work, or did he just not care? He struck me as a man who might have trouble picking up on other people's emotional cues. I could tell he was itching to turn the conversational spotlight on me. I was virgin territory, an unextracted natural resource. The dinner was already intolerable, more gruesome than I'd anticipated. I considered my options. Flight, the most attractive. I could be direct. Do it quick, like tearing off a plaster. How rude would it be just to push my chair back and leave the room? I hesitated too long. Cutting off Edgar's half-uttered question ("and how about . . .") I hurriedly asked Laetitia more about her inscriptions. What kind of thing did they say? Were they extensive, or just a few words? I said *fascinating* a couple of times. The inscriptions sounded fascinating. The Western Zhou were fascinating. She gave me a pitying look. She understood that I was pleading.

"They usually describe the events that led to the vessel's casting, a war, the rendering of some notable administrative service or the performance of a religious rite."

"Fascinating."

"And you? What about these hermetic scribblings of yours?" His blunt white fingers splayed on the table, Edgar had the bland but purposeful look of a farmer at the wheel of a tractor, surveying an unplowed field. "What aspect of the poetic *oeuvre* are you working on, up there in your attic?"

Irritated by the Frenchified sneer of *"oeuvre,"* I told him: lyric poetry, a textual technology for the organization of affective experience, a container in which modern selfhood had come to be formulated, and so on and so forth. I remember I said something about the tyranny of utility and something else about the relentless pressures of self-preservation. I tried to model my speech on Laetitia's, speaking quietly, using a certain amount of jargon, making no wild claims. I hoped that Edgar would be bored enough to allow the conversation to move on elsewhere. Instead, to my dismay, he clapped his meaty palms together in glee. His scoff was physical, an ejection of air.

"Oho! We have a mystic on our hands!"

"I'm actually an atheist."

"If you are, sir, I suspect you're an atheist of a somewhat heretical stripe. I'm afraid I can't give you a pass just because you *say* you're not infected by the virus of religion. While I accept that there is a domain of literary language that uses words in, let's say, a non-denotative way, I am a scientist, and as a man of science, I can't allow anyone to plant weeds in the conceptual garden."

"The what?"

I wanted to say to him, what are you talking about? I wanted to say, I'm not doing anything to your fucking garden. Instead, I stumbled on with my explanation. I tried to sound as technical as possible, defensively striving for a kind of ultra-rationality, the tone of a man speaking to another man out of the firm authority of his disciplinary manhood, but I could hear myself tripping up, giving garbled explanations of ideas that I usually found useful and clear.

Edgar called the waiter and had his wineglass refilled. He toasted me as he took a sip, a gesture that not only failed to be Falstaffian, but came across as actively prim.

"Why don't we leave aside your use of the word *technology*. The idea of writing as a technology does have semantic content for me. But really, even if one accepts the continued cultural importance of poetry, as opposed to some mass medium, say television or social media, even radio, any of which would surely be more powerful and effective—if only in terms of reach, numbers participating—even then one has to ask about the *mechanism* by which poetry would do anything as powerful as, how did you put it, 'reformatting contemporary self-hood'? I assume the use of a computer term is a metaphor, which I may discount?"

He appeared to be waiting for a yes or no. I nodded mutely, in the throes of a sudden physical crisis, a painful muscular spasm that was constricting my neck and shoulders. He took my silence as a sign that he'd already won the argument and could take his time to deliver the *coup de grâce,* allowing himself a few matadorial flourishes on the way.

"I could accept the possibility of a machine consisting of language, words assembled in a particular order which would act, perhaps via the dopamine system, to do measurable neurochemical work. I'm talking off the top of my head here, the exact mechanism is unimportant. But I wonder, wouldn't the words be less a machine than a set of instructions for building one?"

Here, in the absence of some word or gesture from me, he inserted his own preference, doing a little dumb show of a person (presumably me) having a eureka moment.

"Now he gets it! The real machine would be the array of neurons in the brain! So we can rescue *some* meaningful thinking from what you said, but I'm sorry to say that for me the real problem starts much earlier. The 'self' is just a folk notion. I am not trying to humiliate, simply stating a fact. The self is what we might call the elephant in the room when it comes to discussing the value of your sort of, what would you call it, cultural study? Before one starts to make wild claims about how to reprogram something, one is forced to ask, what is it that we're reprogramming? This self that, according to you, changes through history, and can be reconfigured by the unlikely means of poetry? To you, I mean, specifically. What do you imagine you are speaking about when you say the word *self*?"

I know people throw around the phrase "my worst nightmare," but several years earlier I had actually suffered from a recurring anxiety dream about being at a thesis defense, with a panel of sarcastic hectoring men—men like Edgar—as the examiners. When you're angry, you're at a disadvantage. You ought to be marshaling your materials, formulating your case, but you can't concentrate because you're vividly imagining your dinner companion swallowing bits of his wine glass. I spluttered something about Being, the quality I found in myself that was more than the sum of my parts. I used the word *Gestalt*. I couldn't believe the garbage that was coming out of my mouth.

"So is it a little golden chap, sitting at the controls of that big mechanical body?"

"What are you talking about?"

"The self! Where is it? Where is it located?"

"Well, obviously when it comes to lyric poetry, it's in the field of the poem. On the page."

Edgar looked puzzled, and I congratulated myself on executing the postmodernist version of spraying mace in his eyes. Where is the self? What did he think I was going to say, the pineal gland? Recovering, he began to wonder aloud, in a tone that mixed pity and reproach, whether I understood that consciousness was essentially *epiphenomenal,* and my experience of having a self was perhaps not *causal* in the way I imagined. My "self" didn't run things, Edgar told the table, like Poirot revealing that I was the one who did the murder. It was merely a sort of passenger, allowed occasionally to comment on the action. Experimental psychology and neuroscience had rather got ahead of the liberal arts, in Edgar's opinion. My "lyric I" or whatever I wanted to call it, might, he granted, have value in the realm of intellectual history, but only as a poignant artifact of a period that was drawing to a close.

"HE'S AN UNBELIEVABLE ASSHOLE. I mean possibly the most arrogant man I've ever met. And talk about privilege. Unless you're—well, unless you're *him,* essentially, he acts as if he's leading you through a difficult text in a seminar. It was a terrible mistake to come here. I'm trapped. I'm a prisoner in my room."

Rei looked worried. "You didn't start anything, did you? Were you rude to him?"

"God no. I just wanted to get out of there. I didn't even make it to dessert. I told them I had a conference call, and came up to phone you. Darling, I've had to lock the door. I'm irrationally afraid he's outside in the corridor, waiting to carry on telling me about the pointlessness of my life."

"A conference call?"

"I had to say something."

"When do you ever have conference calls?"

"I've had conference calls. Enough, God, you're supposed to be humoring me, not questioning my excuses."

"Honey?"

"What?"

"You're ranting."

"I'm sorry."

"That's OK. It's who you are. I'm at peace with it."

I smiled at her. She smiled back. I felt a little less jumbled.

"So what's been going on? You're in the thick of it, with Nina and everything."

"Don't worry about me. All I want is for you to break through your—whatever. Your thing. Just make the most of your time. Write your book and come back to me happy."

"But this guy is driving me crazy. And it's not just me, you should see the others. They're fucking wrecks, excuse my language. Nina's not around, is she?"

"Paulette's taken her to the library. Don't worry about this Edgar person. Seriously. You're fine. You're going to be fine."

After we ended the call I tried everything I could think of to get to sleep, but I was still too angry. I watched part of a durational Iranian movie, the kind of film that's almost impossible to decipher on a laptop, ten-minute shots of a man walking up a path, long silences as people served and drank tea. When my eyes got tired, I switched to a file of pictures I kept on a thumb drive and masturbated. After a melancholy orgasm I was just as wired as before. I lay in bed, my back and shoulders knotted with undischarged fury, until eventually daylight began to filter into the room. So what if my conscious intention didn't "cause" anything? The force, the *will,* came from me. I was still the one who wanted things, who thought and felt and experienced pain.

For a man who was full of sarcastic little images of what he called the "sovereign self" ("the princeling," the "little golden man," the "wizard behind the curtain" and so on), Edgar was heavily invested in one kind of sovereignty: his own. In theory he was a sanguine population of neurons and I was an uptight mystic clinging on to my childish folk beliefs about the soul. In practice, he was a bully. It wasn't as if I'd even set out to challenge him. I'd been actively trying to mind my own business, keep my head down. Eventually I fell into fitful unconsciousness.

THE NEXT MORNING I went for a walk to clear my head, thinking I'd come back refreshed and write some notes in the Workspace, but although the day was bright and the lake more cheerful and welcoming than before, I couldn't suppress unwelcome thoughts, chiefly the suspicion that I was only annoyed by Edgar because I knew he was right. This "lyric I," this thing I was studying with such seriousness, didn't really exist. Whenever I tried to focus my attention on it, on myself, to experience some version of the exquisite interiority out of which the great poets had forged their art, the fullness that I ought to have found was missing. All I uncovered was confusion. There were impressions, experiences, and there seemed to be a subject attached to them, someone or something to which they were happening. But there was no unity, no proof that this "I" to whom I was so slavishly devoted, who was, now I came to think of it, more or less my employer, the one on whom my livelihood depended, was present in any meaningful way at all.

What did I have to cling on to? There were constants. I always had neck pain. I knew the dates of Rei's and Nina's birthdays. Was that a sufficient foundation for a personality? I could bring my wife's face vividly to mind. My daughter's too. The faces might stop me floating away, but they couldn't make me feel like a "self" with any force or power of action. How could an amorphous blob will anything into being? How could it love? I was a vapor, an incoherent jumble of events inside a sack of skin.

As I walked and fretted, I paid little attention to my surroundings, and was surprised to find myself at the Kleist grave. Someone had left flowers on the headstone. Small blue wildflowers, carefully tied with a ribbon. *Nun, o Unsterblichkeit, bist du ganz mein!* A flight of steps led from the marker to the water. I picked my way down it, wary of ice. Colonized by rowing clubs and villas, the view carried no information, nothing that made it any easier to understand the violence that had taken place there.

Kleist's most famous story, or at least the only one I could remember in any detail, was *The Marquise of O*, which concerned an aristocratic young widow who scandalizes society by taking out an advertisement in a newspaper, inquiring after the identity of the father of her child. In 1808 its publication was a minor sensation, and didn't endear Kleist to the morally rigid Prussian public. What kind of woman doesn't know who she's slept with? The Prussian public knew exactly what kind of woman. An aristocrat's position depended on her name, on the public qualities—honor and reputation—that attached to it. What kind of aristocrat would publicize a shameful secret in a newspaper? The mental state of the Marquise was the story's mystery, its black box. How could she not know such an intimate thing about herself? Was she a liar? An amnesiac? Was she raped? What kind of inner life do you have, if such an event can slip your mind?

I had an answer. Edgar's answer. None. No one was there, no one inside the box. In the story, the Marquise's mystery was resolved and her amnesia explained, I couldn't exactly remember how, but in my mind she'd got wrapped up with a completely different story, the tale of Coppélia, the clock-maker's wind-up doll. A young man falls in love with the doll, projecting his sexual longings onto her lifeless body. The Marquise was a figure like Coppélia, a void with an uncanny human outline.

I came back from my walk shivering, ready to take a hot shower, only to find a cleaner in my room, a slight middle-aged woman whose pinched face was half-obscured by a feathery curtain of hair. We were both alarmed. Before I came in, she'd been near the door, and as I opened it, she was forced to step back. Startled by my entry, she put up an arm as if to ward off a blow and the sleeve of her housecoat rode up to expose a wrist densely inked with tattoos. I stepped aside, trying to look unthreatening, and she sort of melted away. One minute she was there, carrying a caddy of spray bottles, the next she'd vanished.

Her furtiveness was odd enough that I went into the closet and made a quick check on the folder where I kept cash and documents. Satisfied that everything was in place, I locked the door and examined the room. She had folded my clothes, straightened up the books on my desk and carefully lined up two half-drunk bottles of beer next to the sink, as if offering me the choice either to finish them or recycle them. I tried not to interpret this as passive-aggressive. It was oddly difficult for me just then to know that someone had been in my personal space, going through my things. I was entering a period when everything around me seemed to be encrusted in signs. Or more encrusted than usual. I tried to feel nothing in particular about the arrangement of the beer bottles on the counter, or about the housekeeper as an individual, a woman who was probably following a checklist of actions prescribed by her management. I lay down on the clean linen of my freshly made bed and fiddled around on the internet.

An hour or so later, shaved and dressed, I went to the Workspace with the brittle jauntiness of a young revolutionary singing songs on his way to the gallows. I lost heart at the door and fumbled with my keycard in the general vicinity of the reader, telling myself that it didn't work, I couldn't get in, ergo there was no way I could be blamed for not writing in there, for not being *able* to write in there, the Workspace being inaccessible because of a technical problem, no fault of mine. I was about to leave, assuring myself that I'd made every reasonable effort, when Finlay came and swiped me in.

I made my way to my workstation, nodding and smiling at my colleagues as they tried to conceal their curiosity at my arrival. There were at least two people I hadn't met before, and they seemed as interested in me as the others. No one spoke except Edgar, who proclaimed in a booming voice that "the Prodigal has returned." I thought I'd have to endure a routine, some thigh-slapping Renaissance Fayre turn, full of rhetoric and flourishes of wheezy panache. Luckily, Edgar's possession of the moral high ground depended on remaining a Deuterian in good standing, a respecter of the golden rule of Workspace Silence, so he had to be content with shushing himself theatrically, waggling his forefingers over his lips in an awful winsome burlesque.

I sat down at my desk and stared at the wood-effect surface, trying to control my breathing. The Workspace smelled, not overpoweringly, of cleaning products. It smelled of things that generate static electricity and things that dissipate it or prevent it building up. Carpet tiles, rubber mats. Coatings and sprays. I adjusted the height of my seat and powered up the computer. I waved my hand to switch on the light. From my clogged pigeonhole I had recovered a piece of paper circulated by the IT department, listing various logins and IDs and invitations to create passwords. I put it in front of me on the desk. After I had shared my mother's maiden name and a randomly chosen favorite film, I was invited to prove that I was not a robot. Luckily for me the bar was low.

The theory—my theory—was that if I went to work, maybe I would become what I appeared to be: a scholar, part of a common project, a man taking resolute communicative action. I sat and stared at my blank document. Inevitably Edgar turned out to be an aficionado of some kind of keyboard with loud mechanical switches. It was impossible to ignore his workflow, either eerie silence or a torrent of clicks and clacks. Thankfully he was sitting quite far away from me, so there was no chance of accidental eye contact, but it was infuriating that he'd found yet another way to intrude on my peace of mind. Unable to concentrate, I messaged the librarian at the Center to request an edition of Kleist's *Gesammelte Werke*. I stared at my blank document for a while and then opened a browser.

Search: Deuter

Deuter **Center**

Deuter **Chemical**

Deuter**onomy**

Deuter **TiO2**

Deuter**ium**

Deuter **music**

Various portraits. The captain of industry, the philanthropist presenting a prize. A scan of a magazine spread depicting a trade stand, sometime around 1970. Beneath a glowing arch, dolly birds in tight dresses and metallic boots show off an array of consumer products, kitchenware and furniture and fabrics and pharmaceuticals. In another picture, a waterfall of pills tumbles from a spout into a sort of futuristic ewer. In a third there is a Mercedes-Benz, everything—the pills, the car—the same optically brightened white.

I set the portraits of Deuter, the aquiline nose, the commanding eyes, beside portraits of Kleist. Nineteenth-century teenagers had wept over the glamorous corpses of young poets. Chatterton and Shelley and Goethe's Werther. I doubted anyone much had wept for Kleist. From the few undistinguished oils and drawings I could find, it was obvious that he was uncomfortable inside his body. The shoulders were hunched a little too high, the head held self-consciously. The only attractive image of him was by a canny old Swiss who seemed to bathe all his subjects in the same off-the-shelf heavenly light. Even he was forced to admit Kleist's asceticism, the rumpled clothes and violently hacked hair, though he set the blunt-scissored crop over high cheekbones and a fine jaw that weren't matched in other images, and which I read as cynical flattery.

Somehow it seemed impossible to say anything about *Wanderer's Nightsong,* so I spent the day making lists. Quotations, typologies. *Self sufficient (1589); Self-knowledge (1613); Self-made (1615); Self-seeker (1632); Selfish (1640); Self-examination (1647); Selfhood (1649); Self interest (1658); Self-knowing (1667); Self-deception (1677); Self-determination (1683); Self-conscious (1688). Je est un autre* (Rimbaud). *I should have to search for a year to find a true feeling inside myself* (Kafka). I wrote down a sort of light bulb joke about lyric poets, attributed to Karl Kraus. *If you want a window painted, you don't call a lyric poet. He might be able to do the work, but he doesn't.* Not he can't, or won't. He just doesn't. He prefers not to.

Gradually the sun went down. By five-thirty it was already dark. On one side, the Workspace was connected to the house. The other walls were made of glass panels. My workstation looked towards the dark leafy mass of the hedge that marked the boundary. To my right, the driveway led towards the gate and the road. To my left, the garden sloped down to the frozen lake, now invisible but for a few distant lights. Reflected in the glass I could see Laetitia packing up, shuffling papers and powering down her monitor. If I turned halfway round, I could see Edgar's reflected bulk, see the hands moving in time to the irregular staccato bursts of sound. Through the day, I'd grown slightly less aware of the open space around me, the feeling of being marooned on an island. Now it returned. I couldn't be in there any longer. As I climbed the stairs back up to my room, I felt drained. I had no clear memory of anything I'd thought or done.

I couldn't face dinner so instead of going down to the Center's dining room, I left the grounds and ate at a Chinese restaurant a short bus ride away. Its interior was a lurid confection of fish tanks and porcelain ornaments, rendered alien—almost submarine—by blue lighting. It was like walking into a brothel. The collected Kleist had been delivered, a compact four-volume set in a slipcase, each one perfect for slipping into a pocket. I had also ordered several translations of his plays and stories. I took some of these books with me, and drank two or three beers as I ate and read about the young man with the square blunt face, too violent and hysterical to make it in the world. In his own words, he was "absurdly overwrought." Most commentators seemed to believe that he was what would now be termed an "incel," dying a virgin. Born a Prussian Junker and trained as a military officer, he went spectacularly off the rails, crashing out of various prestigious professions and positions open to him through family connections, each burned bridge bringing him a little closer to the lake and the bullet. As a child, he and his cousin signed an undertaking to kill themselves together if "anything unworthy" should happen. Later he proposed suicide pacts to all sorts of people—men and women, passing acquaintances, a friend's fiancée. Always by shooting.

As I read I began to feel slightly suffocated. That face, born to fail. The reek of his melancholy in my nostrils. At one point he challenged the elderly Goethe to a pistol duel, a wildly inappropriate act that cemented his reputation as unstable and faintly ridiculous. You could object that all I had to do was read different books, decide to take another route on my walks. It ought to be easy to forget a dead writer.

BY THE TIME I'd been at the Deuter Center a month, things had deteriorated. By *things* I mean *me,* my state of mind. I still sometimes went to the Workspace, but mostly it was to log time on the Deuter Center's network. One of the more unpleasant surprises of my fellowship was the weekly delivery of a piece of paper, pushed under my door like a hotel bill, with a statistical breakdown of my "activity." Hours spent, documents created, sites visited, and so on. Naturally, the first time this happened, I was outraged, and went at once to see Frau Janowitz, but instead of putting her on the defensive, my complaint about this outrageous invasion of privacy merely led her to pull up the contract I'd signed (without reading) on arrival. Could I not see, she said, where I had agreed to waive all rights to privacy in furtherance of the Center's "research goals"? What were these research goals, I asked. Research into the future development of a transparent public sphere, she said, primly. This was all one word in German. And might she also point out (Frau Janowitz was clearly enjoying herself) that I'd given the Center the right to cancel payment of my stipend in the event that my recorded working hours dipped below a target number during any week of my residency. I had already missed one week's goal, but she was prepared to overlook it. I was new. I was finding my feet.

Her victory was absolute. The situation was impossible (I could not even focus on the word *goal,* it made me too angry) yet I was trapped. I couldn't go home to Rei without having made at least some progress on my book, yet the idea of working under such conditions was intolerable. Not only was I being watched, I was being gamified. Yet if I left the Deuter Center, what would be waiting for me at home? Something had to change. I could not risk bringing my poison back to my family.

My solution was to mark time. I would check into the Workspace with my keycard and try to simulate scholarship. In an agony of self-consciousness, I'd sit at my desk, asking myself the question *does it look like I'm working?* I'd raise and lower the chair, wave my hand at the light, trying to steel myself to write. I'd tell myself that it didn't have to be any good. It just had to be text of some kind. Keystrokes. When I couldn't think of anything, I adopted a contemplative posture, hitting a key every so often. If I was slouching, I tried to fill my slouch with potential, the coiled readiness of someone who might imminently begin to write, might write *at any time,* but just happened not to be doing so. When I sat up straight, I projected an image of transfixed introspection, a perfectly legitimate aspect of the creative process. Having my hands poised over the keyboard felt like too much. Without my hands over the keyboard, I was just a man sitting in a chair, so I would usually lean forward a little, in the manner of someone moving an intellectual project forward, not hesitating or procrastinating, buying time or treading water, but serene, confident, and above all *busy.* Every so often I'd lean back and look "casually" over my shoulder, trying to work out if anyone could see my screen.

I often ate at the blue light Chinese. The restaurant's portions were enormous, and I'd bring back foil trays of leftovers, spooning cold fried rice into my mouth late at night. My desk and bed were dotted with stray grains and spatters of sauce. After a while the room began to smell. Empty coffee cups, beer cans, underwear on the floor—I was creating a teenage midden, fouling my adult nest. It was semi-deliberate, a sort of regression. I didn't know where I was going with it, whether I was playing at collapse or trying to induce the real thing.

Sometimes, to keep up appearances, I had to go to dinner and socialize. To prepare, I drank Scotch. The whisky made me feel raw and a little prickly, ready for the cut and thrust of intellectual conversation. Edgar wasn't always there. When he was, I tried to focus on, say, the grilled fish and the crisp vegetables on my plate, a small pewter tureen of buttery sauce, all the good things the universe had provided. This was not always easy. Edgar was or wanted to be thought of as a gourmet, and somehow he always got very *involved* in the food we ate. I was set on edge by his table manners, the hearty mastication, the uses he made of his clever fingers, tearing and stuffing and cracking and sprinkling and pinching. On the plus side, I'd developed a reliable strategy for warding off conversation. Whenever he started demanding that I justify my work because it didn't meet some Edgarian criterion of relevance or value, I'd claim that "from a methodological perspective" I didn't accept that there was a world outside the text of the poems I studied, that essentially the sphere of phenomena measured in SI units meant nothing to me, so his "concerns" (a good neutral word) had no relevance to "my approach." He now believed that I was an extreme relativist, the kind of zealot who used to stalk university humanities departments in the nineteen-eighties, wearing a leather jacket and quoting Baudrillard. From Edgar's perspective, this was more or less a form of mental illness, and he was shocked and not a little repulsed by it. This curtailed a lot of potentially annoying interactions.

It helped that we had some new colleagues. Alistair, a Scottish economic historian, and Per, a political scientist from Sweden, were white men in late middle age, who dressed almost identically in technocratic smart-casual, slacks and blue blazers and button-down Oxford-weave shirts. They seemed sublimely unperturbed by Edgar, which made him wildly irritated. Often he'd be so caught up in combat with them that he'd barely acknowledge the rest of us. With the eye of Edgar elsewhere, Finlay and Laetitia turned out to be good company. When I asked Finlay what kind of art he wrote about, he replied "anything that doesn't sell," and we both laughed too loudly, drawing attention to ourselves.

One night we listened as Edgar cunningly led his antagonists towards Behavioral Economics, on which ground he'd evidently laid some kind of vicious logical mantrap, designed to impale them and ensure his continued dominance in the tribe. However, they barely seemed to notice his provocations, and by the time dessert was served, Alistair was even correcting his understanding of Decision Theory. Faced with the Scot's placid authority, Edgar seemed ungainly, his mincing hand gestures the wrigglings of a beetle flipped on its back. Yes of course, he kept saying, in a tone of suppressed fury. Of course I'm talking in the most abstract terms.

Listening to Edgar being patronized, Finlay's eyes glittered violently. Laetitia actually became quite animated, telling us about a Vietnamese restaurant she'd found in Mitte which served a superlative *larb*. At a moment when everyone else was safely occupied in other conversations, I asked Finlay how he coped. He told me that he had trained himself not to hear Edgar talking. "When he starts on one of his—I don't even know what to call them—his sock-puppet Socratic dialogues, I space out. The brain is very adaptable. You just have to think of a person as being very very unlikely, essentially impossible, and eventually your frontal cortex just edits them out. Also I check Grindr all through dinner."

"That's what you do in the evenings? Go on the internet and get laid?"

"Sometimes. What do you do?"

"I'm on to Season Two of *Blue Lives*."

"The cop show?"

"That's the one."

"I see."

There was an awkward silence. Laetitia asked if I'd been out

much in Berlin and I told her that I "hadn't got round to it."
She and Finlay seemed confused. Wasn't I desperate to escape
Wannsee? I admitted that I was, and fumbled around for an
explanation. Finally I just said flat out that I didn't really know
why. They let it drop.

Though I hadn't left Wannsee, my walks in the area had
become longer and more strenuous. I would put on my coat
and follow a path round the lake, trudging through muddy
woodland, under winter trees that seemed to set the sky in
relief, their bare branches like cracks in a slab of pale stone.
All along the shoreline there were little beaches and landing
spots. A deep chill slid off the water. It was a place where I
could have lost myself. It would have been so easy to wade out
into the weeds, slipping down a little deeper with each step.

Every day, at least once, I passed by the Kleist grave. The
little four-volume *Collected Works* was now covered with pen-
cil marks and marginalia, a couple of pages stained with oyster
sauce. The more I read, the more I realized that I wasn't dealing with some aristocrat of emotional response, a true poet
in exquisite communication with his feelings. All that nervy
rawness, the excess of violent sentiment, seemed like someone
trying too hard. I don't mean Kleist was a fake. I found nothing cynical in his writing, just panic, self-stimulation, a man
desperately stabbing himself with the needle of his own personality in an attempt to get a response.

One day I was staring at the inscription on the marker,
which now read unpleasantly to me, like a phrase from the
manifesto of an angry young man on his way to murder people
at a Walmart. *Now, O immortality, you are all mine!* The words
are from a play, *The Prince of Homburg,* the speaker a dash-
ing seventeenth-century military commander who is about

to be executed. In a great battle, he has disobeyed orders, spontaneously leading a heroic charge against the enemy. As a result the battle was won, but the Elector is an unusually strict disciplinarian, and the Prince has been court-martialed and sentenced to death. Now, in his final seconds of life, he's gone beyond terror to achieve an exalted state in which he is content—even eager—to die, because he believes that he's going to become an eternal symbol of Prussian honor. Men are leading him blindfolded from his cell. He can see nothing but colors and forms. He persuades himself that angel's wings are growing on his back. *Now, O Immortality, you are all mine!* But there's a twist. Instead of a bullet, the Prince feels a victor's laurel wreath being placed on his head, and the blindfold is taken off to reveal the face of the woman he loves. The whole episode has been a sick joke, a mock execution staged by the Elector and the witty aristocrats of the court. Is this a dream, asks the Prince. What else would it be, replies one of the nobles.

There's a circuit: death is transmuted into glory and glory into love, but the rest of the Prince's life will surely be a letdown, just aimless drifting and *tristesse,* because what could ever top the rush of the last few seconds before a bullet blows your brains out and makes you immortal? The circuit will only be closed when the last connection is made, when love is transmuted back into death. It's the most toxic male fantasy, the orgasmic headshot that will solve all problems in an instant. Poor dumb Kleist, all that pent-up desire to pull the trigger.

I suspect I am not the only person who sometimes imagines kneeling before an executioner in a jihadi propaganda video. I think of what it would be like to be on display, at the mercy of people who hate me, utterly without hope of rescue. I ask myself what it is I would fear most at that moment. Death or pain? Pain is my answer, every time. The sawing motion of the knife, the other exotic ways the bastards might think up to torture me. By contrast, non-existence doesn't seem so terrifying. It also doesn't seem much like an orgasm.

That day I left the grave and walked on for about half an hour, before I emerged out of the forest, back onto suburban streets. A church, an old inn with a heraldic sign. To warm up, I bought coffee at a bakery, where the man behind the counter gave me dirty looks and pretended not to understand my German. I couldn't tell if the problem was me or him. As I drank my coffee, I wandered back towards the Center, passing a couple of dog walkers who nodded and said hello. No one else was around.

As I walked back out onto the main road, a little vintage MG drove past, braked and then reversed back towards me. I bent down to see who was driving and was almost assaulted by the beaming smile of Ulrich or Uwe, the porter from the Deuter Center. He leaned out of the window. He was wearing a tweed cap and string-back driving gloves.

"Hello professor," he said, in his clipped English. "Can I offer you a ride?"

"It's OK. I'm enjoying my walk."

"Where are you going, the Conference House?"

"No. No I'm not. It's OK, thank you. Thank you anyway."

"Get in, I show you something."

I hesitated, not sure how best to get rid of him. I tried making a sort of jaunty farewell gesture and turning to walk away, but he called after me.

"Professor?"

It wasn't possible to pretend that I hadn't heard.

"Yes?"

"Get in."

"No thanks."

"Why not? You're not doing anything else!"

"How do you know?"

"Come on, everyone knows you are having problems with writing. Get in the car, the Conference House will wait."

I was stunned. "What do you mean, everyone knows?"

"Get in."

Something about his bluntness drained me of opposition. I walked around to the other side of the car, opened the door and dropped down into the passenger seat. He turned to me, grinning like a fairytale wolf. "There's nothing in there, you know. A lot of blah blah. Pictures hanging on boards with writing. The Russians took everything, all the furniture. They burned the floorboards for fuel."

"What do you mean, everyone knows?"

He shrugged. "You are never in the Workspace. You are always in your room or walking by the Wannsee. Here you are today, going to the Conference House. This would not be so when your writing was making progress."

"I wasn't going to the Conference House."

He started the engine.

"I save you the trouble. It's very boring. We do something much better."

"What?"

"You will see. Don't worry. It's very close."

We turned onto a side road that led away from the lake into an area of woodland. After a few minutes he turned down a short driveway and parked outside a single-story concrete building, a windowless bunker with a low flat roof. Several other cars were parked outside. There was nothing to identify its function.

We got out, and he retrieved a metal briefcase from the back seat, motioning me to follow him. By the door was a discreet plaque declaring that this was the *Schiessgemeinschaft Wannsee*. The building must have been soundproofed in some way, because as soon as we got through the door, the sound of gunfire was deafening.

Otto greeted the man at the front desk, who looked—with his tightly curled hair, his tracksuit, the cigarette dangling from his lip—as if he'd been frozen at some point during the early nineteen-eighties. He signed us in and we went downstairs to a pistol shooting range, a sunken gallery with baffles on the walls and a big mound of earth at the far end. The whole building smelled of smoke. Two or three positions were occupied by men shooting at cardboard targets.

I was in a trance of suspicion. Ulrich handed me a set of ear protectors and a pair of goggles. His case turned out to contain two black semiautomatic pistols. He laid out a box of ammunition, filled a clip and loaded the guns. He handed one to me. For a moment, I expected him to announce that we would both walk ten paces, turn, and fire.

"Please."

I faced the target, a black-and-white silhouette. I lined up the white dots and squeezed the trigger. Nothing happened.

"The safety," he said. He took the gun from me and flipped a lever on the side. "Try now."

I fired, wide. A casing jumped out of the slide. My second shot was better. I tried to work out if he was surprised. I'm not someone you'd necessarily expect to be familiar with firearms. My mind was full of questions. *How do you know I'm not writing? Do you see the computer logs?* And above all, *Why guns? Why are you introducing guns into this situation?* I started to speak. He tapped his ear protectors, shrugged, and indicated the target.

I shot off a ten-round clip. He took the gun and reloaded it. He took position next to me and emptied his own clip into the target next to mine. In this way, without talking, we each shot off fifty rounds. Finally, he took off his ear protectors.

"So you feel more relaxed now?"

"Sure."

This was a lie. My brain was almost melting from my attempt to work out the angles. I did not for one moment think this encounter was the product of an impulse to be sociable. And a shooting range? A pair of pistols? Every writer knows about Chekhov's gun. It is one of the rules of writing, insofar as there are rules. *One must never place a loaded rifle on the stage if it isn't going to go off. It is wrong to make promises you don't mean to keep.* I was not an actor in a play, so this should have had no bearing on my situation. All the same, it felt as if Ulrich were dropping a hint, nudging a narrative towards a particular resolution.

He drove me back to the Center, swinging the little MG through the front gate and scattering gravel into the flowerbeds. We shook hands and he told me that anytime I wanted to borrow the guns, I had only to ask. I was, he said, a surprisingly good shot.

I went to the library and pretended to flick through an oversize album of pictures of the house and grounds. My eyes skated over a portrait of the man who built it, a Wilhelmine manufacturer of fancy leather goods, gloves and belts and purses. During the Second World War it had been some kind of research institute, and afterwards a club for American officers. Pictures of tennis parties, sailing on the lake. Civilian clothes giving way to uniform. One kind of uniform giving way to another—Deuter, pictured reading in a chair roughly where I was sitting, reading about him—was able to purchase the house from the American occupying forces. I retained little of what I saw. All I could think about was a sound, a single tiny click, the clasp snapping shut on Ulrich's gun case.

Plot is the artificial reduction of life's complexity and randomness. It is a way to give aesthetic form to reality. I went upstairs, lay down on my bed with my laptop open on my chest and carried on with *Blue Lives*. I'd been watching a lot of television drama in Berlin, often several hours a day, retreating from formlessness into soothingly tight plotting. In most ways *Blue Lives* was an entirely unremarkable product. After a lifetime of American police shows I probably wouldn't have devoted yet more hours to watching plainclothes cops brutalize people, let alone spent time on the internet, hate-reading profiles of the "mind behind" the show, had its tone not been so weird, so *off*. On the surface, *Blue Lives* seemed very conventional, but something else was at work, a subtext smuggled into the familiar procedural narrative.

The show's cops were all members of a special unit and they'd lost their moral compass. They were now as bad as the criminals they were pursuing. Everyone—criminals and police—was in high-stakes competition with everyone else, committing acts of appalling violence. When I started watching, the horror of this world had felt safely abstract, so removed from my own life that I could take pleasure in the melodramatic story line.

I'd become very involved with the characters, or if not exactly with the characters, who were quite thinly drawn, then how they dealt with the extreme situations in which they found themselves, their strange combination of recklessness and calculation. They were forced to improvise and make instant decisions, yet had to accept that even the tiniest mistake could be fatal.

That evening, after I'd watched a couple of episodes, my encounter with the porter at the gun range started to seem like just another lurid scene, something happening to a character on-screen. I reheated some takeout leftovers, and ate them as a third episode began to autoplay. I was bored, sick of the car chases and the shouting and the bad blues-rock soundtrack and was beginning to wonder about switching to something else. The protagonist, Carson, was working a case with his partner, Penske, knocking on doors in a project, when they heard a violent domestic dispute. Bursting into an apartment they found a black man and a white woman, both in their underwear, the woman with a visible wound above her eye. Carson, full of chivalrous outrage, pistol-whipped the abuser, a spontaneous outburst that turned into a bloody and protracted scene. As the man screamed and begged for Carson's mercy, Penske took a look around. In a cupboard he found a suitcase with a lot of money, banded up drug-dealer style in thousand-dollar rolls. The two cops looked at the suitcase, then at each other. They made a judgment. This is your lucky day, they told the beaten, disfigured man. They took the money and left.

Their victory soon turned sour. Two days later, the woman who'd been at the apartment was found strangled to death in an empty shipping container. It seemed likely that the drug dealer boyfriend was responsible. Feeling angry and guilty,

Carson and Penske searched obsessively, kicking down the doors of shooting galleries and crack houses. When they found the boyfriend, they took him to an abandoned factory and tied him to a chair. As Carson tortured the man with an electric drill, his face was framed tightly by the camera, a haunted grimace soundtracked by appalling screaming. Usually I could watch dramatized violence, even convincingly shot and acted, without feeling much beyond a sort of defensive boredom and a mild interest in the plot, but something about this was different. I felt—there is no other way to put it—at risk, as if I were present in the room and there would be consequences for watching. It seemed to me that unless I did something to prevent the torture, I would be mentally and spiritually violated by it, by its imprint, its presence in my memory. Carson forced open the boyfriend's bloodied mouth and pushed the drill between his teeth. Although nothing was shown beyond a few impressionistic frames, it was terrible to watch, and somehow I had forgotten that these were not real events and I had only to press the space bar on my laptop to pause them. Carson, whose face was now spattered with blood, looked directly into the camera and spoke. "The whole earth," he said, "perpetually steeped in blood, is nothing but a vast altar on which all living things must be sacrificed without end, without restraint, without pause, until the consummation of things." Then he went back to his grisly work.

The effect was strange and upsetting, doubly so because the line was entirely out of keeping with the rest of the show. Usually the actors never acknowledged the audience and Carson's dialogue consisted of grunts and threats. Sacrificed without end, he said, and his eyes filled with sorrow. It was a different sorrow to mine, the sorrow of the accomplice who fears that watching will carry an unforeseen moral cost. Nor was it the sorrow of the victim whose screams formed the soundtrack to the image of Carson's face. It was the executioner's sorrow, the disappointment of a man who has been initiated into the great mystery of human suffering, only to find that it is just a puerile joke.

Finally the episode ended and as the credits rolled, I slapped the laptop shut before another could start. My breathing was ragged, my heart racing. I kept asking myself what I had just seen. The sense of transgression, of having done something wrong, was very powerful.

People never talk about the insanity of the decision to start a family with everything an adult knows about the world, or about the terrible sensation of risk that descends on a man, I mean a man in particular, a creature used to relative speed and strength and power, when he has children. All at once, you are vulnerable in ways you may never have been before. Before I was a father I'd felt safe. Now I had a child, everything had changed, and it seemed to me that safety in the past was no predictor of safety in the future. I was getting older, weaker. Eventually I would fall behind, find myself separated from the pack.

REI WAS IN BED. I had woken her up. She listened to me talking, her head still on the pillow, her eyes intermittently closing.

"I mean, what security do we have? The only real security is money. Hello?"

"I'm listening. We're fine for money. Honestly, we're OK."

"Are we? Not really. What if one of us got sick? What if things change, if we have to move?"

"Why would we have to move?"

"Have you been online lately? I think this is what Weimar Germany must have felt like. The sense that something was coming. We have to expect the unexpected. A Black Swan event. We don't want to be the ones who hesitated. I mean, Walter Benjamin—"

"It's six in the morning and you want to talk about Walter Benjamin."

"I'm bringing him up because he's relevant. He wasn't a fit man, an athletic man. When he fled he dragged a heavy case of books over the Pyrenees. He took an overdose when he was denied entry at the Spanish border. He wasn't mentally equipped to survive. Why? Because he was a collector, tied to his collection. He was hoping, irrationally, that something would work out and the Nazis would let him stay in his study. By the time he realized how ludicrous a wish that was, it was too late."

"You're talking about the Nazis. I'm going to put the phone down."

"Don't, honey. Just a minute. People extrapolate from what they know. They find it hard to imagine radical change. It's a cognitive bias. Ask yourself honestly, what will happen to people like us if they come to power? They hate us."

"Who hates us?"

"The bastards. It's always people like us who go first."

"Look, I'm as worried as you are. There's actually a fundraiser tomorrow night. A lot of legal people. We're going to back our slate of candidates and make sure the Democrats have the best possible chance on the night. Besides no one seriously thinks it's going to happen. Have you seen the polls? I'm not minimizing whatever anxiety you're feeling, but we'll handle it, OK? We're smart people. If it comes, we'll see it coming."

This was a problem between us, Rei's faith in the democratic process, in the Democratic Party, in the essential reasonableness of the world. To me, the presidential election later that year was only a small part of what I feared. The shift was bigger than one candidate, one country. The rising tide of gangsterism felt global. I saw nothing reasonable about what was coming. Nothing reasonable at all.

Rei yawned. I tried to put it as straightforwardly as I could. "I just—I don't want to spend my last years scavenging for canned goods in the ruins of some large city."

"Would you listen to yourself?"

"Honey."

"I'm going to have to be up with Nina in a few hours. I have to get more sleep."

"Sorry. Of course. I'll let you go."

"Go to bed."

The screen went blank.

I said the rest of it silently, the things I badly wanted to tell her but couldn't: that I was afraid and needed her help, that every day we were alive was precious and ought to be filled with love and honesty, that I was feeling very far away and the distance scared me and I was worried that if something happened I wouldn't be able to protect her and Nina, not just because I was in Berlin and they were in New York, but because I lacked power and money, the only true protection in the world. I lacked so many other things, necessary personal qualities, courage and stamina and strength of will. I wanted to tell her that the future I foresaw was unimaginably bleak and terrible and I was beginning to realize that I'd been complacent, or perhaps just selfish, absorbed in my little projects, my lofty thoughts and scribblings. I had not taken the most vital thing seriously, which was safety. The safety of my family. Without safety, we had nothing at all.

IN 1801, at the age of twenty-three, Kleist had a crisis, brought about by reading Kant, who taught that the human senses are unreliable, and so we are unable to apprehend the truth that lies beneath the surface of things, the famous *Ding an sich,* the "Thing in Itself." This was a huge blow to Kleist, who was planning to gather as much truth as he could while on earth, then transmit his accumulated wisdom to future versions of himself, living "on other stars," eventually producing a perfect and complete man. The discovery that he was probably not even seeing the world correctly, let alone collecting points towards cosmic gnosis, led him into a deep depression.

He tried to distract himself by getting drunk and going to the theater. He wrote to a member of his all-female lecture circle (he lectured, they listened), saying that he had an "indescribable longing" to cry on her breast.

I was sympathetic to the desire for a system. Who wouldn't want to have an answer for everything? But twenty-three is a reasonable age to accept that the world is more complex than whatever map you've made of it, and systems, however metaphysical or abstract, are never innocent. They do the dirty work of knowledge, clearing the ground for action, for taking control. The truth is that the savages should always eat the anthropologist. They should murder the botanist who comes tripping through the jungle looking for the blue flower, because after him will come the geologist and the surveyor and the mining engineer and the soldiers to protect the miners as they work.

There could be no clearer demonstration of this than the use made by Frau Janowitz of the Deuter Center's logs. One afternoon a letter was slipped under my door, accompanying the usual breakdown of my Workspace computer usage. There was a café by the station which had bad coffee and a few greasy Formica tables. I took the letter there to read it. The woman behind the counter had never liked my face. As I settled myself with my barely caffeinated mug of milk froth and opened the envelope, she hovered nearby, cleaning tables, sweeping aggressively round my feet. Written on heavy Deuter Center letterhead, the communication had a legal tone. It itemized how many hours I'd spent in the Workspace (not enough), how many of the communal meals I had attended (not that many) and how many of the public lectures, roundtables and other events I had missed (all of them). I had, she wrote, "exhibited disdain for the ethos of Herr Deuter" and failed to understand the "need for full participation." She was concerned by my "lack of mutuality." If I felt unable "to join in the life of the Center," perhaps it would be better if arrangements were made for me to leave.

I wondered if my situation was irremediable. If I showed contrition, would they give me another chance? The waitress was impossible to ignore and the coffee even worse than usual, so I left the café and headed back out into the chill Wannsee morning. To be fair, I hadn't actually seen a calendar of events. It must have been part of the slew of paper clogging up the pigeonhole with my name on it in the downstairs corridor. I considered walking by the lake, but ended up back in my room. Though the curtains were drawn, just as I'd left them, the dirty laundry had been folded and the snack food packaging and beer bottles made to disappear. My mess hadn't vanished, exactly, but it had been organized. I looked at the books and papers on my desk, carefully piled up and straightened. They seemed diminished, unserious, the detritus of a boy's hobby. Why had I not chosen to do the things that men do? Ordering the world. Exerting my will. Instead I'd built whatever this was, this rat's nest of paper.

I opened my laptop and called home, wondering sourly, as usual, if that connection was monitored, like the one in the Workspace. Rei answered, and the screen framed a rectangle of kitchen: a high-chair, a plastic bowl containing the butchered remains of a scrambled egg, a single snow boot improbably sitting on the table beside it.

"Hello stranger. We're getting ready for a play date."

Nina bounced into frame, wearing the pink tutu that I loathed. She jumped up and down in front of the laptop, then brought her face very close. I realized she was kissing the screen, and this produced an involuntary smile that jolted through my jaw, an almost painful physical pang of love. The screen-kissing became giggly and deliberately disgusting, big licks of the tongue that left smears and bubbles of spittle. Rei scolded her and hoisted her backwards, wiping the screen roughly with her sleeve. I saw that my wife was still in her pajamas. Her hair hung over her face. She squinted at me through her glasses, looking harassed.

"I can't really talk. It's one of those mornings. As soon as I drop her I have to get all the way to the Upper East Side."

"Politics or pleasure?"

"Ha ha. A coffee morning for prospective donors. I have to go and give a presentation, make nice."

"Go magic all those checkbooks out of all those expensive purses."

"Everything OK? You're not sad, are you?"

"No, of course not."

"Don't get sad. I love you."

"Love you too."

The screen went blank.

I felt reassured by this scrap of conversation, and at the same time bleak. Clearly, I ought to accept defeat and leave the Deuter Center at once. I hated being there, no one liked me, and I wasn't doing anything useful, but I wasn't ready to go back home. I wasn't qualified. I hadn't solved myself. I spent an hour or so on the internet, falling down various rabbit holes, before I finally hit on one of the things I was looking for, the source of the strange words Carson had spoken as he tortured his victim on *Blue Lives*. As I suspected, they were a quotation, but they didn't come from some well-known "great book," but a peculiar and recondite writer, Joseph-Marie, Comte de Maistre. Insofar as he is remembered at all, Maistre is usually thought of as a footnote to the intellectual history of the eighteenth century, a rigid medieval mind shocked to find itself in the Age of Reason. He was a contemporary of Kleist, a Savoyard aristocrat flung into exile by the hateful French Revolution, first in Switzerland, then in the backwater court of Cagliari in Sardinia, and finally to Saint Petersburg, where he served as the Ambassador of the King of Savoy to Tsar Alexander I. He was a royalist zealot who hated Jacobins, scientists, Protestants, journalists, democrats, Jews, Freemasons, secularists and various other categories of people that he thought of as comprising "the sect," a Satanic conspiracy to undermine the divinely ordained power of Pope and King. In his writing, he dedicated himself to fighting the pernicious influence of reason and liberty wherever it reared its head. Carson was quoting from a text known as *The Saint Petersburg Dialogues, or Conversations on the Temporal Government of Providence,* which in its time was scandalous enough that it could only be published after the author's death. Three speakers, a Knight, a Senator and a Count, debate questions of morality and politics, laying out the author's bleak worldview—that the earth is a cesspit of corruption, and salvation can only come from abject prostration before God, and before the powerful people that God has established to rule here. Why would the writer or writers of an American police procedural make such a peculiar reference? I didn't know.

I put on my coat and hat, and went out for a walk. I wanted to avoid the Kleist grave, so I headed for the other side of the lake, past a leisure center and down a sandy path into an area of woodland. As I walked through the trees, four or five young brown-skinned men in jeans and padded jackets came towards me over the rough ground. They had the slightly mincing gait of people who aren't dressed warmly enough for the weather, boys laughing and talking, enjoying their power to fill up a space. They passed either side of me, none of them making eye contact. Their conversation faltered, then started up again once they were at a distance.

The woodland ended abruptly and I walked out onto a wintery beach. The icy sand crunched underfoot. The water had the look of black ink. Ahead of me was a long brick pavilion. The Strandbad was famous in Berlin, a nineteen-thirties lido built in the austere style of the *Neue Sachlichkeit,* the New Objectivity, a leisure facility for working people, a surviving fragment of social democratic Utopia.

I walked between rows of two-seater chairs covered in canopies, perfect for sheltering on blustery northern beaches. Some way down I saw a woman sitting in one, reading a book, her feet tucked underneath her. As I approached, she swung her legs nervously to the ground and it seemed to me that she was getting ready to run. With a pang of embarrassment, I recognized her as the cleaner from the Deuter Center.

The gray façade of the Wannsee Conference House was clearly visible on the far side of the lake, and just at that moment I'd been trying to recall the name of the dining room waiter who'd first pointed it out to me. I saw him every day, it was frustrating. That kind of lapse feels worse when it is someone who serves you. Your lack of courtesy seems boorish, an assertion of status. I think it was this minor sense of shame that made me feel obliged to stop and say hello to the cleaner. I intended to walk on with a curt but friendly nod, a minimal form of contact which would have been entirely appropriate, but instead I stopped in front of her and formed my mouth into a brittle smile.

"It's nice to see you," I said, instantly absurd. Why hadn't I just walked on? "Not at work, I mean. It's nice to see you not working."

When she was cleaning, she wore a plastic tabard over her clothes. Now she was wrapped in a long black coat, her feet in heavy army boots. I saw that she'd been reading a book, a little yellow Reclam paperback. As if defending against my curiosity, she slipped it into her coat pocket. The hair she usually hid behind was itself hidden under a thick black woolen hat, and she was wearing heavy-framed glasses, so it was still hard to see what she looked like. A thin face and a prominent jaw. The word *mousy* is overused, but there was something quick and brown and slightly verminous about her.

"Yes, hello," she said. She got up, and for a moment stood straight and tall, facing into the wind. Then she hunched her shoulders, retracting herself, as if to reduce the amount of space she occupied. "Goodbye." I watched her scurrying down the beach and couldn't shake the feeling that she had shrugged on that furtive persona like a winter coat.

I spent the rest of the day watching *Blue Lives*. The man Carson tortured to death turned out to work for La Mettrie, a Haitian drug lord and one of the most feared criminals in the city. La Mettrie's gang was efficient and completely nihilistic. It was made clear in various gruesome scenes that he was prepared to do anything to maintain his grip on power. He was inhuman in his ruthlessness and completely inflexible about the enforcement of his own terrible set of rules. Informers were subjected to medieval agonies. A subordinate who stole from him was mutilated and murdered by the person who had been tapped to take his job, part of a macabre interview process. The pace and intensity of the murders and other acts of retribution accelerated, and somehow, though each lurid scene went by into the past in a fast-flowing stream of images, instantly replaced by the next and the next and the next, it became cumulatively more upsetting to watch. As I autoplayed episode after episode, Carson began to seem almost naïve, his crimes mere dabblings in horror compared to those of La Mettrie. In the projects and row houses of Brownsville and East New York, the Haitian's gang reigned supreme. *Blue Lives* was fixated on the terror of their victims, as if it wanted to subject the viewer as thoroughly as possible to the experience of being at the mercy of an absolute, capriciously sadistic master. And every so often in the dialogue, I would notice another strange phrase or sentence, a line or two of elevated speech. *Man is wolf to man. War is father of all and king of all.* I recognized some as quotations and every one was out of place in a naturalistic thriller. I came to suspect that they were an insider joke, the entire show just an elaborate illustration of some point of view of the writer, something to do with the world's hopelessness. Look at what horrors are possible, was the message. The only rational response is despair.

Carson's wife, Emily, was presented as an innocent, Carson's "one good thing," a traditional working-class Catholic woman who stayed at home in a small town on the New Jersey side of the Hudson, raising towheaded blond twins who looked as if they'd stepped out of an old TV commercial. Emily was Carson's prize. He maintained her in a fetishistic state of purity. Sometimes we saw him making distracted phone calls at softball games or turning up late to a parent-teacher conference, but throughout all his corrupt dealings he managed to maintain a public image of integrity. As far as the world was concerned, he was a white man in good standing, a faithful husband and a loving dad. To his police buddies, his household was a miraculous survival from an older America, a symbol of everything they had sworn to protect and serve.

The wall that Carson had erected around his family began to erode when he and his men raided one of La Mettrie's stash houses, getting away with over a million dollars in money and drugs. Carson now had a storage unit full of La Mettrie's heroin, and The Crew was putting together a deal to sell it to some Aryan Nations skinheads who wanted to finance their ethnically pure homeland in Idaho. They celebrated the deal at a strip club, under a murky blue light that reminded me of the Chinese restaurant in Wannsee.

La Mettrie was not the kind of gangster who had old-fashioned compunctions about getting family involved. One of his men left a grisly calling card at Carson's home, decapitating the pet cat and nailing the corpse to the door. Emily phoned her husband, crying hysterically, just as The Crew were trying to move the money and drugs out of the storage unit. They were understandably tense, expecting to be attacked, and Carson had to leave to deal with the situation, which made him feel that he was losing face. He was angry at his wife, but as soon as he saw the dead cat, he realized what had happened. He persuaded Emily that it was nothing (she had a cloying, almost bovine trust in him) and drove off in his car, snarling with vengeful fury as soon as he was out of her sight.

Unfortunately for Carson, La Mettrie and some of his most barbaric henchmen were already in position, watching his house. The gang lord, slumped in the back seat of a black SUV, turned his heavy-lidded eyes to the camera and began one of the show's strange monologues. "There is no instant of time when one creature is not being devoured by another. Over all these numerous races of animals, man is placed, and his destructive hand spares nothing that lives. He kills to obtain food, he kills to clothe himself, he kills to adorn himself, he kills to attack, he kills to defend himself, he kills to instruct himself, he kills to amuse himself, he kills to kill. Proud and terrible king, he wants everything, and nothing resists him."

La Mettrie leaned past the camera, opened the door, and got out of the car. Followed by his men, he crossed the darkened residential street and made his way round to the rear of the house, where, without the slightest hesitation, he smashed his way in through the patio doors. A cut to a shot of Carson's sleeping children—and then nothing. A little circle started revolving in the middle of my screen. At this crucial moment my stream had dropped, the image had stalled, and no amount of refreshing or restarting would bring it back.

I realized that the technical problems didn't lie with the video stream. I also had no email and my phone had no Wi-Fi connection. Automatically, I got out of bed to reboot the router, only to remember that I wasn't at home and didn't even know where the router was. I was helpless. I experienced a premonition of some kind, a sensation of foreboding. I would have to call the IT department. Outside it was dark. For the first time in hours, I looked at a clock. It was later than I'd thought. I drank some whisky but it was hard to drop off to sleep. My mind crackled with images of home invasion, of masked gangsters and terrified children. I wanted to call Rei, to check that everything was OK, but I knew I was in no fit state to hold a conversation.

The next morning, I ate a bowl of cereal at my desk, com-

pulsively checking the internet connection. I dialed the extension of the IT office. It went to voicemail. They were in. I was
sure of it. Everyone knows that tech support never pick up if
they can possibly help it. I always experience low-level panic
when I'm denied internet access, even if I have no immediate need for it. I tried the number several more times. At last,
feeling like a doomed polar explorer, I pulled on my pants
and prepared to go outside. There was an elevator, but I took
the stairs, figuring that I'd be less likely to encounter other
people.

The basement corridor was empty, but from behind a door
came bass-heavy explosions and the muffled crackle of high-
energy weapons, the telltale sounds of space battle. I knocked,
but there was no reply. I figured Player One couldn't hear me,
so I tried the handle and let myself in to a small but efficiently
ordered office. Shelving lined the walls, stacked with baskets
of cable and audiovisual equipment. The man playing the
game sat with his back to me, enthroned on some kind of high-
backed task chair. He faced an array of screens, one showing
his game, the second what looked to be audio or video editing
interface. A third was tiled with surveillance feeds. The front
gate from two angles, the back door of the kitchen, the rear
elevation of the house looking up from the lake. There were
interior views. Stairways. Other spaces, dark and indistinct.
In one of these, I spotted a white shape, a naked old man walking across the frame, from left to right. You could only see his
midsection—a downward-folded white belly, the little cone of
a penis jutting out of a bird's-nest of hair.

The gamer must have pressed some kind of hotkey, because
all at once his screens went blank. He swiveled round on his
space-age throne and squinted at me from behind a curtain

of long dyed-black hair. We'd met, if you could call it that, when he scanned my iris during my orientation. Since then, I sometimes saw him standing around outside the kitchen, smoking with one of the waiters. He was in his twenties and always wore more or less the same thing—black combat pants tucked into army boots, tee shirts with the logos of obscure metal bands.

"Hello," I said. "I think the internet's down."

His expression soured. As I waited for him to say something, I tried to process what I'd seen on his screen. It was clear that the camera wasn't mounted in a public place. It was located at waist height, perhaps on or under a table, framing a view of a bed exactly like the one I slept in every night. The location was unmistakably one of the Center's guest rooms. And I would have known that bulky body anywhere. It was Edgar.

The gamer was staring at me, as if he'd caught me in some kind of transgression rather than the other way around. Unable to deal with his weird energy, I looked away. The basement office had very little natural light. As if to compensate, there were artificial light sources of all kinds—bright tracks on the ceiling, a novelty lamp in the shape of a rabbit, a string of little LEDs. At the other end of the room was another desk, piled high with neatly stacked hard drives. Until then I hadn't noticed the man sitting behind it. He was older than the gamer and wore jeans with a crisp white shirt and wire-frame glasses, an outfit that made him look like someone playing an architect in an advertisement for financial services. He came round to shake my hand.

"Hello Professor. What brings you here?"

The gamer was already back to destroying the solar system, a pair of massive headphones clamped over his ears. On his main screen a swarm of light attack craft buzzed around a mothership. The video editing interface was open again, and so were the surveillance views, though they seemed different, all the screens showing externals of the house and grounds.

The architect looked at the back of the gamer's chair and gave an apologetic shrug. "Lunch break. So how can I help?"

"I've been trying to call you."

"Oh yes? In general, email is better for us."

"Sure, but the internet is down."

"Where, in the Workspace?"

"Upstairs in my room. I can't get online."

"Ah, yes. We know about that."

I waited, but instead of explaining or offering to help, he picked up one of his drives and turned it over in his hands, squinting at the ports on the back.

"I'm trying to work," I said. "This is kind of inconvenient."

"Of course."

"What am I supposed to do?"

"I can tell you I am sorry for the problem, but I don't think it will be fixed today."

It's always hard to judge tone when people aren't speaking their first language.

"Why not?"

"A technical issue. A hardware issue."

It was no good. Involuntarily I began to project forward into a possible future in which I was screaming at him, trying to make him see how vital it was for me, for my creative process, for my book, a very important book on poetry, you could say important *for* poetry, perhaps even for art more widely, to have uninterrupted internet access. I could feel the present connecting itself to this future, setting up links, exploring the route.

"This makes my show very difficult," I said. "I mean my work. I'm at a crucial stage in my work."

"Of course. May I suggest the shared space? The internet functions very well there. Actually there is a fast line, a fiber optic cable. It is much better than the connection in the main house."

"That's out of the question. I can't concentrate in there. I can't think."

"The connection in the shared space is very good. The rest of the house has a wireless network but we always get problems. It is not easy to amplify the signal so it reaches well everywhere. Under the roof, in your room, is always the worst place."

"I had no difficulty until today."

"I can only say you are lucky. It is very unreliable."

"Let's keep it simple. Just tell me, exactly, when will this new hardware be arriving?"

"Soon, I hope. In the next days."

"Days? How many days?"

He could not say. I went back up to my room, defeated. Because I still had no Wi-Fi, I couldn't do the various diverting and quasi-important things I did on the internet—reading Wikipedia pages, downloading pictures of people in war zones—all the subtle and mysterious components of my not-writing. I was thrown back on my own resources, into myself, or what took place in the space where a self ought to have been. The fate of Carson's children was very important to me. If he saved them, it meant that all was still well. By "well," I meant that it was what I would expect to happen. It would be the conventional narrative move. But if Carson's children died, what then? The show was fixated on forcing me to see shocking images of violence. But it wouldn't show that, would it? Once I would have been certain. Now I wasn't so sure. Of course it would have taken a couple of minutes on the internet to find a *Blue Lives* plot synopsis, but somehow I didn't go down to the Workspace and look. There was an element of self-protection in this. The more I considered it, the more I was afraid that the answer would open a trapdoor and send me falling through into a new level of hell.

I made all this—whatever it was, this mental garbage— very important. I bustled around in it, kicked it about like a pile of leaves, all to distract myself from another disturbing question—had I really seen video of Edgar walking naked across his room? Why would someone want to capture that? I lay down on top of my freshly made bed, with my arms by my sides. This seemed to me a visually unremarkable way of being in a room, a neutral position, postural camouflage. If Edgar was being watched, it was logical to assume that we all were. And by "we all" I meant primarily me. *They* could be watching *me*. I settled on the plural because it seemed unlikely that the gamer would watch a surveillance feed in an office with his manager, unless that manager had condoned or even ordered it. Thus it was more than likely that the surveillance, if it existed, and wasn't just some kind of mental misfire, a figment of my imagination, was being conducted on behalf of the Deuter Center.

Reluctantly, I decided that I had to check. I took a look round my room. I examined the underside of my desk, the frames of the pictures, but I could find no sign of a camera. Even looking felt absurd, the beginning of a slippery slope that would end with me surrounded by splintered drywall and pried-up floorboards. As a last resort I tried reading, but I couldn't even settle myself in the armchair, let alone focus on a book. I sat down at my desk and considered things. It wasn't just the lack of internet, the practical inability to perform the various routines I'd invented to fill my time. Somewhere in his writings about prison, Foucault describes the cells in the Panopticon, calling them "small theaters in which each actor is alone, perfectly individualized and constantly visible." So it was for me, with the possibility that the all-seeing eye of a twenty-year-old gamer was scrutinizing my movements. As long as I sat there, I would be forced to perform myself for him. Everything I did would take place against an imaginary headwind of adolescent gothic snark. I got in bed and pulled the covers over my head.

I must have slept, because when the knock came at my door I was profoundly disorientated. It was morning, at least that's what my phone said. The knock was insistent, official. I was a fool to answer it. As usual, Frau Janowitz was very smartly turned out, in a business suit with a pearl necklace and matching studs. She looked as if she were on her way to make a presentation at an investment bank. How could she fail to notice the smell of stale Singapore noodles wafting about the eminent scholar, the five-day stubble? I was the epitome of middle-aged male dereliction. It was hard to meet her eye.

I saw no way I could invite Frau Janowitz into my room, though it was—relatively speaking—in a good state. The thought of her pacing about, examining my desk and my unmade bed, was too traumatic. So I had to weather her visible offense at being forced to hold our conversation in the doorway. Was I sick, she wanted to know. Would I like her to call a doctor? I assured her that I was in good health.

Frau Janowitz told me that she wanted to discuss the letter she had sent. I said I didn't think that was necessary. Sleeping dogs, I said, trying to keep a pleading tone out of my voice. She disagreed. It was part of the ethos of the Deuter Center that matters "like the one between us" had to be addressed face-to-face. In a Deuterian spirit of openness, she wanted to offer me an opportunity to tell her about any personal problems which might factor into her assessment. I told her that I had no desire to factor anything into her assessment, because I was actually on my way to the Workspace. I had come to the end of a period of reflection and now felt ready to take my research to the next level. I heard myself using the phrase *take my research to the next level*.

"I'm also going to be at dinner tonight."

"That is good."

"Thank you for your understanding. And for your concern. I mean to say, thank you for your consideration."

I was stuck in a loop, repeating phrases that sounded as if they'd sprung from the pages of a business English manual. *I am grateful for your. Your attention to this matter is highly.* It was a tone I hoped might resonate with Frau Janowitz. I wanted her to conclude that we had communicated fully and professionally and now she could leave me the fuck alone. But I couldn't find an elegant way to exit the situation and I was beginning to sweat and feel dizzy, so I muttered a curt *best regards* and closed the door in her face.

Looking at my phone I saw I had two missed calls from Rei. I texted her *don't worry all fine u ok* and since that did not seem to be adequate *can't talk rn explain later,* but she immediately texted back *pls call me,* which I found very stressful. I didn't think I could speak to her. She'd hear something in my voice and pick away and I would find myself, as I always did when we argued, skewered on some barb of logic, repeating I don't know I don't know as I tried to work out how I'd failed yet again to convey how I was feeling. But I told myself to be an adult, and called her number. Though she wouldn't be able to see me, I turned instinctively away from the bed.

"Hello?"

"Hey, it's me."

"So you still exist? You sound very far away."

"Just a moment. I'll change position."

I went into the bathroom. The idea of being watched as I made the call was making me nervous. Even as I spoke, I was scanning the room, looking for places where a camera could be hidden.

"Is this better?"

"Yes."

"Can you hear me now?"

"There's an echo. Are you OK? I've been calling. I left messages."

"I'm sorry."

"Why don't you switch on the video. I want to see you."

"I can't. The internet's down. I'm not sure how long for."

"I just wanted to know if you were OK. Everything's OK, right?"

"I'm great."

"Really? Are you sure you're OK in that place?"

"I'm fine."

"You don't want to come back? Come home, if it's not working out."

"Where's Nina?"

"It's Wednesday. She has dance class. Paulette's picking her up."

"So everything's fine."

"Are you really OK? You sound strange."

"Sure. Just working. Do you have the number?"

"For what?"

"Sorry. For Nina's preschool."

"Sure, but why do you need it? Has something happened? Did one of the teachers email you or something? They usually go through me."

"No. I just—I mean, I know it's stupid. I just wanted to make sure she's OK. That you're both OK."

"We're fine, honestly. What's up with the internet?"

"I don't know. It's like they're messing with me."

"They're what?"

I changed the subject, said something about my book, how I was making progress. There was a silence, then she swore under her breath and I could tell from a series of creaks and exhalations that she was sitting back in her chair at the office, sighing and dragging the fingers of her free hand through her hair, as she often did when she was exasperated.

"When your writing is going well you usually want to talk about it, tell me stories."

I tried for that tone, that elusive upbeat tone. "You're fine. Nina's fine. That's the main thing."

"Why aren't you talking to me?"

"I am. I totally am. Look, I'm glad you guys are OK, someone's calling me. One of my colleagues. I have to go. Love you."

I ended the call. Sitting on the clean Deuter-white tiles of the bathroom floor, I could be honest with myself. I found scrutiny stressful, even from Rei. Particularly from Rei, because I wanted to seem admirable to her, for her to be happy that I was her man. I was obviously not ready to go home. I would have to find some way to stay. I went to the Workspace and watched the cursor blink at the top left corner of my document. Paralyzed by self-consciousness, I tried to relax by inventorying the things I actually wanted to hide. There was sexual stuff, of course. What I liked to do, what I fantasized about, the pornography I sometimes looked at on the internet. Not that any of it was very interesting. My coordinates were unremarkable and my preference was for images that weren't particularly explicit. I'd done some drugs, but I wasn't a police officer or an airline pilot. No one cares about a writer getting high. I'd committed some petty crimes. As a teenager I'd had a phase of vandalism, breaking windows and tearing the aerials off cars. Once or twice I'd shoplifted small objects. The weekend before I went to Germany, as I pushed Nina round a phone store, I'd impulsively stolen an overpriced charging cable. There was no reason to do it. I had the money to pay. What other secrets did I have? I'd cheated on a couple of girlfriends, though never on Rei. I'd dented more than one person's fender while trying to get into or out of a tight parking space and then driven off without leaving a note. To my knowledge, I had never seriously hurt anybody. I had no offshore bank accounts, no hidden second family. I had no insider knowledge about anyone high up in government or business, had nothing to reveal that would move a market or strike a blow against the interests of the ruling class. The paltriness of my secret life was disappointing, and as I contemplated it, I realized that my fear of exposure didn't stem from shame, or even the importance I attached to my little secrets, but from their inconsequence. What I wanted to hide was my ordinariness, the fact that I was nothing special, not very bad or very good, not inventive or daring or original. The tracks on which my mind ran had been rutted over centuries by the wheels of my forebears.

Dinner turned out to be a special occasion. *Schnitzelnacht* was a tradition. Very popular with the foreigners, said the waiter, as if daring us not to enjoy it. There were several new fellows present, and though Edgar was dining in, my hope was that he'd be fighting on so many social fronts that I'd be able to talk more or less uninterrupted to Finlay about some undemanding and not terribly personal topic, cinema or art. We'd developed a habit of doing this, the conversational equivalent of standing side by side flipping through the bins in a record store.

A gong was sounded, and from the kitchen came the chef, followed by his staff. He was a gaunt, angular man, without a trace of the stereotypical sensuality of his profession. He looked as if he subsisted on cigarettes. Greeting us without warmth, he launched into a speech (in English) about the origins of the schnitzel, touching on the struggle for ascendency between the Wiener Schnitzel and its Italian archrival, the Cotoletta Milanese, the disputed involvement of Field Marshal Radetzky (of the Strauss march) who may or may not have ordered Emperor Franz Josef's chefs to dredge a piece of veal in egg and breadcrumbs, and the opinion of certain food historians that the Arabs had brought the schnitzel to Europe when they invaded Andalusia in the eighth century. Personally, he did not find the story of a Moorish origin convincing. As a proud native of Berlin and a Berlin chef, it was natural that he should care most about his native tradition. During the Second World War, when meat was scarce, schnitzel had been made from cow udder. In the East, before the fall of the GDR, it was common to make a dish called Jägerschnitzel, from a kind of spiced pork sausage. Tonight, his kitchen would offer Wiener Schnitzel, Cotoletta Milanese and Berlin pork schnitzel, so we would be able to try all three. Here he ended, and the table broke into uncertain applause.

As we ate our schnitzel medley, Edgar was focused on jousting with Per and Alistair about income inequality, until Per unhorsed him with a statistic—I didn't hear what it was—and he changed the subject to the regressive nature of privacy, wagging a reprimanding finger as if someone had made a dubious and easily falsifiable claim. No one, as far as I could see, had made a claim of any kind—Edgar had unilaterally introduced a new topic—but I'd now spent enough time at the receiving end of his table talk to recognize this as one of his regular tricks. The right to privacy was no more or less than the right to lie, he said. To misrepresent yourself to the world. It incubated fraud and corruption, and despite what liberals claimed it was not some sacred universal that all humans needed in order to survive. The Chinese didn't even have the concept. I was staring at the tablecloth thinking *shut up shut up shut up* when to my surprise, I heard Laetitia correcting him.

"No Edgar, I know that's something people repeat, but it's just old-fashioned Orientalism. The character 'si' which is generally translated into English as 'private' or 'privacy,' has a lot of different meanings. Some are to do with selfishness, so it's hard to talk about it in an altogether positive way. That's all. Nothing more."

"Precisely what I'm saying. Privacy is purely a Western cultural construct, perhaps a product of the industrial revolution or low nuptuality west of the Hajnal line, and so really we can discount it. The implications—"

"No!" Laetitia's voice was firm. "On this, Edgar, you don't get to speak."

Edgar's head swiveled round like a gun turret on a battleship. Laetitia met his gaze. There was something glassy and yet final about her stare. I realized she was more than usually drunk.

"Saying privacy is culturally inflected is not the same as 'having no concept of privacy,' like little ants or robots. I know these distinctions are very trivial to you, but they are not to me."

Seeing that he'd lost, Edgar changed the topic, without missing a beat. People, he opined, had an irrational fear of numbers. Fear of numbers was a malaise, particularly among liberal arts types who didn't have the most elementary grounding in mathematics. It led to all kinds of mystical nonsense. Per suggested gently that not everything was amenable to a quantitative approach. Finlay, who should have known better, joined in, saying that there were good reasons to be skeptical about quantification, for example big data and the intrusion of the state into personal life.

Edgar turned to him and scoffed. "You, sir, strike me as exactly the type who's given to signing petitions and open letters. Free this or that, asking the government to fix things for you. How would you do your diversity surveys if you don't let the government collect information?"

Finlay gave him a sharp look. "*My* diversity surveys?" Edgar stared blandly back, so he continued. "Any fool can see that biases are built into these systems, and unfettered information-gathering is going to be abused. People of color understand that only too well. Why is it so hard for you to accept that we need protection from intrusion?"

The wagging finger made another appearance. "Typical. You're always demanding a government agency or a corporation disclose things to you, but what are you claiming for yourself, in your little basement, the grubby hiding place of your soul?"

"The grubby—Jesus Christ." Everyone looked surprised, and I realized I'd spoken out loud. Edgar made a sour *moue* and turned his attention to me.

"People could be hiding anything."

"Oh really?"

Alistair put a hand on my arm. "Come on, now."

Finlay shook his head. "It's obvious you don't see the racial dimension to this. Black people been struggling for our humanity over centuries now and one of the weapons you always use is to classify us, reduce us to statistics."

"Humanity?"

The word seemed to spark deep in Edgar's amygdala, lighting up some primitive anger node. I don't believe he intended to bring his hand down on the table as hard as he did. The effect was startling, a violent eruption. He didn't notice he'd knocked over his glass. I watched red wine spreading across the starched white tablecloth as Edgar subjected Finlay to a verbal mauling.

"Do people consider you a serious person? You have an actual academic position? Quite apart from your outrageous race-baiting, how can you honestly believe the space of evolutionary possibility is bounded by your fuzzy arts-brain notion of the 'human'? Besides, I thought all you people were post-structuralists or postmodernists or whatever it's called this week. You all hate the human! A face in the sand! Wash it away in the tide and hurrah, let the orgy of perversion begin! Well, here's the damn tide! That's what I'm saying. You ought to be pleased about it, but instead you're just whining. I wish you'd make up your minds."

For a moment we were all stunned. It was so vicious that we didn't know how to react. Finlay was ashen-faced. His hands fluttered up to his tie, instinctively checking the knot. He swallowed and got up from the table. "Well, I'm sorry to break up this lovely party but I have other things to do. There is a major world city on my doorstep and I have friends who are charming and well-mannered. I'm going out dancing. With my friends."

This ought to have been Edgar's opportunity to apologize. He didn't. As Finlay left, he ignored our appalled looks and settled back in his chair, dabbing his mouth with a napkin.

"The problem," he said, in the grave but assertive tone of a pedagogue who has dealt with a churlish heckler, "is that the so-called right to privacy is antisocial. Society has a lot of interests. Preventing crime and terrorism, freedom of expression, and so on. Privacy conflicts with them all, every last one. Our patron, Herr Deuter, understood that."

He went for his glass, presumably to raise it to "our patron, Herr Deuter," and discovered the wine stain on the tablecloth. Annoyed, he craned his neck to see if any of the waiters were in the room.

"All smoking outside the kitchen door, I expect. Same as usual. They congregate out there. I've pointed it out to Frau Janowitz more than once."

That night I could not bring myself to lie in bed, knowing that it was possible I was being watched. Only the bathroom seemed safe. I lay uncomfortably in the bath and thought about Edgar, shuffling around his bed, pale as a grub. I thought about

Otto the porter and his case of guns. On the morning of their suicide, Kleist and Henriette left their inn and walked out to the lakeshore. They ordered coffee to be brought to them at a spot where there was a view from a little hill. The landlord's wife grumbled. It was too far, and so cold. Kleist promised to pay the servants for their trouble, and asked that they also bring some rum. Testifying later to the authorities, the maid who carried the tray described them as looking very happy, chasing each other around and running down the hill to the water like children playing tag. They were happy, I thought, because they'd found an ending, a narrative shape to their lives.

I got out my phone and sent a text to Rei. Things weren't so good with me, I wrote, but she shouldn't worry. It was all part of the process. I liked the sound of "process," which had a plausibly therapeutic ring, as if I were "working through" my problem, or better still, "doing the work." I wrote and deleted several sentences which smacked of self-pity. I told her—in a businesslike tone, or so I hoped—that I wouldn't be in touch again for a little while, but when I did, it would be with good news. As I wrote this, I understood dimly that I was flailing. I had no idea what kind of good news I could produce, what rabbit I could pull from my psychological hat. I sent it and then switched off my phone so there was no way I could receive a reply.

I woke up the next morning before dawn, to find myself lying on the bathroom floor. There was no blind or curtain on the window, and a security light outside gave the walls a faint orange glow. I'd made a sort of nest with my bedding, and as I lay there, unable to get very comfortable, I came to the conclusion that I had no real evidence that the bathroom was any more private than the bedroom. It was just an assumption, a product of cognitive bias.

Little by little, the orange light faded to a uniform pale gray. I heard the distant sound of a train and an amplified voice making an announcement at Wannsee station. The light grew brighter. A car went by on the street outside. Time passed. I may have gone back to sleep. The next thing I heard was a knock at the door to my apartment, a pause, and then the buzzing sound of the bolt withdrawing as a keycard was passed over the sensor. Something heavy hit the door frame and a female voice cautiously called out "Herr Professor?" I couldn't muster the will to respond. After a few minutes, the shy cleaner entered the bathroom carrying an armful of fresh towels. Shocked to see me, she swore under her breath and began to back out again.

"You keep the floor spotless," I said to her, as if that would explain why I was wedged in a corner next to the toilet. She was holding the towels defensively in front of her chest. There was something feral about her posture, a wild creature on alert, ready to flee.

"I come back later."

"Don't go. Please."

Why did I choose her? To be honest, only because there was no one else. I felt no particular connection to her. Almost the opposite. There was nothing in her previous behavior to suggest that she'd be sympathetic to me. But I had to talk to someone, and I didn't have many options. I could have said something to Finlay. He was the nearest thing to a friend I'd made at the Deuter Center, but I didn't know if he'd care to involve himself with the messy underside of my life, and even if he listened without an ironic smile turning up the corners of his mouth, he was unlikely to understand. I did have friends, people I'd known for years, but something happens to men in middle age, to male friendships. You get focused on your work, your family, and somehow you fail to keep up. Before you know it, you haven't heard from the people you think of as closest to you for six months, then a year; you've missed birthdays and new children and house moves and changes of job, and inevitably you wonder if your friend is resentful or angry at you for being so distant, and it feels artificial to phone them and invite them out for a drink and more so if your ulterior motive is to ask them for help, to ambush them by bringing up the creeping sense of dread that has hollowed out your life. When Nina was born, I'd sent round photos and made a post on a social media site, basking in hundreds of messages of congratulation. But little children are exhausting, and on the rare occasions when you're not trying to catch up on work after they're asleep, it somehow feels better to open a bottle of wine and sprawl on the sofa with your partner than to head out to some noisy bar to swap stories about jobs and money with someone you used to do drugs with in your twenties. You tell yourself you're getting on fine without them, these men who used to be your friends, and you are—until you need someone to talk to, someone who knows you, who knows who you used to be before you became who you are.

So I looked up at the cleaner, this slight nervous woman hovering in the bathroom doorway, wondering how to escape from me and the various possible threats I represented, and I put on what I hoped was a charming smile and, in German, asked her name. There was such a long pause that I thought she wasn't going to answer.

"Monika," she said, finally.

"Monika, I know it sounds stupid, but can I talk to you?"

Another drawn-out pause. "OK."

"I think—and I know how this sounds—that I'm being watched."

She stared at me, her mouth slightly open. I thought I saw a flash of anger in her eyes.

"This is some kind of joke?"

"No."

"I want you to know it's not funny."

I was confused. I don't know what reaction I'd expected, but she seemed, of all things, offended.

"Honestly, I just want to—to tell someone, and try to explain, to see if it's—well, to see if . . ." I trailed off inarticulately.

"Who's watching you, here in the bathroom?"

"I don't know. I mean, I don't think they're watching me in the bathroom. It's why I came in here."

Whatever slight degree of certainty I'd possessed had already drained away, to be replaced by a sense of utter pointlessness. I felt abolished, physically wiped out. My German was falling apart, so I asked to switch to English.

"Look," I said again. "I know how this sounds."

She shrugged. "Why do you think it is happening?"

"It's not easy to say. To be honest, I may be losing my mind."

She eyed the tangle of pillows and blankets on the floor.

"You went to sleep here?"

I saw the situation through her eyes. The man in the bathroom, probably drunk or medicated, more or less admitting he was in the midst of a nervous breakdown. She put the towels down on the edge of the bath.

"Maybe you need to talk to someone."

"This is what I'm saying."

"I mean a doctor. A—what is the word—*Psychiater*."

"No. I mean, I don't know. Not yet. I'm not in a good way, but there's something else, not in my mind. Something external."

"I don't understand. What do you want from me?"

"Let me tell you about it, and maybe you can give me some idea—I mean, you know this place. You work here."

"As you say. I have five more bedrooms to clean before lunch, then the offices."

"Please."

"Why is this my problem? I don't know what you want."

"I just—I don't know. You seem like you'd understand."

"You know something about me?"

"No, nothing."

She was on her guard again. The same tone of offense.

"You swear it?"

"Of course. I didn't even know your name until you told me."

"You're not a journalist."

"No. Why would you ask that?"

"You're not writing some shit for an American magazine."

"I don't understand. About what?"

I got to my feet, staggering slightly. Instinctively she stepped back. Again, I realized the difference in our sizes.

"I don't mean to scare you."

"I must go."

"Please don't."

My distress must have been convincing, because she

stopped recoiling. Her thin lips contorted themselves into a sort of wince. "Eat something," she advised. "Maybe this is what you need."

"OK."

"So I have a question."

"OK."

"Are you going to kill yourself? Remember, you have a wife. A little kid, right?"

"How do you know that?"

"I clean up your shit, remember. You have a picture on your desk."

"Oh. OK."

"So tell me."

"No. Of course not."

"Good. So I can go."

She picked up the towels and her bucket of cleaning supplies and clicked the door shut behind her. I had the feeling that I'd been efficiently managed.

She was right about eating. I felt light-headed with hunger, and however real my problems, they weren't going to be helped by an additional layer of low-blood-sugar anxiety. Clearly there was no way I could go down to breakfast, so I pulled on some clothes and walked to the café by the station. I sat at a table by the window and ate a stale pastry, washed down with two cups of coffee. I stayed for a long time, maybe two hours, pretending to read a copy of *Bild* that someone had left on a nearby table, ignoring the waitress's outrage. The headlines were about the refugees, the repercussions of Chancellor Merkel's promise that the nation would handle the influx of people fleeing the wars in Syria and Afghanistan.

Then I saw Monika, making her way down the street outside, hands jammed into the pockets of her big army coat. She
came into the café and ordered something at the counter. As
she waited, she turned round and saw me there.

"You again."

I held up my hands. She took her drink and came over to
my table. "You know, if being in Berlin is making you feel bad,
you should go home."

"You're probably right."

"This has happened to you before?"

"What?"

"Thinking people are watching you. Paranoia."

"No."

"You take drugs?" She mimed smoking.

"No. I mean yes, sometimes, but not really. Not for a while.
You want to sit down?"

She took a seat opposite me, unbuttoned her coat, stuffed
her gloves into its pockets, and unknotted a thick woolen scarf
from her neck.

"Your wife is beautiful. Why don't you talk to her about it?"

She saw my look of suspicion.

"Why not go home to her. Say you are thinking these
things."

"I'm supposed to be making myself happy. That was the
arrangement. I would come here and sort myself out."

She laughed. "You came to Wannsee in the middle of winter to be happy?"

Even I could see that was comical. "I've put too much pressure on her. If I don't find a solution, I think she'll leave me."

"I'm sorry. But why do you think the crazy bastards at the
Deuter Zentrum are watching you?"

"Well, they are, aren't they? Everyone's watching each other all the time. The spirit of openness. Transparency."

"Oh, I hate all that shit."

"Haven't you worked there for a long time?"

"Yes, but I'm not interesting to watch. I'm just a woman who scrubs the toilet."

She looked at the time on her phone. "I must go."

"OK."

"But look, if you want to talk some more, that would be OK."

"Really?"

"Sure, why not?"

And that was how we came to be floating together in the undersea world of the Chinese restaurant the following evening, as the brightly colored fish swam in the tank by our heads and the blue light turned our food ghostly shades of purple and pink.

"Tell me one more time," she said. "You're not a journalist."

"No."

"This isn't some shitty way to get an interview."

"No, why? I mean, I don't want to be rude, but you said it yourself. You're a cleaner. Why would a journalist want to talk to you?"

"You don't know about being watched," she said, as she served herself another helping of greasy duck fried rice. "Not really."

Later, when I tried to write down her story, I couldn't capture it exactly. I made notes, but I didn't catch her tone of voice, the strange quality of her telling, which slipped in and out of German and English, the rhythm of hesitations as she searched for a word or checked to see if I'd understood.

"I'm telling you because I think it will help you," she said.

"No other reason." Then she sighed and shook her head. "No. I'm telling you because it is easier to tell someone who isn't part of it. Not German, I mean."

I wrote it down, not because I wanted to publish it—I have stayed true to the promise I made her, at least until now—but because it seemed important. The events she described were both frightening and close at hand, though they'd taken place in a country that no longer existed, under a system that had vanished into history.

She had grown up in the East. She had been, she said, what they used to call a "Negative Decadent," an enemy of the Workers' and Farmers' State. She lived with her family in Marzahn, in one of the big new housing projects. It was a shitty place, a shitty life. Not just because the people were such assholes, the boys all dumb as planks, drinking beer and living for the next BFC Dynamo game, but because it was shitty to live in a country where everything was run by old men. A whole country, reeking of piss and schnapps and cabbage soup.

ZERSETZUNG

(Undermining)

HER FAMILY WERE HAPPY ABOUT IT. It was a big deal to get one of the new places. The entire district was a building site, a showcase for the socialist future. Her father had put them on the list for a new car. She reckoned she had about five more years before she turned into one of the horrible sows who gave her the evil eye from behind their net curtains when she walked past with her friends. Five years of life. At weekends she'd take the train to Alexanderplatz and hang around with other teenagers. Sooner or later they were always chased away by the police. She hated the ride home. Sometimes, as she waited for her train, she thought about climbing down off the platform, kneeling and touching her cheek against the third rail.

She never got on with school and left to become an apprentice at a textile factory in a town just outside Berlin, which improved things because she could move out of the family home and live in a hostel. It was OK at first, but the boredom was like acid. She had a bad temper, and sometimes got into fights. One day some old piss schnapps cabbage man called her into an office and gave her an official warning. She already had a mark against her because she didn't want to join the Free German Youth.

Every weekend she would take the train back to the city. The first time she saw punks, it was amazing, like being electrocuted, jolted out of her dead skin. A couple sitting in a square in Friedrichshain, like two peacocks. They just didn't give a shit. The boy had a leather jacket and his hair was spiked up. The girl wore a dog collar and her head was shaved so that only a sort of lock or tuft hung down at the front. Monika herself had—you couldn't call it a haircut. At first she didn't even know there was music to go with the clothes. She sort of pieced the whole thing together. Someone had to show her pictures of the bands in a smuggled West German magazine.

She didn't have to think twice. She hacked off her hair, dyed the tufts with watercolors and spiked them up with soap. Then she went back to look for the punks. Why not? She had nothing else going on. Even then it wasn't as if she was really *doing* anything. Taking the train, drinking, wandering around, drinking more, hoping for something to happen. But that was all anyone was doing. It was what there was to do. Soon she knew most of the crew, at least by sight. The peacock couple, everyone. The boys from Köpenick, the idiot with the army greatcoat who stabbed his own leg for a dare. It wasn't such a big scene. Most people just went by nicknames. Ratte, Pankow, the girl everyone called Major. Bored kids. She went to a party where a band played in the attic of someone's house. Fifty of them in there, throwing themselves around, drinking and dancing and smoking cigarettes. It was the greatest evening of her life.

All they wanted was to jump around. You'd think it wasn't a big deal, but it sent the piss schnapps cabbage men crazy. They thought the punks were agents of the CIA. It was the way they looked, mostly. By then lots of people had long hair, but this was something else. Poison from the West, a threat to good order. Not that you could get any of the real punk clothes unless you knew someone who could cross over. They had to improvise, make studs and patches and buttons themselves out of whatever was available. They sat on park benches in their homemade outfits. You couldn't stay still ten minutes without the cops coming.

At the factory she got another talking to, and they told her someone else needed her place at the hostel. It was a punishment, of course, they didn't really bother hiding it. What could she do? Better to lie down on the track than go back to live with her doormat of a mother and her piss schnapps cabbage dad. There seemed to be no third option, so she went into the city and got fucked up on paint thinner and tried to shake her head off her shoulders, pogoing in a courtyard behind a church in Prenzlauer Berg as a band thrashed cheap guitars and a singer rhymed *shit and boredom have no borders* with *everyone is taking orders*. Two cool girls were dancing next to her, jerking their heads and punching the air. When some limp-dick tried to hit on one of them, Monika gave him a shove, sent him sprawling. He was drunk and he got up and came at her, it looked like he was going to take a swing, but all three of them faced him down, told him to fuck off, which he did, grumbling in an old-mannish tone that made them double up with laughter. The last they saw he was passed out in a corner with a lapful of vomit.

We need a drummer, said the girl with the bleached crop. She told her she couldn't play drums. That's OK, she said. It doesn't matter. And just like that, a third option opened up. The girls, Katja and Elli, were living black in a place on Linienstrasse, with a rotating cast of boyfriends to carry furniture and fix things. It was a tenement that had officially been declared unfit for habitation—on one side there was nothing but rubble, on the other a building whose frontage had collapsed, a sort of skeleton that no one had got round to demolishing—but several of the apartments were occupied by young people who didn't have a hope of getting on the list for official housing. That's where they took her to jam, in this building whose frontage was pocked with thousands of wartime bullet holes, and it was sort of understood, without her needing to ask, that she was going to move in. The equipment was set up in their living room. The guitar and vocal plugged into a single amp. She bashed away at someone's borrowed kit. She didn't know what to do, so at first she did everything at the same time, hit with the sticks and stamped on the pedal, making a big lumbering primitive noise. She would get better, but not much.

Then it was the three of them. Katja sang and Elli played guitar. Monika had never met anyone like them, girls from art school who spent their days making things, as if it were a job. They weren't ashamed of being different. They laughed at the idea that they could ever end up as net curtain twitchers, disgusting baby factories doing the ironing while some man drank himself stupid in front of the TV. Katja declaimed her crazy poetry into the microphone, all this gothic stuff about blood and graves and ravens, while Elli threw poses and wind-milled her arm as she slammed down on the strings.

Elli was shy, except when she played guitar. Katja was a social force. She seemed to have an almost-supernatural abil-ity to make things happen. Whatever you needed, whatever plot you'd just hatched in the bar, she would be there with an idea, a connection. It would turn out she'd recently talked to someone or seen exactly the thing you needed discarded in the street, or bumped into someone from the old days—Katja had old days, it was one of the sophisticated things about her—a guy who liked her and could be persuaded to help. One day she breezed in and told them she'd got the band a gig. She said it as if it were the most natural thing in the world, but to Mon-ika the prospect was terrifying. Getting up in front of people, making a spectacle of herself. Of course all three of them were nervous. They all dressed to kill, or as near as they could get, Elli with her cropped hair freshly colored orange, Katja in what Monika thought of as her moth-eaten-bride look, lots of eyeliner, an old black dress and a shawl. Monika couldn't remember what she wore. Why would she? She was the drum-mer. She sat at the back.

In the GDR you needed permission from the authorities to play music in front of an audience. You had to audition for a committee. The official pop musicians were all balding men who'd done their military service and trained at the conserva-tory. Of course no one was ever going to give the green light to some dirty punk girls, so they had no option, really. The gig was a secret, or as much of a secret as something like that can be.

So there were official bands and unofficial bands, but few as unofficial as Die Gläsernen Frauen. They'd needed a name, and of course Katja had one. *The Transparent Women*. There had once been a transparent woman and a transparent man, anatomical models made out of some kind of see-through plastic, technological marvels of the nineteen-twenties that children were taken to see on school trips to the German Hygiene Museum in Dresden. It was a good name, Monika thought, a defiant name. They wrote a song:

> *You want to look?*
> *Go ahead!*
> *Go ahead!*
> *Are you happy now?*

The concert wasn't much. A couple of dozen people in a dusty room, the cellar of a building where some friend of Katja's worked or lived, Monika wasn't exactly clear. They borrowed another amp and found a drum kit that was a little better than the first, though one of the heads was patched with tape, and the cymbals were the kind with leather straps, made to be used in an orchestra or carried in a marching band. The kit's owner had hung them awkwardly from a pair of homemade stands. There wasn't a stage, they just walked out into silence, some scattered clapping. And then they attacked. One two three four, into their first number, which was just Katja shouting "Stupid bear! Stupid bear!" while Elli played some chords she'd copied from a Ramones song. Everyone was surprised, of course—three girls playing instruments—but soon they were dancing. Katja and Elli's art school friends, the kids from the park. A few apprentices from the meatpacking plant hung at the edges while the punks fought in the mosh pit. She battered her kit and it sounded like dead bodies hitting the ground and the guitar and the vocal fed back so the whole thing was just a mess of distortion, you couldn't say what it was, or if it was music exactly, but it had something. Energy. Life.

After that there was another gig, and another. One of Katja's boyfriends had a van and drove them to Leipzig, where they were supposed to play at a sort of festival with three other acts, all totally illegal of course, and when they arrived, the police had got wind of it and the venue was locked up. They slept on the floor of someone's apartment and drove back home.

Of course the factory hadn't lasted, but she needed to do something, it was illegal not to have a job, and after a lot of hassle she found one in the neighborhood, at a little workshop where they electroplated bathroom fixtures. One evening, as she was sweeping up, her last task before leaving, a man in a roll neck sweater let himself in through the door and stood watching her. He had that look. They all had it, that unclean cleanliness.

He offered her a cigarette. He was older than her, but not by much. In some places, he would have been considered hand-some. What are you doing here, he said. This place is not for you. Like a lover, a leading man in a movie. It was absurd. He told her she ought to travel. She had never seen this man in her life before.

What did he want? Nothing bad. He wanted her to be able to stretch her creative wings. He did a little drumming mime. He swept his hair back from his face and lit a cigarette, doing some kind of cool cat business with his lighter. He said he had a car outside, could he give her a ride home? No? Well then, he could take her out instead. He would buy her a drink, hear about her big dreams. She was a girl with big dreams, he could tell. She wanted nothing to do with him. Everything about him was wrong. Go away, she said, but he wouldn't stop talking. Finally she waved the broom, made as if she were going to hit him with it. He laughed. OK, OK, holding up his hands. He didn't take her seriously at all. I left you something, he said. In your locker.

When she was sure he'd gone, she checked. Her little lock was still attached, but inside was something she hadn't put there. A record. It was an LP by an all-girl band from London. She knew them. She had a tape—maybe Elli had copied it from one of her friends—with a couple of their songs on it. They were good, but this album had a sort of soft-porn cover, the three band members topless and covered in mud, like sexy savages. It was supposed to be shocking. As a present from that guy it was just sleazy. He knew so much about her taste and at the same time he'd found a way to leer at her. She thought about throwing the record away, but despite the shitty cover, the band was good, and if she decided not to keep it she could swap it for something, so she put it in her bag and took it home. The way she thought about it, if that asshole wanted to give her a record, it was his problem.

He left it two weeks. Long enough for her to think he'd got the message. He made her jump, of course. He was that type. You could go to music school, he said, leaning out of a car window. Another man was driving, matching her pace as she walked home from work. You could get some time in a recording studio, whatever you want. She could do this, she should do that. She told him to stick his studio up his ass and he made a sad clown face. Honey, don't be like that. You ought to be sweet to me. You wouldn't want anything to go wrong in your life. You wouldn't want there to be any misunderstandings.

You tell them to go away but it's not like they give in. They don't say OK, no problem, sorry to have bothered you. He gave her a time, an address, held out a piece of paper with the details. When she wouldn't take it, he finally stopped the car and came after her. He blocked her path and stuffed the paper into the front pocket of her jeans, pulling her close to him and grinding his knuckles against her belly. She would be there or else he would "spank her bottom." Hearty chuckles as the car pulled away. When she got into work the next day, there were three more records in her locker. She left them where they were. She didn't even want to touch them.

She didn't go to the meeting. She had what she thought of as a perfect excuse. The band was heading out on the road. Ten days of Katja singing *better off dead than getting kicked in the head,* Katja singing *only if I'm dreaming can I say I'm free.* Leipzig, Dresden, Halle. Barns and cellars and old factories. Fuck him, she thought. That pig didn't know so very much about her if he didn't know about the tour. In each place there were young people, floors and couches to crash on, hands to pass a bottle or a cigarette. So, yes, she felt hopeful. There were people like her. That didn't mean their lives were "nice." Or "liberating." Mostly they were tired and scared. They were making do, getting wasted on whatever was to hand. There was always a bad atmosphere when DGF played, an edge of violence. Onstage in Dresden, someone threw a glass bottle at Elli, which hit her on the side of the head. She staggered, then went down on her hands and knees. Monika stopped playing, thinking she was badly hurt, but she was only trying to find the bottle to throw back.

Monika didn't tell the others about the man in the roll neck sweater. It wasn't the sort of conversation you wanted to start about yourself. Rumors had a way of snowballing. It was on everybody's minds, who might be working with the Stasi. Everyone knew someone who had been arrested, or gone to prison. If you said something odd or put someone else in danger, of course there was suspicion. People were just trying to protect themselves. The problem was how hard it was to untangle sinister causes from the ordinary muddle of people's lives. Everyone borrowed or stole things or cheated on each other or got drunk and divulged secrets. Not all of it was motivated by the secret police. Like everyone, she was constantly revising a mental list of the people in her life she believed she could trust. Who was it safe to speak to? When was a conversation really private? A bass player in another band was given a prison sentence because he passed someone an environmental leaflet. Others had been charged with delinquency. There were definitely people in the scene who were giving information to the secret police.

When they got back to Berlin, she knew there'd be a reckoning, but she didn't think it would be so quick or brutal. When she went to work, her boss, a nice old man who'd never seemed to mind how she looked or where she spent her leisure time, told her that he was sorry but he couldn't keep someone like her around anymore. She didn't have to ask what he meant. Could she clear out her locker? Yes, he did mean right away. The records were still in there. She didn't know what to do with them, so she stuffed them into a borrowed shopping bag along with the rest of the locker's contents—her lunchbox, her spare clothes. And of course when she walked out onto the street, the man in the roll neck sweater was waiting with his smirking friend. Two junior piss schnapps cabbage men, leaning on their piss schnapps cabbage car. She tried to give him back the records. He'd had his fun, now he could leave her alone. This time he didn't pretend to find her cute. Silly bitch, did she think she could just mess him around? He told her to get in the car. It was time she understood a few things.

They drove for a short while and pulled into a courtyard, next to a delivery truck with a picture of fruit and vegetables on the side. A man in blue overalls was leaning on the hood. As they drew up, he ground out a cigarette with his boot. They took her from the car and told her to get in the back of the truck. She was confused and they were rough as they pushed her inside. She had a moment to see that the interior was divided into little windowless compartments, before she was shoved into one and the door locked behind her. She was left in complete darkness, sitting on some kind of stool. The engine started and she groped around to see if there was a bar or handle, something to hold on to.

These things are easy enough to read about. Transported in total darkness, brought out into a punishingly bright place, banks of neon strip lights trained down on a garage with reflective white walls. The transition from darkness to dazzling light, a shock designed to induce a physical crisis, to reduce the subject to a state of abjection, nothing but a half-blind animal, stunned and panicking.

An uncertain number of uniformed men, a hand pushing down on the back of her head, forcing her to look at the patterned lino on the floor as they marched her along a corridor.

There was a room. They were quick but thorough, photographing her, taking fingerprints. Another corridor. Lozenges, a pattern of lozenges, scuffed and worn, interlocking geometric shapes picked out in brown on a piss yellow background, ending at a gray cell door. It was actually a relief to be pushed inside. She sat down on a bench, or rather hovered over it with her arms braced, unable to relax. She felt as if she were still moving, still being dragged along. She tried to slow her breathing. Her chest was tight. She didn't normally suffer from panic attacks, but something primitive had been activated, something that was causing her to bare her teeth and pant like an animal. In the cell there was only the bench and a lidless toilet. A low-wattage bulb in a mesh-covered ceiling fixture gave off a sickly yellow light.

They didn't leave her long. A pair of guards entered and told her to stand up. They were young, her own age, spotty-faced boys who couldn't meet her eye. Another corridor, rows of identical cell doors. Who was behind all those doors? The interrogation room was furnished in the style of any other government office. A pair of wood-veneer desks were arranged in a T-shape. At the window hung a dirty lace curtain. The lace curtain was funny, she supposed. The roll neck man probably had a sow wife at home twitching one just like it as she spied on the neighbors.

It was the first time she'd seen him in uniform. He looked primmer than he did when he was roaming around the city in civilian clothes. He had placed his hat neatly on the desk, next to a pale pink file. He didn't look up as the guards brought her in, pretending to read. Sit, he said, waving vaguely at a chair at the foot of the T. He pushed back a strand of his thick black hair, smoothed and patted it with a flattened palm. No, on your hands. Still he didn't look up. She was confused, and he raised his voice. Put your hands under your buttocks, palms down. Sit on your hands. She did as she was told. He opened up a file and made some kind of note.

In front of him he had a telephone, a tape recorder, and another box with a row of buttons whose function was not obvious. In front of her was a microphone. Things were going to change, he said. From now on there would be no time for romantic games. She asked if she were under arrest. No, what made her think that? They were just going to have a little chat. The threat hidden in that bloodless phrase.

He pressed a button on the tape recorder and began. Factual questions. Names and places, information about the band, people she had met in other cities. I don't know, she kept saying. I can't remember. In that moment, she was telling the truth. She really couldn't remember anything. It was something she was good at, practiced in. Partial self-erasure. She could live for long periods as if her memories were not hers, as if they were just images taken from films or books.

He oscillated between unctuous compassion and petulant threats. Had she given a single moment's thought to her family, her friends? Take it from him, the consequences of these things were never limited to one person. She should imagine, he said, that she was throwing a stone into a pond. The ripples would spread out. Luckily for her he had a solution. To what, she wondered, other than the trouble he himself was causing. His solution was this: Together they would write out an agreement. She would confirm her loyalty to the German Democratic Republic and agree to work with the Ministry for State Security. A small thing. Most people would see it as their patriotic duty.

She didn't want to provoke him—she had no sense of the limits of his power, what he could realistically do to her—but as he whined on, a bolus of disgust rose in her throat. All of it, the fake delivery truck, the cell, the blinding lights, just so a repressed little man could issue threats and shuffle papers at his desk. She had to concentrate to fight her nausea, and because speaking made it worse, she didn't speak, didn't say the things he wanted her to say. Again and again she swallowed the words and shook her head and eventually he seemed to run out of steam. With one more twist he could probably have broken her, but he didn't see it. Instead he pressed his call button and ordered the guards to take her back to her cell.

As she sat and waited for whatever would happen next, she tried to divert her mind from the more frightening possibilities, but there was nothing else to dwell on, no way to distract herself. If it got really bad, could she escape? The light fixture would hold her weight. She still had the laces on her shoes. Then she heard the sound of keys and the door's heavy bolt being drawn. The interrogator came in, and ordered her to stand. She caught the sour hormonal stink of her own sweat. He could smell it too. His face was a mask of disgust. Surely, she thought, the smell would be familiar to him, a normal part of his work. Look at you, he said. It's obvious that you're not mentally stable. He expanded this train of thought into a short lecture. It was well known that *Creative Types* were *Susceptible to Psychiatric Illness*. She displayed a lot of *Typical Symptoms* such as *Negativity* and *Receptivity to Antisocial Influences*.

I'm going to throw you back, he said, in a tone of professional regret. She thought she had misheard. Throw her back, like a fish. He stepped aside, making an irritated gesture at the open cell door. Could he offer one word of advice before she left? She ought to go straight home. She wouldn't want people to start wondering where she'd been. That weaselly hint of concern. As if the two of them were complicit in something, a scheme or a love affair.

She was given back the borrowed shopping bag, still filled with the contents of her work locker, and escorted to the front gate. It closed behind her and she found herself on a residential street, facing a row of maisonettes. Behind her was a high wall and a watchtower. She didn't have a way of telling the time, but from the light she guessed that it must have been late afternoon.

She chose a direction that seemed likely to lead to a main road, and began walking. Eventually she found a U-Bahn station, and arrived home at more or less the normal time, as if she'd just finished her day at the factory. As she came through the door, Elli was sitting at the kitchen table smoking a cigarette. Everything OK, she asked distractedly, then squinted at Monika's bag. You have records, she said, brightening up. What did you get? At first Monika didn't understand. Then she felt sick. She'd forgotten about the interrogator's "gifts." Without thinking, she had brought a piece of him home. Mechanically, she dug the records out of her bag and handed them over. Seeing Elli reading the sleeves made her feel guilty, as if she were exposing her to a contagious disease. Her friend's amazed, slightly envious expression told her that she'd made a problem for herself. The records were too good, too recently released to come without an explanation. I swapped them with Peter, she said, the first thing that came into her head, and then cursed herself because this Peter was a close friend, in and out of the apartment all the time. The lie could easily be found out. She had a sudden sense of threat, the springing of the trap set by the interrogator as she left the cell. *Go straight home. You wouldn't want people to start wondering where you've been.* Why should she lie? What was the point? Because he put the idea into her head? But then again, how was she to tell the story without inviting suspicion? Every question would breed more questions. *Why hadn't she ever said anything before about talking to the Stasi? Were the records payment for some kind of service?* She was exhausted and very hungry. She just wanted to forget about everything for a few hours. After she'd had some sleep, she would handle it. She ran into the bathroom, stripped off her clothes, and stood shivering under the thin trickle of the shower.

Her plan was to tell Katja first. She wanted to do it when the two of them were alone, but somehow she never found the right moment. There were always people in the apartment, or they were all out somewhere, watching a band or with a big group at a bar. As the days went by, a sort of skin or scab grew up over the memory of her arrest. Why pick away at it? Little by little she fell into a kind of magical thinking, as if the reality of what had happened to her depended on its being *told,* put into words. Instead she swallowed it, forced it down into the pit of her stomach and barred its way back out with the gate of her teeth.

Elli had a boyfriend, whose name was Kurt. Yet another musician, a bass player. One morning Monika was lying in bed when Kurt put his head round her door. Had she seen his notebook? He'd left it on the kitchen table. She propped herself up on her elbows and said no, she hadn't, and just at that moment she spotted it, or rather they both spotted it simultaneously, lying on top of the beer crate where she kept her clothes. There was no reason for it to be there. They had all been at a party.

She'd come in and gone straight to bed, just fallen in drunkenly through her door without even turning on the light.

Kurt was more quizzical than angry. If you want to read my secret thoughts, he said, you could just ask. But the notebook was just the beginning. Over the next few weeks, all sorts of small personal things went missing or were moved around in the apartment. Someone took 100 marks from the pocket of Elli's leather jacket. Katja's photos were left out on her bed. No one came out and made accusations, but these small crimes and clumsy invasions of privacy put everyone on edge. Who would leave a used sanitary towel by her bed? Or tear pages out of Elli's books? A bad atmosphere grew up. Katja and Elli became conspiratorial, exclusive. Sometimes Monika thought she was going mad. Was she actually responsible, doing all these things without knowing? Elli had begun to look at her sideways. Katja too. Deep down she knew there could only be one answer. The bastards could be blatant when they wanted, or so subtle that it was hard to decide if they'd been there at all. Each time she felt sure of what was happening, she came up against the simple fact of its absurdity. Why would they go to such trouble, just to play petty pranks? And yet it was the only plausible answer.

Then came the fight at the church. Even the old tchekists of the secret police only dared to go so far against the Lutherans, and some pastors made use of this latitude to do political things, such as letting punk bands play in their halls. The pastor of a church in Friedrichshain was a bearded young man who painted abstractions and believed in turning swords into ploughshares. In return for letting the band use his space, he asked the three girls to sit in on what he called a peace circle, a group that met every week to talk about current events. There were perhaps twenty others. An older woman, some kind of professor, gave a lecture on the horrors of nuclear war. Most of the members were older than the girls. Monika did not say anything in the discussion, just looked around the circle, trying to spot the informer.

On the night of the concert, there was a good atmosphere, at least at the beginning. Another band played before DGF, and the crowd was excited, whooping and cheering as they waited for them to come on. A few people had even crossed over from West Berlin for the show. Katja introduced her to an English guy who was dressed, for some reason, in a Weimar-era postman's uniform. He'd brought some tapes of underground industrial music as a present. He said he wanted to take the three of them into a studio. Though he was obviously trying to score with Katja, the offer seemed to be genuine.

The church hall had a proper stage, and they were standing in the wings, waiting to go on, when some skinheads arrived. Not a few. Twenty or thirty. It was 88 Tommy's birthday and they'd all been in a bar. Everyone knew 88 Tommy and his idiot friends but tonight there were more of them, a lot of faces she didn't recognize. DGF went into their first song and right away the skins pushed their way to the front. They started spitting and making obscene gestures. From further back, someone threw a bottle. Monika was protected behind the kit, but at the front it was bad. Katja was jabbing at shirtless men with her mike stand, warning them to keep back. During the second song a couple of guys started Sieg-Heiling and one of them got onstage and pushed Elli down into the crowd and after that it was chaos. As if at a signal, the stage was full of skinheads throwing punches, kicking over the PA, beating people. She cowered behind her kit, unable to see what had happened to her friends. When she spotted an opening between the scuffling bodies, she ran for a side door.

Almost as soon as she got outside, she was grabbed by two men in bureaucratic raincoats who smelled of cigarettes and hustled her in the direction of a waiting car, talking loudly about how they were "here to protect" her and "get her to safety." The street was full of people who had come outside to get away from the fight. The men made such a noise, raising their voices. They drew everybody's attention.

Pastor Daniel was in the crowd, holding a handkerchief against a wound on his forehead. He frowned as he saw her go past. She tried to shake the men off, but one of them jabbed her in the small of her back with a fist or a stick, a quick discreet attack which caused a flash of intense pain. While she was incapacitated, they more or less picked her up and threw her onto the backseat of a car.

They drove her to a hairdresser, of all places, nearby in Lichtenberg. The lights were on in the shop even though it was almost midnight. She could do with a makeover, said one, laughing. Mousy little thing like her, she should have a little more pride in her appearance. They took her to the back of the shop where, of course, the roll neck man was waiting, natty in driving gloves and a new brown leather jacket. He was taking pride in his appearance, swiveling on a salon chair under a plastic dryer hood. Have a seat, he said. Don't worry, you're safe now.

She could have defied him. She could have said, pig, when did I ever ask you to keep me safe? She could have said, I know you don't give a damn about me, so cut the shit and tell me what this is really about. Instead she flopped down onto a chair and almost in a whimper, the whimper of a frightened little girl, a beaten dog, she asked why he had to make it so obvious to her friends. And as she heard herself she understood what he'd done, how completely he'd won. He'd made his abuse into a shared secret, a cozy secret that had alienated her from her friends, and she was disgusted with him and with herself for falling for it and with the sordid world that made such a thing possible.

He was using his indoor voice, his forked tongue. He told her he admired her loyalty to her friends, however misguided. He made offers. Perhaps she needed money? He might be able to organize a stipend. She told him to do whatever he wanted. She was exhausted. She'd had enough. He pretended to be offended. He had, he said, a sworn duty to uphold the law. He took that seriously. Did she not take that seriously? Surely, after such a disgusting display of violence, it would be obvious even to someone as obtuse as her that negative decadent elements were at work in her little milieu.

She threw up her hands. So why the hell had he arrested her, instead of them? He claimed not to understand. Them? The skinheads. The ones who did the violence. She couldn't believe how little he seemed to understand. Skinheads? Did he really not know what they were? He asked her to describe them. Ah yes, he said. Ah yes. So did these animals have names?

Tommy.

He smiled and took a little pad out of his pocket. Tommy. Very good. So what else did she know about this Tommy? A last name, perhaps? Where did he live? And then she saw what he was doing, getting her to give him information, reporting to him, and she had a feeling like looking into a pit. No, she said. Just that. No. He pretended to be surprised. Wasn't this Tommy one of the real criminals, the ones she thought he ought to be focusing on? Well, then, surely she should be happy to assist. I'm not working with you, she told him. I'm not one of your creatures.

There was a rustle of plastic curtain beads. I know one thing about you, said a voice behind her. She swiveled on the chair and there he was, as if she'd magicked him into being. 88 Tommy the skin, a few spots of red near the collar of his white tee shirt. He grinned a doughy grin. He looked drunk. There was more blood on the leg of his jeans. I know one thing, he said. You're a shit drummer. She was so confused that she just sat there with her mouth open. She could not put it all together. Roll Neck's smirk. Tommy's presence. His easy, casual air, leaning in the doorway, scuffing the sole of his boot against the floor.

Roll Neck let her take it all in for a minute. We have many people helping us, he said. In all sectors of society. So, it was late. Perhaps he ought to let Tommy drop her off? Someone should see her to her door.

You could come and meet the boys, said Tommy. Roll Neck thought that line was hilarious. Meet them? All of them? No, no Tommy, she wouldn't like it. He grinned at her. Maybe she would like it. She seemed like the stuck-up type to him, but maybe he was wrong.

Maybe, said Roll Neck, they should play a game. If she agreed to work for him he'd give her a head start. She didn't understand. He gestured to Tommy, and then to the door. Say yes and she would have five minutes before he unleashed the beast. Tommy looked angry at being called a beast, but he didn't say anything. An expression crossed his face, a brief collapse of his drunken smirk. Maybe, she thought, Roll Neck had something on him too. She stood up, without speaking.

She didn't give him her promise. Then she turned and walked to the door.

Once outside, she started running, convinced Tommy was coming after her, but after a few blocks and a few turns she realized she was alone, and allowed herself to slow down. Eventually she had to stop and rest, propping her hands on her knees, coughing and spitting into the gutter.

When she got home she found the apartment full of people. The atmosphere was unfriendly. They squinted at her through a haze of cigarette smoke. So who were her friends? She tried to explain as best as she could. Yes they were cops. Of course they were. They'd been harassing her. She'd never given them a thing. She'd found out that they were working with Tommy. That part of it people seemed to believe. Tommy with the pigs. But why hadn't she said anything before? There was only so much of it she could take before it got to her. All the stress and fear. She told them all to fuck themselves and shut herself in her room. After a while, Katja followed her. I would be so sad, she said, to think that you could ever do something like that. Monika promised her it was nonsense. On my mother's life. You don't give a shit about your mother, Katja said.

The next day Elli came back from hospital. She'd broken her arm when they threw her offstage. Accusingly, she showed the cast to Monika. Was that supposed to be her fault too? When she next got Katja alone, Monika broke down. You know me. You know I would never. Can't you make them see. Katja looked so beautiful. I would do anything to prove it to you, Monika slurred. I would follow you anywhere. To the grave. They'd both had a lot to drink.

Pastor Daniel had found out that Monika needed money and offered her some work as a gardener. When she turned up, you could tell that he was suspicious. There was a lot to be done in the church grounds, he said. He supposed he could use her. A couple of days later, she walked home after a day in the garden, dressed in old clothes, mud on her boots, to find everyone waiting for her in the living room, not just the band members but most of her close friends, people from other bands, the pastor himself. They had set up a sort of courtroom. They sat round the walls. One of the kitchen chairs had been pulled out for her and placed on the rug.

Elli went first. Monika had been with some policemen after the fight at the gig. She claimed they were harassing her, but many people in the room had seen pictures that told a different story. What pictures? From a folder (so formal, so like the people they were not supposed to be like) Elli produced a grainy black-and-white photograph of her talking to Roll Neck outside the electroplating factory. It must have been taken from far away. Who gave her that? She kept asking, but Elli carried on. There were a lot of reasons to be suspicious. Monika had just attached herself to their group. She had no friends, except the ones she met through them. Had she been ordered to worm her way in? Elli wasn't afraid to give her opinion. Monika was a snitch. She should leave.

She acted tough, but Monika had been in fights. She was like a charging bull, unable to stop herself. It was over more or less immediately. One of the boys held her back. Elli was already on the ground, screaming about her broken arm. The kitchen chair was splintered. She could hear herself shouting, as if from very far away. Take that back, you bitch. Take it back.

What hurt most was the way Katja looked at her. As if she were a bug or a spider. With a feeling like icy water Monika understood what her future would be. It was like being slapped awake from a beautiful dream. These people had picked her up and invited her in. Elli was right, without them she had no one. They had been her people. And now they were telling her to go.

They didn't even let her stay there that night. She was told she could come back for her things in the morning. She didn't know where to go and it was late and the weather was warm, so she slept in a park. That was what she did for a couple of days, hung around in the park, until she was so tired and hungry that she fell asleep on a bench in the middle of the afternoon and woke up to find it dark and a couple of cops shaking her. They put her in a cell overnight, and told her she'd be charged with vagrancy. She really didn't care. She didn't see what difference it made.

In the morning they let her out and Roll Neck was waiting on the street, looking like the cat that got the cream. I thought we'd lost you, he said. That would have been a shame. She let him put her in the car. She knew she smelled bad and she didn't care. They drove to Prenzlauer Berg, through the streets of war-damaged prewar tenements, and as they got closer she could feel the horror creeping up. She realized where he was taking her. There was a line of police vans parked round the corner from their building. He drew up behind them. The thing is, he said, if you'd cooperated when I first asked you, all the people asleep in there would still be your friends. You'd be in there sleeping too, instead of out here. It wouldn't have had much of an effect on your life. A chat every week or two. A cup of coffee. Things would have gone on much as normal. And instead all this has to happen. Why? Because you gave us no choice. Order must be kept. Now please watch. He gave a signal to a man who blew a whistle. In ones and twos, dozens of police officers jumped out of the vans and doubled round the corner.

In the year or so since she'd been living at the band house, more people had moved in. The building had turned into a little community. Roll Neck got out of the car and opened the rear door. Come on, he said. She refused. He told her not to test his patience and began to stroll across the street. She followed him, her feet like lead. The police had herded the tenants down into the courtyard. They stood there, shivering in their night clothes, listening to the sound of their apartments being searched, bangs and crashes echoing in the stairwell. People she knew, Katja and Elli among them, stared open-mouthed as Roll Neck walked her in from the street. Surrounded by high gray walls, he stuck his hands in his pockets and began to whistle, a jaunty little tune to accompany him as he ambled about, exploring. She followed behind, because staying in the courtyard would have been even worse. He visited almost every occupied apartment in the building, blandly unconcerned by the destruction going on all around him. Monika watched policemen pull out drawers, tip books off shelves as Roll Neck peered around like a tourist in an old church. She was friends with a photographer who lived on the floor above them. They had poured chemicals on his negatives and smashed his developing equipment. In the stairwell, policemen carried typewriters and boxes of documents, the materials the environmentalists across the hall used to make their newsletter. Finally, he pushed open the door of Katja and Elli's place. She saw the pile of kindling that had been their living room furniture, their clothes ground underfoot. The basin and toilet had been smashed, and water was pooling on the bathroom floor, which was covered in unsleeved records, grimy with boot prints. She looked out of the window. From the other side of the courtyard, she heard the sound of glass breaking, someone crying.

AT THIS POINT, Monika found it impossible to go on, and went outside to smoke a cigarette. She was gone for so long that I thought she might have left, and went out to find her. We carried on talking standing in the cold, between a pair of large ceramic dragons.

As she stood in the apartment that had been her home, Monika felt completely dissociated, as if she no longer occupied her body. It was self-protective, she supposed. A way of distancing herself from what was happening to her. How could I understand what it was like? To be looked at with such hatred by the people in the courtyard, people she cared about? To feel that you had betrayed them so thoroughly. Roll Neck walked her down the stairs, half-supporting her. And when she broke down in the car afterwards, when she began shaking and screaming, he spoke kindly to her, rubbing her back and offering her a handkerchief. He knew it was unpleasant, but he had to make her see how things were. This was how the world worked. He would have liked her to be useful in Berlin but there were other places too. He would find her somewhere else to live, give her a new start. He made her feel grateful to him. Then he took her to an office where she wrote out a document, a declaration that she was loyal to the GDR, and was cooperating with the State Security service of her own free will. And so it was done. She belonged to him.

Up until then Monika had been very thorough in the way

she told her story, never missing a step, filling in details in response to my questions. Now she became vague, skipping over large parts of her life, describing things in the most impressionistic way. She was tired, I think. She had been talking for hours, and the staff of the Chinese restaurant had long since started folding napkins and cleaning silverware, making the place ready for the next day's service. But there was something else, a reticence that I identified as shame.

She moved out of Berlin. The Stasi used her in other cities, where she wasn't known. She was taken to places where the band had played and told to get back in touch with people she'd met when she still belonged to herself, when she was, as she put it, "still a person." In a few cases the contacts had heard rumors about the police raid and wanted nothing to do with her. But others welcomed her, gave her a meal or somewhere to stay, and she paid them back by making reports, reports that caused trouble for them, opened up the possibility of harassment, or prison. She hung out in coffee bars and parties in Karl-Marx-Stadt, in Dresden, in Weimar. She tried all sorts of tactics to keep her sense of her own decency alive. She tried to give as little information to her handlers as she could, to keep the things she said neutral, just gossip, tidbits that sounded useful but wouldn't harm anyone. She soon found out that this was futile. Harm was everywhere. It spilled out as soon as she opened her mouth.

Roll Neck would meet her in hotel rooms or private apartments. There was always somewhere to which he had the key. He usually brought a bottle and would badger her to drink with him. She usually refused, until one evening she was sent to a poetry reading at a private apartment in Leipzig. The poets were good people and she felt shitty enough about reporting on them that when Roll Neck was debriefing her she said yes to the offer of a glass. Later on, when everything was blurry, she let him take her to the bedroom and do what he wanted. She was aware, from a great distance, of Roll Neck's white body, his grinding and whimpering, his ragged breathing next to her on the pillow after he came. She felt almost tenderly towards him. After all, he was the only one. The only one who knew her, who listened to her, who cared if she lived or died.

By this point, she said, she felt she had no inside. She was a sort of hall or public gallery that people could walk about in as they pleased. Gradually Roll Neck found her less useful. The targets she was supposed to observe became suspicious. They could tell something about her was wrong. She was drinking more and more and one night she got into a fight at a bar and used a heavy ashtray on another woman, who was badly hurt. A broken nose, a cracked skull. She was arrested and charged with assault. Roll Neck did nothing to help. He told her that the situation was her own fault. She hadn't been trying. He washed his hands of her. She was sentenced to eighteen months in the women's prison at Hoheneck, a grim red-brick fortress on a hill above a Saxon market town. It had a bad reputation and the reality was worse. Sleeping in a dormitory. Up at five for labor, sewing tablecloths and bed linens under signs extolling order and cleanliness. There was never a moment when she was unobserved. She couldn't sleep. She stopped getting her period. Her hair fell out. The prisoners used to make lipstick out of spit and matchheads. They smeared the paste on their mouths so they could feel less like sickly ghosts.

After she got out, she moved to Potsdam and eventually found work in a factory canteen. She served and swept and scrubbed and tried her best, as far as possible, never to speak to another living soul. Then one day she arrived to find the canteen workers gathered round a radio, listening as if their lives depended on what the announcer was saying. Hadn't she heard? The borders were open in Hungary. She didn't believe it. She thought it must be a ruse, a way to entrap traitors. From then on things moved very fast. In Leipzig the demonstrations got so big that the police had to stand aside and let the people pass. Every day the end was closer. The GDR began to collapse. People were packing and leaving for the West. Not her. She wasn't fooled.

It was impossible to believe that the whole system would fold just like that. And besides, they were still watching her. She was not sure who it was in particular, whether it was a coworker, a neighbor, or one of the people who stared at her in the line at the bread shop. When the minister announced that all travel restrictions had been lifted, she hurried back to her room. It seemed unwise to be on the street. She sat on the bed and listened to the radio, as the country she had grown up in vanished like a conjurer's illusion.

Everything happened without her. The dancing on the wall, the champagne, the banners hanging in the stairwells of the occupied Stasi buildings. She didn't even visit the West until almost a year after the change. A day walking around the other side of the city, looking in the windows of the shops. She went into the KaDeWe, the big department store, and rode the glass elevator up and down. When she came to the food hall, the luxurious displays of chocolate and fruit and delicatessen goods, she couldn't take it anymore and hurried away. She did not belong in such a place.

Soon enough, the secrets started to come out. Researchers were looking through the Stasi files, trying to reconstruct documents that had been hastily shredded or burned. Victims wanted to talk about who had done what. There were ugly scenes on the TV, media denunciations. Friends found out the truth about friends. Heroes turned out to have feet of clay. Maybe it was a sign of her naïveté, or her isolation, but it didn't occur to Monika that any of that would touch her. After all, who was she? Nothing. Nobody.

She didn't recognize the man who came to the door, until he reminded her that he used to write a fanzine. Then she remembered him, one of the Köpenick boys. He used to wear a dog collar and an army shirt. Turned out he'd done well in the new Germany, learned the tricks. He was now a journalist for a big weekly news magazine. Out of his writing he'd squeezed a watch and a fancy tape recorder and a little VW Golf parked on the street outside. He wanted to put certain questions to her, accusations of an unpleasant nature. Documents showed that she had been an informer. She'd put people in prison. Go away, she said. She had nothing to say to him.

You can tell them to go away, but they don't. Though she never read what he wrote, her neighbors did. They began to spit on the ground when she walked past and let their dogs do their business outside her door. Someone pushed a note through the letter box, calling her terrible names. By that time she had another job, quite a nice one, serving lunch to children at a Kindergarten. One day one of the teachers told her that "someone like her" had no business near children. They didn't fire her. They didn't have to. She packed her things and never went back.

Through all this, she had doubts. Everyone said that the Stasi were gone, but was it really true? For her they'd simply sunk underground, into the walls and the floorboards, the fabric of things. Objects still moved around in her apartment. She'd find the tea in the coffee jar, her books in different orders on her shelves. There were unexplained setbacks. A stolen bike, lost parcels at the post office. All of it was suspicious. The texture of her reality was soft, spongy. She couldn't trust that it would take her weight. She often wondered what had happened to Roll Neck. Sometimes it was as if he were still with her. At any time he might walk in, smirking and carrying a bottle of cheap booze. And then quite unexpectedly she saw him, standing in the cold selling pickles at a street market. He was wearing a cap with ear flaps, and his breath was spilling out in a frosty plume, and somehow the sight of him, wrapped in his hat and scarf, offering samples to the shoppers, was pathetic. It was like a balloon bursting. Finally she could believe that it was gone, the thing whose face he had been. She hurried away before he could spot her. That night she cried as she hadn't done in years.

Little by little, she made a life for herself. One with small dimensions, but safe and sustainable. Objects stopped moving around. No one hid in the doorways or followed her when she was on the street. Sometimes at weekends she packed a little picnic and went to the lake, or took a bus out to the countryside. Then came the revelations about Katja, and everything was difficult again. Naturally, with the fall of the wall, Katja had become an important person. It was inevitable, a woman with her charisma. After her days in the band, she'd been part of the movement for democracy. She'd written poetry and made speeches and chanted slogans. At the reunification ceremony she'd even been invited to sing a song at the Brandenburg Gate. She was an artist, an activist, a victim of the Stasi, a national symbol of resilience in the face of oppression. She'd just published a memoir when they found her file, and for Monika it felt like the night of the skinhead attack all over again, when she'd turned round to find Tommy standing in the doorway. The shock was just as great. The feeling of disorientation.

Looking back it now seemed to Monika that her best memories of Katja were actually invented. She was usually kind, but it was the sort of kindness that cost nothing. She'd always won so effortlessly, and no one had ever thought to question how she did it. Now it seemed so obvious, the ease with which she could get hold of things, make things happen. Monika could barely process what was in the articles, couldn't draw it into the circle of her imagination, so she made an appointment at the office which handled the Stasi archives. She was only allowed to read the material that pertained to her, but that was enough. Katja had been recruited by the Ministry for State Security at high school. She was described as "highly motivated," and "committed to the cause of socialism." She had reported everything, worked as hard as she could to undermine the influence of the decadent West. Most of Roll Neck's cruelties—the way he'd pressured her, the guilt he'd made her feel—served no useful purpose at all, because Katja had already been telling them everything. It was even more perverse than she'd imagined. In a secret ceremony, during the time that they were in the band, the MfS had awarded Katja a medal and the rank of captain. Finally Monika understood the purpose of parading her in front of her friends on the day of the raid. It had been to protect Katja, to divert suspicion from their real asset.

So what was left, after all that? She had nothing of her own. All her intimacies were on file in numbered paragraphs, all the movements of her soul. There were things she'd forgotten, or blocked out. A report dated soon after Roll Neck started poisoning her life, when the others had begun to be suspicious: *Monika E claimed not to be a coworker with the MfS. She was intoxicated and revealed homosexual impulses* . . . She had been drunk, that was true. And she'd wanted to make Katja believe her, believe that she would never ever betray her trust. When she'd tried to kiss her, Katja had gently pushed her away.

This time she read the newspapers. A tabloid printed a picture of Katja holding up a hand to ward off a photographer. There were other pictures, interviews with people they had known in Berlin, all saying how shocked they were to discover the truth about their famous friend. Everyone was shocked about Katja. Her, not so much. There was a brief revival of interest in DGF, the three-piece band with two informers. Monika moved again, though that didn't stop a journalist finding her and following her down the street to ask about her Stasi "colleague." After a month or two things died down again.

And that, she said, was more or less that. She did a lot of drinking and got sentimental tattoos and tried to work out what she would say to her friend if she ever saw her again. Ten years after reunification, someone found Katja in a small South German town and persuaded her to give an interview for a TV documentary. Monika barely recognized her. She'd got fat, and her hair was badly dyed. The bohemian disorder of her youth had become an ugly jumble. She was breeding dogs, or rabbits or something. Animals for pet shops. She said she didn't regret what she'd done. She'd followed her heart. So what if things had changed around her? She'd turned out not to be right about the world. That was true of many young people. Who could see into the future? A few months later, Monika saw Katja's face again, in a newspaper obituary. She had gone out to the Wannsee and walked into the water. She had taken a lot of sleeping tablets and filled a backpack with rocks.

There Monika stopped. Not much of an ending, she said. Not really an ending at all. I told her I thought I understood. That was why she went for walks by the lake—to feel close to her friend. She looked bemused. Why would she want to feel close to Katja? She was a Stasi bitch. She put some money on the table to pay for her share of the bill, and got up from the table. She told me I was sentimental. I was trying to help you, she said. But you're soft and selfish. The world will chew you up and spit you out.

AN APOCALYPSE

●

AS A CHILD I experienced myself as a ghostly event in the world. It came first, this "self," before everything, before thought or action. It was the place where *I* was, my present moment. As I got older, one thing that never changed was the conviction that exploring its luxurious particularity would keep me busy for the rest of my life, that I would never finish thinking myself through, and at a minimum it would be an honorable project, useful or at least absorbing, and however else my circumstances changed, it could never be taken from me. In Berlin, that came to an end. Now, what I think of when I think of my "self" is the atrocious waste of my years.

To explain, I have to write about Anton. Firstly, what he was not. He wasn't some kind of hallucinatory plus one. He never spoke to me or appeared to be physically present after the last time I saw him in Paris. That said, when I was on the island, I was also convinced that it was only a matter of time before he showed up in person. All the signs were there.

I thought it was clever of him to use the island. He'd obviously walked the topography and knew precisely where to send me. The way I looked at it, since I knew what he was doing, and had no way of getting out, the best thing was to wait. I thought we would confront each other in some kind of third-reel showdown. Holmes and Moriarty, the Jets and the Sharks. I thought I knew where it would happen. At the northernmost point, following the path round the cliffs.

Each time I try to find a point of departure, a place to make a stand and defend this part of my story, some narrative tentacle emerges out of the swamp, and I have to stagger back. I'm certain about some of the things that took place in the last days before I left Berlin. Others I suspect may have been interpolated wholesale into my memory, not figments of my imagination exactly. Not *my* imagination. Memories that derive from an external source. There is a third category, in between the two—the indisputable or at least subjectively experienced facts and the cuckoo-like alien fabrications. I think of them as shufflings—rearrangements or deformations of material that was already there. To speak about Anton in a way that has any chance of being meaningful, I have to mix up these different levels, to walk out on a metaphorical rope bridge with many missing slats or supports, willing myself to believe that my feet will not meet thin air.

I am not sure in what category to put my conversations with

Monika. Our relationship really was as brief as it appears in my notes. There was certainly no sexual charge. We sat down, I listened to her story, she told me I'd misunderstood, then she left. We never spoke again. I find it surprising that she told me so much about herself, given that she'd spent much of her life in hiding, and had reason to be wary of strangers. Nevertheless it is all there, in a transcript I made in Berlin.

I do know that I really attended the party at the Konzerthaus, because I've seen a picture of myself there, one of dozens on a photo agency website. In it, I'm standing next to Anton, looking ill at ease. There is a woman too, a famous Russian model. The caption: *Irina Titianova, Gary Bridgeman and friend.*

It came about because of Finlay. He found me. I was walking back to the Deuter Center, the evening after I had heard Monika's story. I had spent the day walking agitated circuits of the lake, unsure what to do. He was with a young American woman I didn't recognize, a film-maker well-known in some scene or circle that I didn't follow, at least that was the impression I got from the way he introduced her, the slight emphasis on her name, a hint that I ought to recognize it and be aware of her work.

It was done out of pity. Finlay forced me to admit, again, that since my arrival in Berlin I hadn't once left Wannsee. His friend, who lived in one of the fashionable districts, Mitte or perhaps Kreuzberg, was appalled. We could get him in, she said, and Finlay agreed that they probably could. Ignoring my questions about exactly where they could get me in, they escorted me back to my room and instructed me to change. When I reemerged in a jacket and a crumpled dress shirt they assured me that I looked great, and besides, where we were going everyone would be too drunk to really care. They were in an expansive mood, raising their voices and making cutting remarks about this and that, and after a while I realized that they were high and I was part of a gesture, a dig at the organizers of whatever event we were attending. It seemed to be a fancy party, something they wanted to be at but not part of, to keep at an ironic distance. I wasn't sure how I felt about this and made the first of several attempts to back out, but they wouldn't take no for an answer. They had excess energy and needed me as an audience, or at least a receptacle, a sort of garbage can for their gestures and theorizing.

They linked arms and half-carried me to the S-Bahn station, and we got on the first train that came along, the two of them jabbering at each other as we rode through the suburban night. Out the window, the darkness assembled itself into a city. A glimpse of elegant buildings in Charlottenburg. Yellow high-rises at Bellevue. At the Hauptbahnhof a three-piece Roma band got on and made an unlovely race out of "When the Saints Go Marching In." As we got out at Friedrichstrasse I experienced something like awe. The lights of bank buildings shone through the glass of a canopy held up by steel struts and giant concrete shafts. I felt like a peasant visiting a temple, gawping at giant banners advertising Ritter chocolate and Social Democracy. To be among so many other citizens, bustling along the platform, riding up and down on the shining escalators!

We walked out of the station and crossed Unter den Linden, passing the flagship stores of international brands. It became clear that the party we were going to was for a movie star's foundation, and had something to do with the film festival, the Berlinale. In the darkness I caught a flash of pink sparkles, and saw a little girl in a parka and a pair of glittery tights, clutching on to the hand of a man who looked to be in his late twenties. He was holding out a paper coffee cup, begging for change. As we drew near, he caught my eye, and looked away. He didn't ask us for money.

We turned the corner onto the Gendarmenmarkt. Finlay was telling me something about how the buildings had been destroyed in the war, how the streetscape was fake, virtual reality something something, but I couldn't concentrate on any of it. The young father had recognized me. And I'd recognized him. What were they doing there?

We reached the party venue, and saw the famous Neo-classical façade of the Konzerthaus incongruously covered in orange life jackets. Finlay saw the bewilderment on my face and explained, as you would to a country cousin unused to the ways of the city, that the life jackets had been used by refugees, and the famous artist Ai Weiwei had recovered them from beaches on the Greek island of Lesbos.

We had to pass under a rubber boat and a banner with a hashtag and I saw two women in ball gowns, smoking cigarettes, keeping warm in the February chill with the kind of foil blankets that are given out to disaster victims or runners at the end of a race. Finlay said his name to a young man with an earpiece and we were ushered into the aftermath of a charity banquet. The concert hall was a confection of gilt and white, and dozens of tables bore the wreckage of a big dinner. Seemingly everyone was wearing the foil blankets. They littered the floor. Men in black tie had knotted them like superhero capes. They were draped across the backs of chairs, jauntily wrapped like high-tech shawls around women in backless gowns. The guests had drifted away from their tables, members of the donor class like strange tropical birds, shy and awkward in the presence of humans, being soothed and coaxed by professionally gregarious service providers, friends or advisors or coaches. We had just missed some kind of award ceremony. Here and there, Plexiglas trophies were being passed around, winners having their hands shaken, modestly expressing surprise. A waitress came with a tray of shots and I drank two, one after the other, staring numbly at the foil-wrapped crowd cosplaying as refugees.

At the weekends, the Deuter Center's dining room was closed, and though a few basic necessities were provided in a communal kitchen, fellows were basically left to fend for themselves. The supermarket was a fifteen-minute walk, slightly uphill, just far enough to be worth taking a bus if the weather was bad. One day I had wanted to stretch my legs and for once there was no wind, so the cold was bearable. I trudged up the main road, which in Kleist's time had been a newly paved highway linking Berlin and Potsdam. In the supermarket I filled a trolley with bread, gherkins, cheese and fruit, basic things that didn't require preparation. I liked cooking well enough, and my room had an electric ring and a microwave, but somehow at the Deuter Center I was never able to bring myself to do anything more taxing than breaking a plastic seal. In the drinks aisle I picked up a bottle of Scotch, added some beer, a lot of salty snacks, and went to the checkout to pay.

I didn't feel like walking back, and so I sat down under the shelter and opened a bag of chips. Across the road was a hamburger franchise, with signs in the parking lot advertising German twists to its menu. You could get a burger in a pretzel bun. You could get pickled cabbage. Behind the restaurant was a row of dumpsters and a small play area with a plastic slide and a garish polka-dotted horse on a spring, made for a small child to ride. A little girl in a hot pink parka stood beside the horse, maybe three or four years old, about my daughter's age. She wasn't playing, just standing there, her face framed in an oval of fake fur. I looked around for an adult, concerned that I couldn't see one. Maybe her parents were eating and had sent her out to play. I wouldn't have done that. It was winter and she seemed too young to be unsupervised with a busy road nearby. Still, she didn't look distressed. She just stood, looking vacantly into the distance, patting the plastic horse with a little ungloved hand.

As I watched, the lid of one of the dumpsters wobbled and a man climbed out, piking his upper body over the lip and swinging his legs to drop heavily down to the ground. He was younger than me, but the maneuver still cost him some effort. He was wearing a down jacket, sneakers and acid-wash jeans. He'd retrieved a plastic trash bag from the dumpster, and he squatted down and opened it, transferring some of its contents into a backpack. The little girl stood watching him, rocking from foot to foot. These were the people I had just seen again on Friedrichstrasse.

It was the year they all came, more than a million refugees crossing Europe, massing at fences, drowning in the Mediterranean, hunted by vigilantes in the Bulgarian woods. On bright days in Wannsee you would meet them by the lake, the lucky ones who had made it to Germany, families pushing buggies, groups of young men taking selfies and horsing around. They had been housed all over Berlin, and the authorities were struggling to cope. On lampposts around the lakeside colony were stickers with English slogans: *Refugees Welcome. No Borders.* Other stickers asked *Wieviel ist zuviel?*

"How many is too many?" Around the station, I'd seen some Antifa kids wearing shirts saying *Kein Mensch ist Illegal*—*No one is illegal*—and *FCK AFD,* an insult directed at the new right-wing party whose supporters had spray-painted *Mut zu Deutschland*—Courage for Germany—on the side wall of the Chinese restaurant.

The father took his daughter's hand and together they crossed the road to the bus stop where I was sitting. Seeing a car, he tugged on her arm, encouraging her to break into a run. They made it to safety, the pack bouncing against his shoulder. As he lifted her up and put her down on the metal bench beside me, we made brief eye contact and exchanged nods, the freemasonry of dark-skinned men who meet in white places. From their looks, I guessed that they were Syrian or Iraqi. He knelt down, and handed her something from his backpack. It was a hamburger, wrapped in paper. The little girl opened it carefully. She was a mournful creature, with a narrow face and big brown eyes. She pushed back her hood so she could eat, and I saw a head of frizzy brown hair, partially tamed by a plastic barrette. She ate slowly and contentedly, savoring each bite. The burger must have been stone cold, the previous night's surplus thrown out at the end of the shift, but she didn't seem to mind. Her father stared down at her with such tenderness that I had to look away for a moment and collect myself.

When I looked back, the father was watching me. His expression was beyond defiance, a sort of exhausted appraisal of my reaction. He knew that I knew he was feeding his daughter from the trash. He was expecting to be insulted, was already protecting himself against my display of disgust. I rooted around in my shopping bags, and found a tub of cashew nuts. I asked, in English, whether I could give them to the girl. He nodded. She put them beside her on the bench and carried on eating her burger.

After a few minutes a bus came. The man scooped up the girl, still eating, and carried her up the steps in the crook of his arm. With his free hand he showed some kind of pass to the driver. Though it was the bus I was waiting to catch, I didn't follow. I sat there, rooted to the spot, as the doors closed and it pulled away. The tub of cashews was still sitting there.

At the party, I moved with Finlay and his friend through the crowd. I met a former child soldier turned rapper, and a Swedish artist who was there with her film editor boyfriend and wanted me to know, in confidence, that she felt uncomfortable. The money, she said. They bid so much. She showed me her program. At the charity auction, someone had won a recording date with Pussy Riot. Someone had won a case of 1989 "Fall of the Wall" Château Mouton Rothschild, with a label painted by Georg Baselitz. Finlay took me away and we got drinks at a champagne bar. Downstairs was another bar, and side rooms with dancing and cabaret. We watched burlesque dancers and a magician, introduced by a Weimar-themed MC. I was still thinking about the man and his daughter. I was visualizing myself outside in the cold, shaking a paper cup. How often had that man and that girl slept in the open, on a station platform or a beach? How often had it been a matter of life and death to hold on to daddy's hand?

There were more drinks and another chain of introductions—to a familiar-looking actor, an executive from one of the big European film distributors. Finlay's friend floated us adroitly between conversations, and then somehow she and Finlay vanished, I think to do more coke, and I was left to make small talk with a Swiss festival director. By this time I was quite drunk, so I told her my theory that Kleist suffered from what we would now call PTSD, having fought at the age of fifteen in a Prussian infantry regiment during a war against France. He had what are clearly manic episodes. He once disappeared in Paris and was found near Calais, trying to persuade a conscript soldier to swap places with him so he could find death as part of Napoleon's planned invasion of England. The festival director said she was sorry but she'd seen someone she absolutely had to talk to. Her target was part of a nearby group, and she reached out and squeezed his upper arm, not letting go until she'd drawn him towards us.

As we were in a crowded space, the festival director was obliged to introduce me, and I shook the hand of a white American in his late thirties, "the writer Gary Bridgeman." There was an exactness to his appearance, an aura of calculation that put me on guard. About my height, he looked physically fit, with three-day stubble and a hint of product in his fashionably cut hair. The festival director moved her body slightly sideways, subtly edging me out as she began to tell him flirtatiously why he simply had to do a panel at her event. I couldn't catch precisely what was on offer, it was obvious that he didn't want it. As she pitched, his face took on a mask-like rigidity. She was insistent, she really had him in her sights, and I watched him realize that he needed to find a way to shake her. Briefly he made eye contact with me, and he must have seen that I knew what he was thinking, because he used me to execute a nasty but undeniably virtuosic social maneuver, which commenced with a brush of his fingers against the festival director's cheek. As she reacted to the touch, visibly offended and—I thought—also a little aroused, her hand floating involuntarily to her face, he broke into a huge grin, as if responding to something said or done just behind her right shoulder, some phantom outbreak of wit. Between the sudden invasion of her personal space and the anxiety that she was missing out—or worse—that she'd lost her social bearings entirely and had somehow embarrassed herself, the director was momentarily disorientated. She turned to her right in a dazed arc, looking for the source of the inaudible *bon mot,* and in that window Bridgeman dipped left towards me, grasped my shoulder, steered me through a gap between two waitresses and out into a sort of pocket or bubble of open space. Keep walking, he said. Pretend to find me funny. His accent had a Transatlantic indeterminacy. The strange Brownian motion of parties spat us out into a corridor, laughing in a way that was fake at first, and then genuine, at least on my part, as I realized how rude we'd been. Two cheeky boys running away from mom. Only when we were standing at the bar did it dawn on me that I knew exactly who he was. And I was afraid.

When you come face-to-face with someone you've googled, you feel instantly sly and underhand. I'd seen a picture of this man riding a motorbike through the Mojave Desert. I'd seen him on the cover of one of the Hollywood trades, posing against a burned-out car. *Disruptor: How Gary Bridgeman's Violent Vision Transformed TV.* For that he'd been styled as a war reporter. Tactical pants and boots, a khaki bush shirt, a pair of dark glasses pushed up into his hair. A spray-painted mural was visible behind the wreckage, as if he were filing from the front line of the race war. He had a camera around his neck. He had a fucking notebook. Everything about that picture had annoyed me. And yet I'd spent so long watching his show. Hours and hours, watching his show.

We toasted each other with whatever cocktails we'd just grabbed from a passing tray. "Man," he said, "did we ghost that bitch." I winced at "bitch" and mimed dejection to cover myself, grimacing and holding up my drink in a what-can-you-do-about-it shrug. "Well, I guess we're not going to Switzerland."

He laughed. "That was so, so wrong." We introduced ourselves and he told me to call him Anton. I never did find out if it was a middle name or something completely assumed. We talked about some innocuous topic, I can't even remember what, because I was mentally and physically reeling, drunk but at the same time hyper-alert, my nervous system sending notice that it was about to trigger fight-or-flight.

"Are you feeling OK?"

"Sure. I'm just a little light-headed." I tried to pull myself together. "I have to ask, are you the director of *Blue Lives*?"

He shrugged. "I directed a couple of episodes. I'm the creator and show runner. You've seen it?"

"I guess you could say I'm a fan."

"You guess?"

My strained laugh was surely a tell. A silence began to build or congeal or perhaps spawn between us. I broke it by blurting out a question.

"So why are you interested in the Comte de Maistre?"

It didn't sound natural. It just wasn't the sort of thing people say. It's not always a good idea to start a serious conversation about someone's work, particularly in the middle of the kind of party where half the room is trying to persuade the other half to come back to its hotel. Anton pretended not to understand. "Sorry, who did you say?"

This was when I knew I'd stumbled onto something weird, because he was so obviously lying.

"Maistre."

"Never heard of him."

"Come on. You quote him."

"I do what?"

"You quote a lot of things in *Blue Lives*. Heraclitus. Schopenhauer. Emil Cioran. That's not exactly standard for a TV cop show. And as far as I can see you don't talk about it in interviews, so it's probably not just so you can look intellectual."

"Somebody's paying attention."

At first, when the little wheel began to rotate in the center of my screen and no amount of reloading or reconnecting would get the video up again, I was desperate to find out what happened. Later a tinge of relief crept in. La Mettrie was the personification of the thing I lay awake worrying about: the darkness, the outside. Carson had invited the darkness into his world through his own corruption. It had arrived to swallow up a weak, helpless, arrogant man. I didn't care what happened to him. My anxiety was focused on the children. If they were murdered, I didn't know what I'd do.

It wasn't that I thought Carson's children were real, or even particularly well-drawn. They were Anton's puppets, marionettes in his theater of cruelty. At the same time, I can't claim that I was watching in a dispassionate way. I identified instinctively with the family whose house was being broken into. The door was my door. The children were my children. In stories, at least the kind of serial dramas that are financed and streamed by big American networks, the outcome of this situation is never really in doubt. Carson will arrive in the nick of time and his children will be saved. But *Blue Lives* had demonstrated, again and again, that its vision of the world was utterly cold and merciless. In that show, it was perfectly possible that the children would die. And if they died, would Anton make the viewer watch? Would their terror and pain actually be shown on-screen? Again the answer ought to have been obvious. No network would ever allow it. To show such scenes would go against all established norms of decency. But I didn't feel certain. I didn't think it was likely, but it didn't seem impossible either, and that in itself was frightening. If that particular norm had shifted, then what else had changed? What other lines were nihilistic young men like Anton now dreaming of crossing?

What I wrote, my faltering accounts of the things I thought and believed, reached a few thousand readers in the tiny milieu of people who bought and discussed books of cultural essays. Anton's work had an audience of millions. *Blue Lives* wasn't big as far as TV shows went, but it had more reach than I could ever dream of. Not that I had anything to say that would be of interest to millions, and I was comfortable with that, or at least reconciled to it. At a certain point I'd accepted that I could only communicate in my own way, which is to say by generating a sort of paratactical blizzard of obscure cultural references and inviting my reader to fall through it with me. This is almost by definition not popular, and though I have no interest in being recondite for its own sake, I also have no gift for simplicity. So my issue with Anton's TV show wasn't jealousy, or not exactly. And it wasn't mere curiosity, a bland expression of interest in some phenomenon passing by the porthole. *Blue Lives* felt threatening. Threatening to me, to me personally, to who and what I was, to the people I loved. I understood that this was an excessive reaction to a TV show.

"So what is it you want to ask me?" Anton seemed suddenly bored. For a moment I thought he'd break off the conversation. But he didn't, and since I'd started, I felt obliged to go on, to pick my way into the thicket. What was it I wanted to ask?

"*Blue Lives* has a very pessimistic tone."

"That's one way to put it."

If I'd stopped then. I could have gone to the bathroom. I could have turned and walked out of the party into the cold night air. I was free to do those things. One of the knots I find hard to unpick about my encounter with Anton is how much of what happened to me in the following months would still have happened without him. It may not be important, ultimately, or not important to anyone but me. Still, I would like to know. It would help.

I heard the familiar note of hysteria in my voice, and tried to fight it. "So that's it? Is that what you believe? That it's just a war of each against each. That we're living in hell?"

He shrugged and did a sort of movie-mogul drawl. "If I wanted to send a message, I'd use Western Union."

"Come on."

"Whatever's on your mind, just let it go. It's entertainment. You're taking it too seriously."

It is infinitely annoying to be told what to take seriously and what not to. What sense of my priorities can some stranger have? None. So why say it? Anton's ironic tone compounded my irritation. "But you've slipped in all these literary allusions. That's a lot of trouble to go to, if it's just entertainment. I mean, how did you even get the studio to agree?"

"I don't know what you mean by trouble. You're a writer, you know how it is. Bad writers borrow, good ones steal."

"That's not the whole story."

"Isn't it?"

"Why Maistre? You're not just saying you were lying by the pool and happened to pick up the *Soirées de Saint-Pétersbourg*."

"You actually know about Maistre? You realize we're probably the only two people in this building who ever even heard of the guy."

"That speech. The one about the whole earth being perpetually steeped in blood. You left out the end."

He held up his hands. "Before you get into—whatever it is, I want to know is this, like, your specialist subject? You teach eighteenth-century something or other?

"No. That is, not in particular. I'm not a specialist. I don't really have a specialist area."

"So, a generalist."

"Yes."

"Who wants to talk to me about an eighteenth-century French aristocrat."

"Exactly. I played back what you have Carson say. A few times, actually. With the screaming. I don't know how you handle that, by the way. In the edit or whatever. Over and over again."

"They're real screams."

"What?"

"Just fucking with you. Go on."

"OK. Sorry. I mean, right. You left out the last lines. In the *Soirées*, Maistre talks about the earth being a sort of sacrificial altar, with every living thing being butchered forever, on and on, until what he calls the consummation of things. That's where you cut."

"Yeah. As you say, it's hard getting the weird shit past the execs, and that speech was already quite long."

"Really? That's it?"

"What can I say? You have to know which battles to fight."

"I—well, I looked it up. Maistre continues the sentence 'until evil is extinct, until the death of death.' So yes, the world is an abattoir, but he's not saying that's the end of it. That's not the meaning of life. There's redemption. He was enjoining his readers to obey God, because their only hope of salvation from the earthly meat grinder was Heaven."

"I don't understand."

"The meat grinder. That's it, for you. That's all there is."

"You're calling me out for this? Because I left out the redemption?"

"No."

"Good, because that would be unbelievably lame. Although maybe not if you were a Christian of some kind. Are you?"

"What?"

"A Christian of some kind."

"No."

"You do strike me more as the secular type. A believer in progress, religion of the liberals."

A waiter was passing with a tray of drinks. I swapped my empty glass for a full one. "You don't want something to hope for? Something to work towards?"

"What? Why would I need something to work towards? Jolly as that sounds."

"Because . . ."

I trailed off. I had the hollow feeling in my chest that usually meant I was missing something. I was too drunk to construct an argument, or even really follow one. I knew I sounded hopelessly naïve. I wanted to say something about how human beings should always be ends, and never means, how we have rights by virtue of our agency. I wanted to tell Anton that his nihilistic TV show made a mockery of human dignity. The following day, through the acid mist of my hangover, it would all present itself to me in an orderly sequence.

Anton was still laughing at me when we were interrupted by a sallow-faced man in a tux and an LA Raiders cap who clapped him on the back and began to administer a sort of one-handed shoulder massage, bobbing his head up and down to the music like a nodding dog toy. "Hey!" he said. "There you are!" And again. "There you are." His face was doglike too, which accentuated the effect, thin and jowly, the sort of bloodhound countenance that is doomed always to look disappointed, even if its owner is animated by stimulants.

Anton shrugged him off. "What up, Greg."

"Me and Irina are going to try our hand at the roulette wheel. You want to come?" He had a woman with him, tall and professionally beautiful. I registered her as a semi-familiar face, like many other people in the room. The whole party was swimming in a sort of amniotic fluid of celebrity.

Anton shook his head. "I'm heading out pretty soon. Going to get something to eat."

"Seriously? We just had a five-course meal. You want a bump? Get you back in the game?"

"No, I'm good. I'm going to go. I'm meeting some people."

"I don't understand you. Why would you want to leave? Did you get to meet Irina?"

Anton smiled. "Hi Irina."

Irina smiled back. Greg obviously felt he was getting somewhere. "Irina, can you believe this guy seriously wants, what is it you want? What kind of food is worth leaving this lovely party and this unusually attractive company?"

"A döner."

"That's a kind of sandwich."

"A kebab."

"You are out of your fucking mind."

"No. That's what I want. I might take this guy along with me. We're having a very interesting conversation."

Greg turned to me and stuck out his hand. "Hi. Greg Novak." I shook it, but he'd already launched back into his conversation with Anton. "I don't understand. You got a fucking tapeworm? We just ate. And before that the canapés. I saw you with the fucking canapés. You were raping the fucking canapés and now you want to go get fucking Lebanese food?"

"Turkish."

"Hold on."

Greg raised a finger and stepped away to take a call or do some other business on his cell phone. For a moment Anton and I were left standing either side of Irina, who really was very tall. That was when the photograph was taken. No one wanted me in the shot, least of all me—I must have looked like a monkey trying to climb a tree—and the photographer was motioning me to step aside so he could get one with just the supermodel when Greg walked into frame and someone wearing a headset popped up next to Irina and she disappeared, actually vanished, or so it seemed to me, as if she'd been raptured. The photographer had no interest in a picture of three non-celebrity men and moved on. Greg confronted

Anton with all the grace of a child whose ice cream had been knocked on the floor.

"You asshole. You let them get her back."

"What did you think I could do?"

"Thirty seconds I leave you. You could have been charming. Made fucking conversation until I could take the reins again. I had a fucking connection going."

"Dude, she's married."

"She is?"

"To the guy who owns LVMH. Or Formula One. I forget which."

Anton let Greg process his disappointment and turned to me. "You're hungry, right. You look hungry."

I did actually feel hungry.

"Yeah, you're hungry. Follow me of your own free will, for I have opened the book of secrets." He said it with a sort of ironic courtly flourish, but this odd phrase had the same unsettling tone as the speeches in *Blue Lives*. I got the feeling, dulled by alcohol, that his words had hidden barbs, and the joke (if there was one) was at my expense. But I left the party with him. I got my heavy jacket from the coat check and went outside. Greg trailed along behind us like a small boy being taken to visit relatives.

As we trotted down the steps, Anton began to wave at one of the drivers who'd lined up their cars on the street, hoping for a fare. I spotted Finlay under the portico. He was wrapped in a foil blanket, sharing a cigarette or a joint with someone. He waved and gave me a thumbs-up. I waved back. I saw his friend leaning up against the other side of the pillar, making out with a waiter. I got into a taxi with Anton and Greg.

Anton read the driver an address in Kreuzberg that he

looked up on his phone. Greg turned round from the front seat to remind us again that we'd "lost Irina." "Where are we even going?" he asked.

"I told you. To get a döner."

"On our own?"

"Some friends of mine will meet us there."

Greg turned to me. "This fucking guy. Seriously. He knows people everywhere. Every fucking city we go to."

"What do you do, Greg?" I asked. "Do you work with Anton?"

"I'm a producer."

Anton smiled. "Greg's rich. Or as he likes to say, *fucking* rich. And he always wants to have a good time. That's the only reason I keep him around."

Greg laughed heartily, though there was nothing in Anton's tone to suggest he meant it humorously. He finished with his phone and looked out of the window. We traveled through the city in silence.

"You get it, right?" It took me a moment to realize that he was talking to me. "It's Carson's show. His journey. He starts off as just another schmuck, but as time goes on he learns the truth about the world. He's initiated into the mystery of power."

"You mean he tortures people."

He sighed, as if indulging a difficult child. "I thought you said you'd read Maistre."

I shrugged.

"Pop quiz: on whom does all greatness and all power rest?"

Drunk as I was, I knew the answer. It was the most famous passage in Maistre's writings. "The executioner."

"One point to you. You can't have a state without the threat of violence. It's the only way to get people to obey. The executioner *is* that threat. He's the one who wields the axe."

"So what are you saying? We need Carson, because he's the executioner?"

"The executioner isn't a criminal, he's a priest. The scaffold is his altar. Everyone worships there, even if they pretend they don't. Killing in war is fine—we admire soldiers, we give them parades and medals—but the executioner does something just as important, and the only emotion he inspires is fear."

"Carson's a corrupt cop who robs and tortures suspects."

"Go ahead, call him names if it makes you feel better. But you rely on him. You know you do. You fear and hate him for doing something that you can't do, that you secretly know has to be done. Society needs fear. It's our dirty little secret."

The argument got confused. I said that what Carson did was morally wrong and Anton accused me of being "one of those people," so I asked what kind of people and he told me the kind who say morality when they mean politics and politics when they mean morality. Most of what I called politics was, in his opinion, just squeamishness. There were people who acted, and people who wrung their hands and behaved as if they were going to act at some point in the future, once they'd sorted out what was *moral* and what wasn't. Their so-called morality was just paralysis. In truth, they'd delegated their power of action to others, men who weren't frozen rabbits, who could do what needed to be done. I told him he sounded like every other writer guy, secretly fretting that he wasn't a man of action. If he really wanted to be a fireman or whatever, why didn't he just go and fight fires instead of making TV shows?

It was the first time I saw him angry. He sniffed something

about my "censoriousness" and withdrew into himself. We drove for a long time in silence. Greg paid the driver and we got out on a dim street lined with concrete apartment blocks, pocked with satellite dishes. Breaking their ranks was a single-story arcade of little stores and cafés. We found an awning saying *Okacbaşi,* a steamed-up window. Greg shoved his hands in his pockets and said no fucking way was he going inside. "Nothing in there for Greggy but food poisoning."

I hesitated on the sidewalk. I wondered how far it was to the U-Bahn. Anton could tell that I was about to slip off the hook. "Don't be a pussy," he said. "Come inside or stay in the dark." So much of what he said had that particular tone, that suggestion of double meaning. Come inside or stay in the dark, as if he were about to initiate me into a mystery, offer me the red pill. What the hell, I thought. I was hungry. As we walked in, we were hit by heat and smoke and the mouth-watering smell of lamb cooking on a charcoal grill. The room was decorated in blue and white tile, and packed with men sitting on plastic garden chairs, smoking and drinking beer and watching a football game on a screen mounted on the wall. A harassed-looking waiter took us to the back, where a table with no view was still free.

As we sat down, Anton's friends arrived, a couple in their thirties. He was heavyset and bearded, his features squashed together in the middle of a broad, high-cheekboned face. As he took off his cap I saw that his hair was shaved into a foppish undercut, much like Anton's. His partner was the kind of well-groomed blonde you see a lot in New York, rigorously skinny, fashionably but conservatively dressed, in the way that Rei had once characterized to me as "calculated to appeal to the crucial forty-plus finance demographic." She kissed Anton's cheek. They put their hands on each other in a way that suggested prior intimacy.

"Why this restaurant, Anton? Are you making a joke?"

She spoke English with a German accent.

"Exactly, Tara. A little joke."

"I walked in and I felt relieved to have Karl with me."

"We're all lucky to have Karl. Hi Karl."

"Hello Anton. You don't really want to eat here, do you?"

"Sure I do."

Karl shrugged and Tara made a face. They spent a few moments stripping off coats and sweaters, gloves and hats, all the heavy layers needed to function outside in the Berlin winter. We sat down under a tourist calendar with a picture of the ruins of Ephesus. Anton threw an arm round Tara's shoulders and introduced me. At first sight she had the look of a Victorian doll, her pale heart-shaped face framed in ash-blond hair and decorated with a little pointy nose, rather red from the cold. She said hello with a condescending half-smile, and I responded as—I regret to say—I am programmed to do to a certain kind of woman, a woman who is performing superiority and desirability, demanding a tribute of attention. I twisted my mouth into a raffish grin and heard myself make some half-joke about her dislike of Turkish food, which she let fall without a hint of amusement. Karl asked me what I was doing in Berlin, and to my surprise seemed to know all about the Deuter Center. That building has an interesting history, he said. There is a wartime bunker under the house that I've always wanted to see. I was curious to know more, but he started telling Anton something, leaning over the table and using a low voice. I couldn't hear much, but he was obviously unhappy. Anton shook his head. This is all stuff for Paris, he said. We can deal with it then.

The waiter threw a couple of laminated menus down on the table and started laying out bread and *cacik* and olives. We ordered beers, which came almost at once. Cheers erupted around the room as a goal was scored. I tried again with Tara. Was she in the film business too?

"I'm a journalist."

I asked what kind, who she wrote for, but she just shook her head. "I can barely breathe in this room," she said. "All this sweat and smoke." Her edge of dislike was a challenge, and once I would have tried to harden it into a flirtation, to force her to find me charming. Now I just felt depressed. I wished I was with Rei. She would have liked that place.

Greg was vaping and looking at his phone. "What are we even doing here?"

Pensively Anton wiped a piece of bread through the yogurt dip. "You'd hardly believe you were in Europe, right Greg?"

"I don't get it. We could still be at the party. There was crazy pussy, a dance floor, open bar. And you want to come and sit in a toilet with fucking al Qaeda."

"But I guess this is your kind of spot, right? Multicultural and whatnot. Diverse."

I realized Anton was speaking to me. "It's not really diverse. Everyone's Turkish except us."

Karl snorted. "It's very nice when you're the person adding diversity in your own country."

I was saved from having to answer by the arrival of the waiter. I ordered a döner, everything on it. Anton said he'd have the same. None of the others wanted to eat. The tension at the table was palpable. Anton hammily mimed concern and turned to me. "What are we to do? Karl seems to feel uneasy. Perhaps we should be concerned. Unlike us writers, Karl is a man of action. He's the kind of guy who—well, if he'd been born a few hundred years ago he'd have been bathed in Ottoman blood at the gates of Vienna."

"So why did you come here if you knew he didn't like it?"

Anton laughed and nodded, as if I'd won a debating point. Karl sat with his hands in his lap, staring into the middle distance. Greg looked at his phone. For a while Anton and Tara spoke about something innocuous, a car that she wanted to buy. The food arrived. A Berlin döner is a beautiful thing and as it was set down in front of me, I was reminded that I was very hungry. I ate with relish, gulping beer, drunkenly spilling sauce and shredded cabbage on my plate. After a while I noticed that Tara was watching me with palpable disgust. Anton was scrutinizing me too, picking vaguely at his own sandwich with a fork. I felt as if I were doing something unclean, snapping and nosing at my food like a dog at its bowl.

"What?"

Anton laughed. "So you like kebab."

"Yes."

"But we have a problem. Greg thinks it stinks."

Greg made no eye contact with me, examining his phone as if this had nothing to do with him. Anton continued. "Greg's another crusader. He's from LA, like me, so we essentially grew up knee-deep in Jews, but we both have a feeling for our heritage. And here's another thing. My friends have an aversion to being told what to do. To having things forced on them. Karl doesn't like his culture being polluted by immigrants. Tara doesn't want to have to worry about rape. Greg just doesn't like spicy food. The question is do Greg and Anton and Tara have a right to their preference?"

"What preference?"

"To live a life without kebab."

I kept my tone even. "So that's it? That's your big reveal? Plain old-fashioned racism?"

They all broke out laughing. All four of them, as if they'd just heard the punch line to a joke. Anton made a sweeping gesture. "And there it is! We are ruled out of play. No need to listen to us anymore." He turned to Tara, whose expression had hardened into a grimace of contempt.

"So, Tara. Do you feel ashamed? Are you going to change your ways now you've found out you're a racist?"

Tara shrugged. "Well Anton, racism is just another word for exercising choice and I choose to be with my own kind."

Their tone was artificial, like a pair of TV announcers sarcastically reading an autocue.

"And you, Karl?"

"Shit, Anton. I don't even know this guy."

"OK." I got up, staggering slightly. "Fuck you and fuck your friends. I'm out."

Anton looked disappointed. "Oh come on. Don't you have any more than that? I brought you here because I thought you might have some fight in you. I wanted to hear you explain why kebab is so great and tasty. Why Tara should feel good about being skewered by an Arab."

I wish I could say I fired back a devastating retort. To tell the truth I was too stunned by the sudden blast of hostility. I just wanted to get out of there, to disengage. I started putting on my layers of clothing, feeling absurd as I pulled a sweater over my head and hunted for my scarf and gloves.

"Can we go somewhere else, now?" asked Greg, as if oblivious to the tension.

"Sure Greg," said Anton. "Your weakness," he added, turning back to me, "is that you're always surrounded by people who think just like you. When you meet someone who your silly shame tactics don't work on, you don't know how to act. I'm a racist because I want to be with my own kind and you're a saint because you have a sentimental wish to help other people far away, nice abstract refugees who save you from having to commit to anybody or anything real."

"I feel sorry for you," I said. It did not feel like a strong comeback.

I made my way through the crowded restaurant and pushed open the door. Outside, the cold cut my face like a knife. I found a single taxi waiting at a rank and fell asleep in it on the way back to the Deuter Center. I woke up to find myself being driven around in the Grunewald, the darkness of the pine forest absolute and disorientating. It was impossible to tell if the driver was genuinely lost, or just clocking up the fare. After a testy conversation, he found the right road, and deposited me outside the Center's gate. Ulli or Uwe the porter buzzed me in, and I dragged myself up the main stairs to bed.

I woke up late the next morning wracked by a vicious hangover that wasn't alleviated by water or painkillers. I needed to think, and after so many weeks without leaving Wannsee, I suddenly couldn't stand being there. In the face of an icy wind, I trudged to the station and took a train back into the city. I got off at Hackescher Markt and drifted around Mitte, eating a bowl of *pho* at a Vietnamese restaurant and then holing up in a bland but low-lit café where I could pretend to read Kleist as I watched the well-heeled young patrons check their social media accounts. My hangover gradually loosened its grip and for a while I was happy. I couldn't really remember why I'd shut myself away in the suburbs. As long as you have walking-around money and are capable of following basic behavioral norms, anonymity is yours in a city, or if not actual anonymity then its ghost, what remains of it for us. No one in the café expected anything of me, and I didn't care what they thought of the way I looked or dressed. I didn't feel on edge. It was as if I'd suddenly remembered how to exist in the world.

I turned over what had happened the previous night, trying to put a good complexion on it. An unpleasant experience, an event without consequences. I was ashamed that I'd allowed myself to be manipulated by Anton and angry that (as far as I could see) he'd invited me out for the sole purpose of humiliating me in front of his friends. I suppose I'd wanted to provoke some kind of confrontation with him, I'd foolishly imagined that I'd be the inquisitor, haughtily demanding answers about the bad politics of his TV show. Instead I'd been blindsided, caught off balance. I didn't want to admit it, but the things he'd said hit home. Was I just a squeamish intellectual, incapable of action? Was my capacity for human relationships so stunted that I replaced real people with abstractions, "deserving" refugees who I'd never have to meet or interact with?

A good-looking young man came into the café wearing a military peacoat, his hair styled in the same nineteen-thirties undercut as Anton and Karl. I felt suspicious of him, and realized that this was yet another sign that things had changed. When had I stopped assuming that a fashionably dressed man in his twenties, in a cosmopolitan urban neighborhood, would hold liberal social views? Now I was wondering if he went on the internet and posted about throwing people out of helicopters. The barista found him attractive. She kept glancing in his direction as she made his coffee. In a past age he might have made a good model for a propaganda picture. The handsome young soldier, the explorer, the mountaineer. Would it matter to the barista whether or not he *knew where he was from*? Was she looking for a man with *pride*? A man who wanted *to secure a future for his children*?

As I rode the S-Bahn back to the suburbs my mood worsened. All the equanimity I'd accumulated during my day in the city began to drain away. It was mid-afternoon and the sun was already low in the horizon as I walked up the driveway, the gravel squeaking under the soles of my boots. I had a sense of jeopardy as I held my keycard up to the reader. The porter came out of his lodge to meet me as I stepped through the door.

"Sir, I'm glad you're back. Professor Starhemberg and his colleague are here. They're in with Dr. Weber."

"Who?"

"Your guests." I must have looked puzzled. "The historians? You invited them to tour the house?"

It must have been obvious that I had no idea what he was talking about. Filled with foreboding, I went upstairs to the director's office and knocked on the door.

"Come in!"

Dr. Weber was standing behind his desk with two other men, examining one of the framed Chinese paintings on the wall. All three turned round as I entered. Dr. Weber smiled and nodded and so did Anton and Karl, who were both wearing thick-framed glasses, theatrical "intellectual" props. Anton grinned ironically. Karl's smile vanished like a set of shutters coming down on a shop. I was so appalled that I just stood there, my mouth opening and closing like a fish.

"Come and see!" Dr. Weber's tone was warm and hospitable. He was obviously enjoying himself. "I hang it here because it doesn't receive so much direct sunlight."

Anton stepped aside to make room for me, just the faintest hint of irony in the courtly sweep of his open hand. My mind raced, trying to game out the possibilities. What were they doing? Was the point to embarrass me further? Did they want something from me? Money? I didn't understand.

"I wasn't expecting you," I said, carefully.

Anton nodded sympathetically, speaking in the tone of a concerned friend. "I didn't want to bother you with the arrangements." It was clear that whatever game we were playing, for the moment we were going to keep it secret from Dr. Weber.

"I find this rather moving," Dr. Weber said, unwilling to be diverted from his show-and-tell. "It's a copy, sadly, but a good one. A leaf from a Ming Dynasty album called 'The Garden of the Inept Administrator.' You see him. He has been, what is the phrase? Put out to grass." Pleased with his idiom, he paused. I peered at an ink painting depicting a pavilion in a garden enclosed by a high wall. Inside the pavilion, a man knelt at a desk, attended by a smaller figure who I assumed was a servant.

"There is a poem that goes with it, mostly about the banana tree. How tall it has grown."

I followed where he was pointing and saw that there was indeed a tree in the foreground, with the broad leaves of a banana, curling over the pavilion's pitched roof. In front of it was another object, dark and irregular, almost as tall. Vegetable or mineral? It was hard at first to say. Then I saw that it was a huge scholar's rock, taller than a man. Dr. Weber turned to me. "If I do not often give these tours, it is only because people don't usually ask."

"Tours of your collection?"

"No, the building."

Anton smiled unctuously. "After our fascinating conversation last night at dinner, I took the liberty of having my assistant contact Dr. Weber's office. You'd mentioned the Center, and as you know, my colleague and I both have an interest in the conduct of academic research under National Socialism. Dr. Weber was kind enough to offer to show us around."

Dr. Weber furrowed his brow. "Of course we keep no archive here. There is no institutional continuity with the National Socialist period."

Karl nodded sagely. He must have imagined that his pompous expression made him look smart. I wondered how Dr. Weber could buy the idea that these two were history professors. Karl was wearing a ridiculous wide-lapelled corduroy jacket that looked several sizes too small. It was bunched up under his armpits and stretched tight across his back. Greenish tattoos spidered up over the collar of his shirt. Weber was too wrapped in his tour guide persona to notice any of this. He led the way out of his office, talking in a steady stream.

"The body you're interested in, if I understand correctly, is the Institut für Nordforschung, which occupied this building. It was set up in 1936 and dissolved towards the end of the war, when resources became scarce."

Anton pantomimed extreme attention, as if daring Dr. Weber to notice his insincerity. "This research into, I'm sorry, what was the word you used?"

"Nordforschung. You would translate it as something like

'research into the North.' But this concept of North was more spiritual than geographical. Mystical nonsense, I'm afraid."

"A shared destiny among Northern Europeans," suggested Karl.

"That would be the sort of language they used. From what I understand, there were some credentialed archaeologists and linguists involved, but of course by then there had been the purge of the universities. Loyalty oaths, preference for those with early party membership and so on. These men were enthusiasts for the National Socialist cause. I've looked at a few of the publications. They were no more than propaganda."

"You have them?" asked Karl.

"No, of course not. As I said, there is no institutional continuity with that time. It was the antithesis of what Herr Deuter wanted to achieve. Come, let me show you what we do have in the library. You may be interested to see the signature of Bundeskanzler Adenauer in a book he presented to Herr Deuter."

In the library Weber told various stories about the house, mostly illustrating the wisdom of Herr Deuter, who seemed to exist in his personal pantheon somewhere between Willy Brandt and Lao Tzu. Anton played the part of the fascinated historian. Karl seemed sullen, pent up. It popped into my head that he might be armed, and once it had taken hold, the thought was hard to shake. He seemed like a man who was about to do something, to break the tension with a knife or a gun. It seemed impossible that Weber hadn't noticed the insanity of the situation. Occasionally Anton looked over at me, a sly grin floating over his mouth. "The North," he murmured. "The idea of North. It's very moving, in a way, what happened here. Machine-age Europeans who were longing for Ultima Thule."

I looked at him sharply. For the first time, I thought I saw some doubt creep across Weber's face. Anton saw he'd overdone it, and hedged. "Not everyone has that feeling, I suppose."

"I am interested to see the bunker," said Karl.

Weber brightened up. "Ah yes!" He made a vague hand gesture at a camera high up on the wall. Almost at once, the porter appeared.

"Can we unlock the bunker, Uwe?"

"Yes, of course, Herr Doktor."

Uwe, I thought. That's his name. Uwe.

We followed Uwe downstairs and walked along the corridor past the IT office. He opened a door and stood aside, gesturing us to step into a small storeroom lined with shelves of office supplies. At the back of the storeroom was a second door. He unlocked it and reached inside, switching on a bright light.

"Please."

Weber led the way down a flight of stairs to an extraordinary space, like something from a dream. Our footsteps echoed as we walked across a huge, completely empty room, with concrete walls, floor and ceiling. A featureless box, the air cold and damp. What made it so strange was its brightness. Every surface was painted white. Strip lights lined the ceiling, many more than necessary. Dazzled, we all squinted, shielding our eyes.

"Deuter white," explained Dr. Weber. "It was his specific instruction."

"Why?"

Anton scoffed. "Because he was afraid of shadows."

Dr. Weber smiled. "Yes, that's a good way of putting it. He wanted to banish the darkness of those years."

"What did they do down here?" I asked, not really wanting to know the answer.

"Oh, nothing very scandalous. Sheltered during air raids. The Nazis built these bunkers under many of the houses round the lake. When there was bombing the Institute held its meetings and cultural program down here. I can show you a photo."

He'd brought a book with him, some sort of local history publication containing old photographs of Wannsee. He flicked past pictures of boating parties on the lake, grainy pictures of interiors. I saw the dining room, recognizable but full of heavy dark furniture. Finally he found what he was looking for, a photo of a man speaking to an audience of uniformed military personnel. The caption: *A lecture takes place underground: Reichsdramaturg Rainer Schlösser speaks on "Kleist and the Nordic spirit of honor."*

We stood and looked at the picture. The speaker was gripping the side of the lectern and gesturing with a closed fist, in the approved rhetorical style.

"Over here you see more or less the only unusual thing about this room."

Weber walked us over to the spot. Set into the concrete floor was a brass arrow, about two feet long. It was plain and unabstracted, with a barbed head and detailed lifelike fletching.

"It points due North."

Karl turned to Anton. "You see? I read that this was here."

Anton nodded, and at once, as if at a signal, they both turned smartly to face in the direction indicated by the arrow, and held up their right hands, as if swearing an oath. "I am the Magus of the North," intoned Anton, as if he were uttering the words of a spell. "I have opened the book of secrets."

"I am the spear bearer of the North," said Karl. "I am the complete man."

Weber frowned. "What is this? What are you doing?"

Anton relaxed his posture. "No amount of light will banish the shadows," he said, his tone conversational again, laced with irony, though the words themselves were still portentous. "The shadows are your history."

Weber was angry now. "I must ask for an explanation."

"Don't take things so seriously, old man."

"Why do you speak like this?"

"Yeah," I said, suddenly disgusted by the whole stupid business, the deception, whatever occultist idiocy I'd just witnessed. "Tell us, Anton."

Weber turned to me, accusingly. "Who are these people? "

"I'm sorry," I said. "I actually didn't invite them here."

"They are your friends."

"They aren't my friends."

Anton did his sad face again. "That's cold, dude. Seriously."

"Oh go to hell."

Weber was furious. He turned to Anton. "This is a place that has fully faced up to the past. We acknowledge it, of course, but there has been a decisive break. I don't know what you're doing but I find it tasteless. Your flippant tone, your humor about this, is misplaced, more so from an American."

Anton shrugged. "I guess that means it's time for us to leave."

Uwe the porter was hovering. He and Karl were making hostile eye contact. We all began to move. I could not wait to get upstairs, out of the dazzling light. As soon as we were out of the storeroom and the door closed behind us, Dr. Weber said a curt goodbye and stalked off down the corridor.

"Looks like you're in trouble," said Anton, cheerfully. "Shame, because your poker face was holding up so well."

"Why did you come here?"

"Karl's into this esoteric stuff. The hollow earth, the spear of destiny, all that. Me, I just wanted to mess with your shit."

"Please," said Uwe. "It is time for you to leave."

"Sure, man. Just a minute." He gestured at our surroundings. "You know this is all bullshit, right? Reason, technocracy and a coat of white paint. It's just a front, my friend."

"Please," said Uwe. "No more."

"Underneath, these enlightened liberals enjoy all the same dark age shit as the people they condemn. All the obscene shit. They call it humanitarian intervention, but it's just a chance to play Abu Ghraib."

Uwe placed himself in front of Anton, who raised his hands in a gesture of pacification. He spoke to me over Uwe's shoulder.

"They're better at hiding it. That's the only difference."

Uwe touched Karl, steering him towards the door. Karl reacted badly, snatching away his arm and squaring up to Uwe, who took a step back and adopted a fighting stance.

Anton giggled at them and turned to me. "You know what the best part is? I'm going to be living rent free in your head from now on. You're going to think about me all the fucking time. Come on, Karl. Time to go."

And with that, they left. I stood at the front door with Uwe and watched them sauntering insolently down the drive, their hands in their pockets.

"Personally," said Uwe, "I am surprised. I didn't think you were a Fascist."

"What? God, no. Of course not. I'm nothing to do with those guys."

"I'm different from a lot of people here. I was in the army. I'm not so judgmental."

"No, seriously. I met them last night."

"But I think others will have problems with it. Dr. Weber, for example."

"What do you mean, problems?"

"I think after today you will not be able to stay."

I had a bad night. The only person I wanted to speak to was Rei and I absolutely could not call her. I couldn't think straight. I barely slept. Sometime in the early morning I went to the station and caught the first train into the city center. I spent the day wandering around, I don't exactly remember where. I was consumed by the shock of everything that had happened, the ruthless disruption that Anton had visited on my life. His invincible sarcasm, his constant hints of transgression. Everything he said sounded like a dare, an outrage that was taken back as soon as it came out of his mouth. I meant it, I didn't mean it. Sorry, not sorry. I was conducting a constant dialogue with him, with some version of him I'd conjured for myself, all the while knowing that this was exactly what he'd predicted. *Rent free in your head.* The stress this induced in me was intolerable. Rage was eating away at the core of my being. As I came back to Wannsee, the late afternoon sun was already low in the sky. Long shadows. Frost on the ground. I needed a sign, a talisman, something to ward off Anton. What would clear my confusion was a baseline, a piece of firm moral ground. I needed to remember why I believed the things I did, and why I had a right, even a duty, to defend them. At the station I got on a bus that took me over the bridge and past the blue-light Chinese. It dropped me near a set of iron gates, kept open so that people could pass freely in and out. Beyond them a paved driveway led towards an undistinguished Neoclassical villa.

If you say the name *Wannsee,* Berliners may think of the lake or the Strandbad, but for everyone else, the immediate association, if any, is with this house, the venue for a conference held in January 1942, where SS-Obergruppenführer Reinhard Heydrich presented his plans for the extermination of the Jews of Europe. I paid an entrance fee and went inside. To my dismay I found an empty shell, completely without character. I knew at once that I would find nothing to help me. There was little or no furniture, and in the absence of any meaningful connection with the past, the freshly painted rooms had been filled with images and wall texts narrating the events that led up to the conference and the terrible consequences of the policy that was agreed on there. I found a photograph of the interior as it had looked when it was still a private house, with tapestries on the walls and Persian rugs on the floor. At the time of Heydrich's meeting it was a guesthouse for the State Security Police, expropriated from its former owner, who had been generously allowed to donate it to the Nazi government after his arrest for fraud. At the end of the war Soviet marines were billeted there, and in succession it housed American officers, an adult education center and a school hostel, changes that explained why there was nothing left to see.

That afternoon the house was disconcertingly busy with British teenagers, two or three different school parties being shown around by guides. They walked around solemnly, all behaving in, I suppose, much the same way as me, talking in lowered voices, receiving the terrible information. I had been directed to join a tour, but couldn't face it. I needed the house to do something immediate, something primal. I wasn't in any condition to follow the whole grim story, from the medieval blood libel to the Eichmann trial. I felt distracted and claustrophobic.

I was retracing my steps to the front entrance when my way was blocked by yet another school group, dozens of young people squeezing through a narrow corridor. I had to step back into an alcove that housed a display about the Nuremberg race laws of 1935. As I waited for the group to pass, I read about the consequences of the law criminalizing extramarital sex between Jews and gentiles. In various places, local Nazis had staged carnivalesque public humiliations, dragging mixed couples through the streets. There was a photograph of a man and a woman flanked by policemen, surrounded by a crowd of gawkers, mostly children. The man wore a curling paper sign saying "Ich bin ein Rassenschänder." The words were underlined as if they'd been written out for a school exercise: "I am a race defiler." The woman beside him looked crushed. Her head was bowed, her hands clasped contritely in front of her. He gazed directly into the camera, at me.

A gap opened, and I was able to slip through the crowd and out the front door. Though the sun had set, I walked around the grounds for a while, peering vainly across the dark lake in the direction of the Strandbad and the Deuter Center. I left the house and wandered down a side street that led to the water, where I found a large bronze statue of a lion, apparently captured during a war with the Danes.

I was staring up at it, feeling the chill sharpening in the air, when a flash of color drew my eye back to the road. I recognized them at once, lit up in the glow of a streetlight, the refugee father and daughter walking down the street. The little girl was wearing the same bright pink parka that had drawn my eye when I first saw her in the play area behind the restaurant. The father was setting a fast pace, perhaps because of the cold. His clothes—a thin jacket and jeans—weren't warm enough for the weather, though the little girl, trotting to keep up with him, seemed properly dressed. They turned away from the lake, along a road with houses on one side and woodland on the other.

I followed them, keeping some distance behind. After a few minutes, they crossed the street and seemed to disappear into the woods. When I reached the spot where they'd vanished, I saw a driveway and some lights visible through the trees. I walked down a slight incline and a large concrete block came into view, a sort of bunker, eerily lit by yellow sodium lights. There was nothing to say what the place was, but much later I found out that it dated from the Second World War, part of a Luftwaffe training complex that had been hidden in the woods to deter Allied bombing. People were milling about outside the building. Boys played football on the cracked concrete of a parking lot. A group of old men sat on green plastic chairs, bundled up in heavy jackets, smoking cigarettes and drinking little glasses of tea. A security guard in a fluorescent yellow vest leaned against a wall, engrossed in a tabloid newspaper. The father nodded a greeting to the tea-drinkers and took the little girl inside. I hesitated, expecting to be stopped, but when I followed them into the building, the guard didn't even look up.

I passed through a set of swinging double doors like those

in a hospital, and found myself in an enormous room, bigger than a gymnasium, with peeling magnolia walls and a high ceiling supported by metal beams. The space had been partitioned with sheets of plywood to form dozens of cubicles, each one with a number spray-painted on the side. There were people everywhere, sitting or lying on camp beds, feeding babies, charging cell phones around long tables festooned with extension cords and power strips, the whole scene taking place under a hard white fluorescent light that made everyone, young and old alike, look haggard and drawn. It was a world of noise and plastic water bottles, pervaded by the smell of chlorine. A man pushed past me, a toothbrush clamped between his teeth like a cigar. Along one wall was a line of portable toilets, and a second line of plastic sinks where women were washing clothes. Beside me, near the main door, two men began some kind of altercation, gesturing and raising their voices. Others gathered round to reason with them. I could see into the nearest cubicles, where bunk beds were curtained with sheets and blankets.

I looked around for the father and daughter, but I couldn't see them. Along the wall above the toilets ran a sort of gantry or walkway, reachable by a ladder. A few teenage boys were up there, leaning on the rail, looking down at the spectacle below. I climbed up and joined them, scanning the room until I spotted the father in the doorway of one of the cubicles. As I climbed back down, I was suddenly gripped by intense emotion. It was physical. An inflation, a rush. I was the Prince of Homburg! Immortality was all mine! I knew what I would do. I would make a gesture, not a grand one, nothing showy or egotistical. Something pure and true. A small act of charity in a fallen world.

As I had these thoughts, I could feel Anton's adversarial presence, an imp squatting on my shoulder. I don't believe in possession, though the language of possession is the best I have to describe it. Some part of my own personality had broken away and dressed itself up in Anton's clothes. I walked down one of the narrow corridors between cubicles and Anton pointed out how absurd I was, like a pop singer in a charity video, passing fashionably through a crowd of the global poor. I ignored him and found where the father and daughter were staying. A stenciled number, a blue plastic refuse sack hanging by the door. The little girl was lying on a camp bed reading a Donald Duck comic, the father sitting next to her, one foot up on the frame, cutting his toenails. Seeing me, he looked startled. He got up and came to the door, the clippers still in his hand. Now watch, I said to Anton. This is an authentic connection between two human beings. And at that moment I did not know what to do. All I could think of was to take out my wallet. I only had a fifty-euro note, which didn't seem enough. I want to give you this, I said. Anton sniggered. The man waved his hands, shook his head. I felt in my pockets for more money, but couldn't find any. I held out the banknote to him, pleaded with him to take it. No, no, he said. No. He looked around nervously.

All at once I saw that I'd come unmoored. I was embarrassing myself and frightening him. It wasn't how I meant it to go. Money wasn't the meaning of what I was doing, just the easiest and most direct way to help, to make my commitment clear. I realized that he thought I wanted something in return for my fifty euros, and at that moment we both looked at his daughter. No, I said. My God, no. I saw you walking on the street. You looked cold. This is for you to buy a coat. Go, he said. No want. Anton pointed out that you couldn't really get a coat for fifty euros. Look, I said. Take mine. I was wearing a thick goose down parka. I took it off and handed it to him. He didn't know what to do with it, just held it in front of him at arm's length, like a man asked to dispose of the corpse of an animal. Why not give him your boots too, Anton suggested. I was unlacing them when the security guards came. *Was machen Sie hier?*

It was a confused and difficult scene. The father talked rapidly in Arabic. He pointed to his daughter. No, no, I said. You have the wrong idea. Anton said that for the right price, he'd probably change his mind. Those fucking ragheads didn't care. I should just offer him more camels. The security guards told me I had to leave. I said I wanted to help the people. All the people. I had the right to help, to reach out to another human being. They could not deny me that. They said they would call the police. I told them I didn't give a damn about the police. Then I was outside in the cold, holding my winter boots in my hands, my feet growing numb as moisture seeped through my socks. In the scuffle I'd left my coat inside.

I was limping back down the road towards the lake, shivering in the freezing night air, when a police car pulled up. The policemen asked me what I was doing and I said I was existing, just being in the world. They asked if I need help. I said I didn't need help, I didn't want anything from anyone, I wanted to give to people, not take, but they got out and blocked my path, and I thought they'd taser me, gun me down, it's what would have happened in America, but for some time they just stood there, apparently unwilling to act. I realized how cold I was, already my legs were numb below the knee, and so I got in the back of the car and allowed them to drive me back to the

Deuter Center as I coughed and wheezed and laid my cheek against the cold glass window.

Inside they sat me down with a cup of hot coffee and wrapped a blanket round my shoulders. Someone found me a dry pair of socks. They were thick woolen hiking socks with a diamond pattern. I looked down at my unfamiliar feet. The room was unfamiliar too. Located in a wing of the Center that was not usually accessible to the fellows, it seemed to be some kind of staff lounge. While Frau Janowitz and Dr. Weber negotiated with the police, Uwe had been set to watch me. He sat in a corner, pretending to read a magazine, occasionally looking up with a sly smile.

"I told you there was nothing to see at the Conference House," he said. "You should have believed me."

Dr. Weber came in, followed by Frau Janowitz. He was dressed for dinner, and had clearly been called back from some engagement to deal with me. How was I feeling, he wanted to know. Any suicidal ideation? Frau Janowitz checked her phone and made no eye contact. I said I was fine, all I wanted to do was rest. Dr. Weber wanted to know if he should phone my wife. He thought he should let her know. I forbade that absolutely, and I must have been more vehement than I intended, because Uwe put down his magazine and came to stand next to his boss, as if preparing to intervene. Things were very jumbled. I asked some questions about the history of the house that Dr. Weber didn't seem willing to discuss. Yes, it had been built by a Jewish family. All these houses had a complicated history. Why hadn't it been returned to the heirs? He didn't know. He did not see why it was relevant. Please could I focus? I seemed to be having some kind of crisis. Surely I would agree that it was not appropriate for me to continue my stay at the

Deuter Center. This was not the right place for me in my current condition. Frau Janowitz would make herself available to assist me in planning my travel. What, he wanted to know, was I doing at the refugee accommodation? The police said I had been accused of taking an unhealthy interest in children.

This made me very angry. Uwe raised his hands and moved to stand in front of Dr. Weber. I said I wasn't going to hurt anyone, but this was very bad. Surely he could understand. To be accused of that. He had, he said, my best interests, and also the best interests of the Center to consider. It was a question of reputation. I told him if he cared so much for reputation, he might look into the conduct of his staff. It was not ethical to put cameras into the bedrooms of guests. I didn't know German law, but I would be very surprised if what they were doing was legal. He said he had no idea what I was talking about.

I told him I was more concerned with the future than the past. He smiled and nodded, as if to reinforce this positive-sounding sentiment. He said he thought my wife would be very happy to have me home. Frau Janowitz returned with the news that she'd booked me a seat on a flight leaving for New York in the morning. Uwe escorted me back to my room, and though there was nothing so crass as a guard outside my door, I knew that if I tried to leave, he would be watching.

THE FRENCH PHRASE is *l'esprit de l'escalier,* and there doesn't seem to be an exact equivalent in English. Staircase wit. It's an idiom that evokes the eighteenth century, the Paris of the Age of Reason. The *philosophe* has left the party, and is almost on the street when he thinks of the precise thing he should have said, the *mot juste*. With every fiber of his being, he wants to go back up, to say the words that have belatedly come to mind, to destroy his celebrated opponent's position and reap the dazzling social rewards. He wants his wit to be recognized, but he can't turn back time. It is already too late.

Take that regret, the fleeting moment after the door has

shut, muffling the music and the sound of conversation, and raise the stakes, introduce the possibility that there is an existential risk to losing the debate. Of course an argument at a party isn't any kind of action, neither can it bring about some particular version of the future, nor prevent it from coming to pass. That is mistaking the map for the territory, ascribing a power to words that they don't possess, the power to bring into being the thing they name. Yet by allowing myself to be humiliated by Anton and his friends, I honestly felt I'd triggered a disaster, not just for me but for everyone and everything I cared about. In the future that was drawing me towards it, the future that I had failed to refute, there was nothing but horror. I couldn't accept that. I couldn't allow it. I had to make up for what I'd done, my failure to find the *mot juste*. At the time, I would have reacted impatiently to anyone who said I wasn't thinking straight, that my decision to follow Anton to Paris wasn't motivated by the coldest rationality.

I didn't board my flight to New York. Uwe drove me to the airport, and helped me check my bags. He walked me to the security line and said goodbye, telling me that I should look after myself, he was sorry things had gone so badly for me. I can't remember what I said. I may not have said anything. He watched me until I was almost at the desk to have my passport checked, then turned and walked away. As soon as he was out of sight, I ducked back under the tape, went over to one of the airline ticketing desks and bought a seat on the next flight to Orly.

I sat at a bar near my gate and drank a shot to steady my nerves before I made a call that I'd been putting off. Rei had left eight messages, all of which I'd ignored. She took a long time to pick up. As I listened to her phone ringing, Anton sniggered silently at my nerves. I said hello in my best and most natural voice and she asked what was going on. "Tell me you're OK. That's all I want to know."

I said I was. I said I couldn't really be more specific. I said it was hard to explain.

"You've really freaked the Deuter people out, whatever you've done."

"They called you? I told them not to call you."

"Why wouldn't you want them to call me? They said you were found wandering around at night with no shoes on."

"I wasn't wandering around. That makes it sound— whatever. I knew what I was doing."

"So what's wrong? You're about to get on your plane, right."

"I don't know. Maybe I made a mistake."

"What do you mean, a mistake?"

I spun out a long silence. I heard the irritated tremor in her sigh.

"Honey, I'm at the office, and I'm kind of slammed. I really want to talk, because I'm worried about you, but let's do it face-to-face? I have to be in court in under an hour."

"I do need to talk to you."

"Call me when you land. As soon as you land."

"How's Nina?"

"She's fine. Missing you."

Another long pause.

"Look, it'd be great if for once you remembered what it's like for me when I'm here."

"Please. I'll tell you what it's about."

"Really?"

"It's just . . ."

I trailed off again. I wasn't sure why I was forcing the issue. I wasn't even sure that I had anything to say.

"OK," she sighed. "Two minutes. I'll close my door."

A pause, then she got back on the line.

"So what's on your mind?"

"I need to ask you something. It'll sound strange, but humor me."

"OK."

"Why do you believe in human rights?"

"That's what you want to talk about?"

"Yes."

"Jesus, I thought you were finally going to be real with me. I thought you were going to tell me what's been up with you all these months."

"I'm trying. Please."

"I just don't have time for any more— Oh, forget it."

"No, go on. Any more what?"

"Any more bullshit, OK? You're over there. You're supposed to be writing your book. I've spent so long trying to coax some sense out of you, and now I'm hearing you've been— I don't even know what you're doing."

"I'm sorry."

"God, it drives me crazy. You're sorry. You're always sorry. I just want to find out how to help you. You drop all these hints about your dark existential crisis, but what do you actually want me to do? Is it that you just like to have someone worrying about you? You want to keep me on the hook?"

"No. Of course not. I'm trying, here. I'm trying really. I wouldn't ask if it wasn't important."

"About what?"

"Human rights. Why you believe humans have special rights."

"I really have no idea. Why are we even talking about this?"

"Please."

"It's what I do. I practice human rights law. It's my job."

"Which you do because you really believe, deep down in your heart, that people have an inherent dignity, because they're human."

"Do we have to?"

"Please. It's what you believe, right?"

"Of course."

"But why?"

"Why do people have rights?"

"Yes."

"Because they're people."

"But why are people important? Why are we more special than, I don't know, an eagle? Or a coral reef?"

There were sounds in the background, and I heard her say to someone, just one minute.

"I have no idea, honey. I have no idea why you're more special than an eagle or a coral reef. But you're scaring me. So please call me back the minute you land. Make sure you call as soon as you get in. Now I have to go. I have no choice. People are waiting for me."

"Isn't it just a fiction, though? Just something we tell ourselves?"

"No."

"We say all these things. That we have consciousness, that we feel things so deeply. If we still believed in the soul, maybe. Do you believe in the soul? I can't believe I've never asked you that."

"We're human. That's enough. I'm going to hang up, now. Please, just call me from arrivals. You're scaring me. As soon as you get in, OK?"

The line went dead. I sat with the phone in my hand, feeling as if I'd let slip some terrible secret. Not to feel human. To walk around concealing your own emptiness. This was how the horror had crept in, how it had poisoned the future. And I'd not said the thing I most wanted to say: that I was sorry; that my negligence was culpable, and it had left her and Nina without the means to survive what was on the horizon; that though I was afraid, I was completely unable to make myself understood, not to anyone, but particularly not to her. All I really wanted was for her and Nina to live without fear. That would have constituted success for me, giddying, impossible success. I knew that were I to confess my jumbled apocalyptic terrors, it would make Rei afraid, even if—particularly if— she didn't believe a word of what I was saying. She'd be afraid of what it meant about me, or at least more afraid than she already was, and she would mistake my fragility—of which I was only too aware—for the content of my message. I needed her to understand that the most pressing problem was not my mental state but the state of the world. The danger was objectively real. There was no guarantee that the needle of crisis, which had always pointed away from us, at other families in other places, would not swing in our direction. I wanted to tell her that she shouldn't worry about me more than necessary, that she should focus her energies on making preparations for herself and Nina. I wanted to say that I wasn't coming home.

IN A TAXI, heading into the center of Paris, I worked my phone, trying to find some trace of Anton's presence in the city. All I had was the overheard snippet of conversation with Karl. *This is all stuff for Paris. We can deal with it then.* I hoped that he wasn't coming to do something private, some dinner or closed meeting that wouldn't be searchable online. I got lucky. A premium vodka brand had commissioned "Three Short Films on Inspiration" and was presenting a screening at a cinema in the Latin Quarter, followed by a Q&A with the subjects, a dancer, a creative director, and Anton. I'd given the driver the address of a hotel near the Gare du Nord, the first place that had come up on a booking site, but now I diverted him to the cinema, even though the event wasn't for two more days. I asked if he knew a cheap hotel nearby, but he said I was in the wrong part of town. I got out anyway and walked around, trying to attune myself—that's how I thought of it—as if I were a receiver, a sensitive piece of technology that could pick up Anton's presence through some kind of occult magnetism. As the taxi drove away, I realized that I didn't have a suitcase with me. My bags must have been unloaded from the New York flight. They were probably in a storeroom at Tegel.

Eventually I found a hotel, the Prince something or other, the most down-at-heel in a row of similar establishments on a steep street behind the Odéon. I rented a tiny garret room, accessed by a rattling elevator about the size and shape of a vertically oriented coffin. I went online and reserved a ticket for the screening, then went back out onto the Boulevard Saint-Germain and bought underwear and toiletries. I didn't really regret losing my luggage. It almost seemed like good luck, a shortcut to asceticism, to the total focus I would need in order to complete my task.

Rei was leaving agitated messages on my phone. I couldn't bring myself to listen to them. Ignoring a string of emails with all-caps subject lines, I sent one to her telling her not to worry, that I was in no danger, just "taking some time to think." I didn't say where I was. Then I spent an hour scrolling through videos of Nina, watching her chatter and play at various ages, forwarding and rewinding her three years of life to persuade myself that I was keeping faith with her and Rei, and even if I couldn't speak to them, they were on my mind. I wished I could send a transcript of my thoughts, a log or spreadsheet. *Hours spent thinking of:* Total of boxes C1 to C16. The woman who took sudden unscheduled naps all through her pregnancy, who I used to find asleep on the sofa, or her yoga mat, even once nestled among hangers and plastic wrapping in a pile of dry-cleaning left on our bed; the baby girl I'd carried in a milk-stained sling, whose head I'd surreptitiously sniffed as I walked to the supermarket, woozily intoxicated by new fatherhood. I haven't left you. Not in my heart. See, I have receipts.

The room was covered in busy rose chintz. It was easiest to be in there with the light off, but in the dirty yellow glow of the bedside lamp it was bearable. Without moving, I could explore the streets of Paris, looking for Anton in the crinkles and folds of the rose petals, the interlocking patterns of stems and thorns, traveling without moving like one of Dr. Weber's opiated Chinese sages. Sometimes the walls closed in and I had to walk the streets for real, looking in the windows of bookstores, examining the permutations of the city, its vast potential for meaning. There was a synagogue nearby, with armed police standing guard outside. Throughout the *quartier,* on walls and doorways, someone had written a phrase, perhaps a political slogan, in black marker. *Europe en danger.* These things were clues, signs of the new dispensation.

Even so, when the evening of the screening came, I wasn't ready. I lay on the bed inside my box of roses, exploring the possibility of not moving. If I just stayed still, the event would take place without me. The audience would find their places, the films would be shown, Anton and the others would speak, the audience would leave, some janitor would sweep between the seats, lock up and switch off the lights. The wave that was rising up towards me would peak, and then fall away.

But what then? *The only way out is through.* The words—a

catchphrase of Carson's heroin-addicted partner Penske in *Blue Lives*—had been repeating on a loop as I walked around Paris. *The only. Way out. Is through.* Again and again. If I didn't find Anton, I would be in limbo. If I wanted to live, to make it back to Rei and Nina, I had to get dressed and leave my room. Outside, the city was going about its business. The hotel was only a few minutes' walk away from the cinema, and as I arrived, a small crowd was already waiting to get in. I hung at the fringes. The filmgoers were young and dressed in flashy branded streetwear. I'd been wondering who'd pay to go and watch advertising (the tickets, while not expensive, were not free) and now I had my answer. Would-be beautiful people with disposable income, people who were trying hard, a desirable demographic for a liquor brand. While they waited, they vaped and peered at their phones. Across the street, workers were setting up a bar in a hotel courtyard, ready for the after-party.

The doors opened. I showed my ticket and took an aisle seat near the back. Though I looked around, I couldn't spot Anton, then, just as the house lights were dimmed, he came in through a side entrance with several other people, who all took reserved seats in the front row. I felt dizzy, nauseous. I should have left. The CEO of the vodka brand climbed onstage and made an introduction, thanking numerous people. My stomach cramped. I wanted to go to the bathroom. Anton was in two places at once, superimposed. In the front row, oblivious of my presence, sitting behind me, sniggering. You almost shit yourself at the sight of me, he whispered into my ear. You can't tell me that's not funny.

The first film was about a contemporary dancer, who took inspiration from the natural world. There were close-ups of her muscular body, interspersed with shots of plants and insects. She wore costumes with hard, inflexible elements. Shields and carapaces. She did not like soft and pretty things. It was important to her that people understood this. She was not a soft and pretty dancer. The second film was a scroll through the socially mediatized life of a man with a job at a fashion magazine, the kind of publication with a small circulation and a large budget for parties and promotions. He took pictures at the parties and had his picture taken. He frolicked in exotic locations and was served fine food and drink. It was hard to say if all these things were his inspiration or only some of them or whether he himself was the inspiration, inspiring and taking inspiration from himself in an endless autocatalytic loop.

The creative director's soundtrack of chillout EDM changed to a swelling Romantic orchestral piece, something familiar that I wasn't immediately able to place, and Anton appeared, standing on cliffs overlooking a Northern sea. To the sound of a plaintive flute, he hiked past a dolmen on the shore. He chopped wood outside a chic modernist cabin, alone on a hillside covered in gorse and heather. Then, abruptly, the entire mood changed. A hard cut to some kind of science-fiction scenario, menacing liquid machines assembling themselves, all chrome and kung-fu metallic clashing sounds. Back to the sea. The rise and fall of Anton's axe, the sun glinting on the blade. In voice-over, Anton laughed. "I wouldn't say it's them and us, exactly. I think if you value human-embodied intelligence, you may want to take defensive action. But are you really attached to that monkey body? What's so good about it? Why not defect?"

Cut again to Anton on the cliff. Now he'd taken off his shirt. He was doing yoga. He had a tattoo on his side, curling up under his rib cage, letters in typewriter script that suddenly animated, unpeeling from his body to fill the screen:

```
           I suffocated in the universe,
        I wanted to leap into the infinite
```

Now Anton stood in the graveyard of a ruined church, next to a Celtic cross. He turned to look at the camera and his eyes flashed with a cosmic red glow. Abruptly the scene solarized and eighties synthesizer music took over. "Around us," he said, walking towards the camera, a fuzzy outline against an inverted black sky, "Capital is assembling itself as intelligence. That thought gives me energy. I'm growing stronger by the day." Cut to Anton on-set, surrounded by lights and camera equipment. He was talking to the actor who played Carson in *Blue Lives,* showing him how he wanted him to swing an axe at another actor, who lay on the floor, covered in fake blood. Anton raised the axe high. It was the same axe he had been using to chop wood. A real axe. He was about to bring a real axe down on the actor. Cut to a shot of a total eclipse of the sun, a computer animation that turned black and abstracted itself into a spinning wheel. The soundtrack doubled down on cosmic synthetic chords. Dissolve to Anton at the wheel of a small boat, navigating between two islands. Scudding clouds. A gull overhead. "This is what drives me," he announced, looking to camera. "You can sail over the horizon as a pauper and return with wealth and power beyond your wildest dreams. You can be Cortés. You can be some man's younger son and go to the other side of the world and burn your ships on the beach when you get there because either you're going to sit on the throne or die trying. My people go west in wagons, building roads behind us. We see a mountain, we plant a flag on top of it. We don't accept limits. My inspiration? It's in the blood."

Again we saw Anton at the cliff edge, posed in Warrior One. A drone-mounted camera spun around him, drinking in the spectacular scenery. An orchestral swell. *Fingal's Cave,* maybe. Fade to black.

The lights went up and the host bounded back onstage to enthusiastic applause. Chairs were arranged in front of a branded backdrop, and the three subjects were invited up to discuss inspiration. Where did it come from? How to get more? The dancer and the art director were francophone, but Anton had a translator, a young South Asian woman. Anton sat and listened, his head tilted towards her, as the others spoke about what a great experience it had been to work with the brand's creative team. He was dressed in black, in jeans and a biker jacket made of some kind of technical-looking fiber, not leather, something that seemed as if it would retard flames or block a knife thrust. When the host turned to him, he spoke about his "program of self-optimization." He worked out and took a lot of supplements, but when it came to bodies, he was platform-agnostic. Whatever the substrate, carbon-based or not, he thought the future belonged to those who could separate themselves out from the herd, intelligence-wise. In fifty years' time, many humans would be surplus, just so much unproductive biomass warehoused on some form of universal basic income. Everything important would be done by a small cognitive elite of humans and AIs, working together to self-optimize. If you weren't part of that, even selling your organs wasn't going to bring in much income, because by then it would be possible to grow clean organs from scratch.

It wasn't clear what this had to do with the theme of inspiration, and it certainly wasn't the light and optimistic tone the host had hoped to strike, so he hurriedly turned to the dancer and asked her something about beetles. She'd worked extensively with beetles. She was interested in the way their limbs moved. Was that right? Anton sat placidly, the faint hint of a smile playing over his lips. After a few more minutes of conversation that pointedly excluded him, the host asked whether there were any questions from the audience. An assistant appeared in the aisle and scanned the room, looking for raised hands. There weren't many. People wanted the talking done so they could get to the bar. I forced myself to stand up from my seat. My heart was racing and my legs felt weak. I was given the mike.

"Question for Anton. For Gary, I mean."

I'd practiced what I wanted to say, repeated it as I lay on the bed in the rose-patterned room. At the sound of his name Anton frowned. I spoke slowly, trying to control the tremor in my voice, pausing to give his translator time.

"I think you've made it clear what you believe. In your film and your remarks. That the future looks like most of us fighting for scraps in an arena owned and operated by what you call a 'cognitive elite.' And I want to say I think the purpose of *Blue Lives* is to soften us up for that. To prepare us to accept it. You want to terrorize us into accepting that this world is inevitable."

Anton shielded his eyes to see who was talking.

"Oh, it's you," he said.

"Maybe you could arrive at a question?" asked the interviewer.

"I suppose what I'm saying is why are you promoting a

future in which some people treat others like raw material? That's a disgusting vision."

Anton laughed. "I'm sorry it gives you sad feels, but I think it's how it's going to be. Some people will have agency and others won't. I'm not saying I like it or I don't like it. I didn't express a preference. Despite your outraged tone, all you're doing is describing your own preference, which, when you think about it, is more or less irrelevant when assessing the truth or falsity of a prediction."

The translator did her work. One or two people hesitantly clapped. I was aware of at least one cell phone camera pointed in my direction. Now I was off script. Everything felt a lot less clear. I had to say something.

"Come on. This is such bullshit."

There was a murmur of disapproval. I could sense people around me shifting nervously in their seats. No one translated what I had said, and the host made a gesture to someone at the back of the hall. The assistant was hovering and trying to grab the microphone.

"You're not some aloof observer, describing objective facts. You're working to make this come true and I think—I think something ought to be done to stop you."

"Done? What do you mean, done? By who?"

Before I could reply, the assistant had lunged forward and plucked the microphone out of my hands. The host pointed at another audience member, who began asking the Creative Director how he coped with the pressure of meeting so many famous people. He jumped in eagerly. It turned out it was overwhelming at first, but you got used to it. After a few minutes of blather, the host wrapped things up, and invited the audience to cross the street where there was a vodka bar and a

DJ who'd be playing "inspirational sounds." As the audience filed out, I hovered by the stage, hoping to catch Anton as he walked off. Seeing me, he shook his head.

"Fuck off, man. I don't have any more time to give you."

"Two minutes."

"No."

"Come on, you turned up at my work. You wore a disguise."

"Is that why you popped up here? You want me to debate you?"

"I see you, that's all I'm saying. I know what you're doing. I came to tell you that you're on the wrong side."

"The wrong side of what?"

"History."

"Jesus, for this you flew to Paris? Cultural Marxism has filled your brain with worms."

The host was hovering nearby. "Is everything OK?"

Anton nodded. "I'm fine." He looked me up and down. "You, on the other hand. You don't look like you're in a good state."

"Yeah?"

His mouth twisted in a nasty half-smile. "Here's all you need to know about your situation. I'm several steps ahead of you. I will always be several steps ahead of you. Why? Because I'm smarter and I know how the world works and I'm not a loser or a fuck-up. You are broken and naïve and I'm so far into your head it's almost comical. From now on when you see something, you need to understand that you're seeing it because I want you to see it. When you think of something, it'll be because I want you to think about it."

"What's that supposed to be? Mind control? Are you trying to hypnotize me?"

"You might want to think of it as a curse."

I had to laugh. The pompous expression on his face. Like he was imparting serious information. He wagged a finger angrily at me. "I am the Magus of the North. I have opened the book of secrets."

The host quickly steered Anton into the flow of people crossing the street to the party. I followed, but I had been pointed out to the security guard at the door and he barred my way. I hung around outside for a while. Eventually I got bored of it. So Anton thought he'd got in my head? I tried to scoff, to feel deep down in my heart how ridiculous that was.

AFTER THE FILM SCREENING I went back to my hotel room and ate a Lebanese sandwich, sitting on the bed and dropping salad over my laptop. I had no plan, no idea what to do next. I assumed Anton would go to Los Angeles. In an interview he'd mentioned living most of the year in Malibu. I started looking at flights. I'm not sure what I intended to do. Stake out his house, I suppose, a continuation of what I was already doing online. Eventually I fell asleep. The next morning when I woke up the first thing I did was reach under the bed for the laptop. The hotel wasn't the kind of place that had room service, so sometime later I had to go outside, but I fell into a rhythm that lasted several days, scouring *Blue Lives* fan sites for details of Anton's personal life—family members, an address—only leaving the room to get food. I soon had aerial photos of his house, a folder of red-carpet pictures. There was no wife and children, no girlfriend who appeared more than once or twice among the various dates on his arm. Gradually I realized that in forums that discussed his work, there were several users with similar punning names, cross-posting what I came to call the Starhemberg content, material completely unrelated to television fandom. As I clicked through from *Blue Lives* trivia to Flat Earther tracts or archives of nineteen-eighties body modification pictures, it seemed to me that I'd stumbled on something significant.

Waldeinsamkeit was the name of one blog. *The feeling of being alone in the woods.* The header was a winter forest painted by Caspar David Friedrich. The owner had no bio, just a thumbnail of a shining sword and the text *the grail is undiscoverable but our whole lives are a perpetual search for it.* There were posts about German history, astrology and biodynamic agriculture. There was a long discussion of medieval manorialism and kinship structures. Some posts were signed *Seeker* but most were by *Earnest Star Mountain,* who often linked to them from a *Blue Lives* Facebook page. It was part of a constellation of names that I had begun to recognize: *E. Berg, Vonn Berger, Rudy Stormberg, Ernesto* or *Neto* or *Ernest Stürmberg* or *Starnberg* or *Net70 Stormbug* or *Starcraft* or *Starhaven* or a number of other Tolkienish variants. *Harberg Stimrod* was one. *Starbuck.* I found these names in all sorts of contexts. Blogs on bodybuilding and science fiction. A site that collected photos of Savitri Devi. Two years previously, *Erno Hermberg* had written a catalogue essay for a show at an obscure East London

art gallery, vaporwave updatings of a German symbolist illus-
trator. There was a review of a horror comic called *No One Will
Ever Find You Here,* hailed by *Rudy Berghain* as "the ultimate
in nihilist tentacle aesthetics." All of these accounts, with all
these esoteric interests, were also posting on the *Blue Lives*
internet. What was it Uwe had said, telling me that Anton
and Karl were waiting in Dr. Weber's office? *Herr Professor
Starhemberg and his colleague are here.* At some point it clicked
that all these screen names were plays or variations on "Ernst
Rüdiger von Starhemberg," the name of the Austrian general
who held off the Ottoman Turks in the siege of Vienna in 1683.

At first I thought it was straightforward—Starhemberg was
Anton—but it seemed beyond the power of a single user to
generate so much content, even if he was working full-time.
There were posts about firearms, robotics, anime, piracy, political theory, sex. The accounts had very different profiles. The
Vegan Heathen, hiking barefoot through Idaho. The Dutch bit-
coin entrepreneur. The MMA fighter turned proselytizer for
the Great Replacement. They linked to pages of self-published
occult tracts, crudely made gas oven memes, sound files of
dirge-like martial ambient music, a collection of scientific papers documenting Chinese experiments in human embryo se-
lection. There were Starhemberg posts leading to forums for
preppers, wargamers, Euroskeptics, heavy metal fans, tattoo
artists, collectors of militaria. *What is falling should be pushed,*
declared *Ernst Sternheim* on the Instagram of something called
the *New Resistance Fitness Club. The biggest impediment to ac-
celerating human progress is the precautionary principle,* argued
Ernesto Estrellamonte in an essay titled *Down with Homeostasis!* published by an online journal calling itself the *Agora
for Syncretic Politics.* So many figures capering at the bonfire,

eager to bring on the cataclysm. But how many figures, really? How many were real? I came to the conclusion that Anton—because, surely this was him—had to be running some kind of troll farm dedicated to circulating the Starhemberg material. To what end, I couldn't say.

I stayed on in Paris. It seemed as good a place as any other. I moved hotels a couple of times, ordering room service and racking up online charges. In the offline world, things were loose and jumbled. At the first hotel, some money went missing from my bag and I got into a shouting match with the manager. I argued with the front desk clerk at the second hotel because people had been in my room and moved things around.

When I got kicked out of the second hotel, I rented an Airbnb, an airless *deux-pièces* near the Buttes-Chaumont park. I ate supermarket microwave meals and tried to function with as little human interaction as possible, concentrating as hard as I could on solving the problem, as if I could even have stated coherently what "the problem" was, this question that, were it answered, would make my family safe again. Starhemberg was like quicksand, the deeper I went, the harder it was to get out. What would Anton do if he felt he was under threat? I wondered if I needed to hide my location. I had no training or specialist knowledge. I withdrew cash from ATMs in other arrondissements, and used it to pay for everything I could. Even I knew that every time I used my card I'd be visible to anyone with access to banking databases.

Eventually I stumbled on something that felt significant, audio of an Identitarian panel discussion that had taken place in London the day before the film screening. The timeline worked out—Anton could easily have been there. It was posted on a European civilization reddit popular with white nationalists: a closed meeting, the location unidentified. A speaker introduced by the moderator as "creator, visionary, and important figure in the Western canon, Ernst, Graf von Starhemberg" rambled about a conspiracy to exploit a genetic predisposition towards openness and altruism that he claimed was characteristic of Northern Europeans. Through the power of Frankfurt School theory, wily Jews had guilt-tripped Scandinavians, Britons and other Nordic altruists into inviting black and brown immigrants into their homelands, immigrants who were themselves predisposed, through generations of customary cousin marriage, to give preference to their relatives, and thus were incapable of the fair dealing that was the foundation of Western democracy. His conclusion was not just that the immigrant populations were inferior and should be expelled, but that democracy itself ought to be abandoned for something more muscular. The West should be led by those with the will to counter the genetic replacement of white Europeans, which was otherwise inevitable. This would involve abandoning the pretense of equality and the sentimental muddle of Human Rights. "We must accept," said the speaker, "that not everyone can have full personhood. Autonomy is not for all. Some are destined to wield power, others to be wielded. Ideally we want something that has the same utility as a person—that can do all the labor a person can do—but to whom we don't owe the same moral obligations. We will eventually be able to build or grow such servants ourselves, but in the medium term we must use the ones we have, the ones over whom we hold dominion, like our ancestors did before us."

The speaker had an unplaceable accent, sort of Eurotrash American. It was not Anton's accent, or at least not the accent he spoke in when we met, or in the video clips and interviews I'd watched online, but the more I listened, the more convinced I became that it was him. There was something about the ironic way Starhemberg elongated the vowels, something performed, camp.

Was Anton controlling Starhemberg, the founder of some cell dedicated to pushing out far-right content? I had no doubt that this was the murky water he swam in. Judging by the accounts that posted on *Blue Lives* threads, he had a lot of fans in the subcultural far right, and as someone working in the creative industries in Los Angeles, it would certainly have damaged his career if he were exposed, so a pseudonym made sense. I couldn't tell if there was anything real at the heart of it, any spontaneous energy. Many of the Starhembergs were bots, amplifying and circulating content to drive traffic and game the big algorithms. There were profiles that did nothing but like and repost the posts of other Starhemberg profiles, in an endless automated circle-jerk.

One night, as I followed the forking paths of the Starhemberg content, I began to find my own picture. The image had been taken when I confronted Anton at the screening. I was holding the mike, speaking and gesturing with my free hand, my eyes wide and my mouth hanging open in an idiotic "o." I looked angry, slightly unhinged. The picture was given various captions, mostly satirizing hysterical "social justice warriors" as brainless authoritarians who shouted and screamed. A popular one just had the word "RAAACIIIST!" in all-caps.

I tried to work out who'd started it, and sure enough, the earliest variant I could find was posted a few hours after the screening, from an account called *StabRag1683* that put out a steady stream of content, mostly GIFs of gory scenes from old

Italian horror films. I wasn't posting to the boards and forums I was watching, so I didn't think there was any way for Anton to know that I was paying attention to Starhemberg, but as soon as I saw the memes I knew they were not only *of* me, but *directed at* me, a taunt or joke. *From now on when you see something, you're seeing it because I want you to see it. When you think of something, it'll be because I want you to think about it.* I knew it wouldn't be long before they doxxed me. They would find out where my wife and child were sleeping, behind a flimsy front door.

One night I was looking at a subreddit devoted to Nazi polar mysticism where a prolific poster called *Rudi Stroembourg* was insulting anyone who knew less than him about Vril energy. To my surprise, as he rambled on about Hyperborea and Miguel Serrano, he made passing reference to a "mongrel book" that included an essay on sunsets that was "little more than a porridge of half-understood concepts drawn from the great German Romantics." Though he didn't say so explicitly, I knew the book he was talking about. It was mine. I checked on the big sites and found, just as I suspected, that they were all carrying the same newly posted one-star review of *Seven Types of Vacancy,* focusing on a chapter I'd titled "Wasting Light."

User: *Erno Strindberg*

*Would be improved by actual thinking

This is the work of a writer whose modest intellectual abilities have been scattered to the winds by the most degraded type of postmodernism. In this mongrel book, rootless cosmopolitanism finds its aesthetic correlative in shopworn irony. Among the low points are a flaccid discussion of French New Wave cinema, in which the writer inhales the last fumes of 1968 and strikes postures intended to impress us with his radicalism, and an essay on the figure of the setting sun in Western art that tilts at being a critique of Eurocentrism and the notion of decline, but loses its way in a porridge of half-understood concepts drawn from the great German Romantics. Seen from the cliff top, with the sea wind in your face and the ancient stones close at hand, there is no challenge here, just cowardice and confusion. True wisdom arises out of primordial fear, which is fear of the unknowable essence of things from which all authority derives. The author of this collection of platitudes is neither smart enough to intuit that essence, nor self-aware enough to know how afraid he ought to be.

It was unpleasant to read, of course, in the way of any bad review, but more importantly it was surely by Anton. The language was unmistakable. The reference to the cliffs and the sea and the ancient stones would have been proof enough. I might be a coward, confused and intellectually limited, and he might stand on the high cliffs of ancient wisdom, regarding me with pity, but he was definitely regarding me. The more I read and reread the review, the more disturbing I found its tone of mystical threat. He was issuing a challenge, telling me where to meet him.

After the screening, the vodka brand had put the film up online. I watched it again, frame by frame. The narcissistic cliff-top yoga, the Modernist hut. I took grabs of the scene in which he chopped firewood. In the background you could see a stretch of water, and beyond it a mountainous island or peninsula. The footage had been shot during the golden hour, and the sun was visible, setting over the sea in front of him, so I could tell that he was more or less facing west. It was most likely somewhere in Europe. I tried to get a good look at the dolmen, only briefly visible as he walked past. It was an irregular pile of stones and on second viewing I wasn't a hundred percent sure it was a man-made object. To me the scene seemed like the west of Ireland, maybe Brittany or Scotland. I supposed it could also have been Scandinavia, perhaps some island in the Baltic. If the dolmen was just a pile of stones, that would open it up. New Zealand, South Africa, Patagonia. Or it could be a place that didn't exist at all, altered or generated entirely in post-production.

Eventually I found a sort of gazetteer, a site whose contributors painstakingly listed all manner of ancient remains around the world. On a page of amateur photos I saw something that looked very similar to the dolmen in the film, tagged with the name of an island off the west coast of Scotland. I searched for more photos, and found one that seemed to show the cliff top where Anton did yoga. Then in the background of a snapshot of someone's birdwatching vacation I saw the hut or bothy where Anton had chopped wood. It was unambiguously the same place.

I went straight to the Gare du Nord and caught a train.

Twenty-four hours later I was on another train, heading from Glasgow into the Highlands. We sped past lakes and mountains, bathed in the golden light of Anton's film. The landscape shimmered. Across the aisle, a man in Scottish formal wear, a kilt and a jacket with silver buttons, sat at a table, listening to music and drinking his way steadily through a six-pack of beer. I felt as if I were traveling into the afterlife.

I stayed the night in a room above a pub near the port, and the next morning caught a ferry, a small boat just big enough to take a dozen passengers. We made our way out to the island in light rain, spray scudding across the bow, seabirds wheeling overhead. The boat was not full, just me and three young local men in overalls who spent the journey chatting to the captain in the wheelhouse. I checked and rechecked the backpack resting on my legs. Bivvy bag, waterproofs, water bottle, dried fruit and nuts, a flashlight, binoculars, a vicious-looking camping knife with a serrated edge, the largest one the Glasgow shop had in stock. In my pocket was my phone. I took it out and turned it over in my hand. Holding it over the water, gradually, as if by accident, I relaxed my grip until it slipped out of my fingers. Not a thing I'd willed. Not a choice.

A stone breakwater protected the island's little harbor. By the dock was a snack bar and a little store, where I bought canned food and gave a vague answer to the girl serving behind the counter when she asked where I was staying. I headed uphill from the dock, along a well-maintained single-track road which took me through an area of woodland, past two or three houses and a school. No one was around. Once a delivery van passed me, otherwise all was quiet. The road climbed up onto a high moor, grazed by sheep. I walked until I reached a kind of saddle or gap from which I could see down to a little bay, where a scattering of farmhouses lay in the lee of a range of high cliffs.

There you are, I said to Anton.

As the road began to slope down I turned off it and crossed a boggy field, scrambling up the rocky hillside. From there I could get a better view of the dale, the good land sectioned into strips of pasture by dry stone walls that ran down to a beach of grayish sand. On the other side of a channel was another island, purple crags crowned by mist. I walked further up onto the moor. Below me, a steep hill choked with bracken gradually became a cliff. Near its foot, well above the highest of the farmhouses, there was a glint of glass. I trained my binoculars on the spot and saw an angled roof, a solar panel. Anton's bothy.

I couldn't be sure if he was there. I didn't want to take the risk of going too close, and I didn't want to approach from the road that ran along the shore. By that time it was mid-afternoon. We were far north and there were still many hours of light. I retraced my steps, came down off the moor and then skirted the base of the cliff, diving into the bracken some distance above the bothy. I proceeded slowly, army-crawling so I couldn't be seen. By the time I'd worked my way round to a position just above the hut, I was wet and cold. The bothy was a neat little hut of tarred wood, with firewood stacked under a tarp by the side wall. The cliff loomed over me like the judgment of God but I kept watch, looking for anyone coming or going, any sign of life.

As I waited, the sky cleared and over the water a sunset began that made the clouds look like falling petals. I felt unbelievably calm, a feeling that persisted until, without warning, my mind was peeled open by an ecstatic vision, a flood of elation at the peachy orange light that became anxiety, then pure terror as I saw sunlight glinting off a reflective surface, turning high in the air. A satellite, a drone. I threw myself down on the ground, clawing the dirt, squirming in the petri dish of the sky's empty regard. Maybe there'd been no one up there before, but now we'd built it. Out of neediness, pathetic craving for daddy's attention, we'd built *Him* to watch over us, to witness our abjection. A black disc passed over the sun and began to spin, just as it had in Anton's film. Exposed on the hillside like a hare under the eye of a raptor, I understood for the first time the extent of the malevolent energy Anton had directed towards me, how completely I had put myself under his control. Stupid, stupid, stupid. I was trapped in a game, a simulation, some sadistic overlay on the real world that he had devised specially for me. In a state of abject terror, I zipped myself into my sleeping bag to shut out the light.

The night was interminable, one of the worst of my life. The next morning I woke up exhausted and hungry, the sleeping bag soaked through. I was sick of everything, and maybe it was that irritation, the wish to push against things rather than surrender to them, that grounded me. In any case, something about the day felt less treacherous, more solid and plausible than the one before.

By then I was more or less sure that no one was in the bothy. I army-crawled closer but the ground exhaled a freezing mist that made me shiver and I thought to hell with it and stood up and swished my way downhill through the bracken. I peered through the window of the hut and saw bare board floors, a stove and a bed raised on a platform. A strip of decking faced the sea. The door was locked. I checked around for a key—and found one under a large rock that sat at the center of a sort of mandala of sea shells.

There were no signs of recent occupation. A gas bottle was connected to a pair of cooking rings, fixed to a chest-high shelf. Another shelf under the bed held a few volumes on natural history and a torn map. There was a table and a chair, a little cupboard containing a few basic cooking things. I fumbled with a tin mug and a saucepan and a jar of instant coffee, shaking with cold.

I took my coffee outside to the deck and sat for a while, feeling the warm breeze on my face. Gradually the chill went out of my bones. I took off my jacket and sweater, then my boots and socks, my feet emerging like alien creatures, bloodless and damp. The sight of the island across the sound was infinitely calming and I surprised myself by beginning to laugh, first silently, then out loud as I realized the irony of the situation: Anton had found the kind of privacy I'd been looking for at Deuter Center, somewhere to be alone with himself, free of judgment and observation. For a while, I got lost in the possibilities. I would stay a month, a year, experience the passing of the seasons, write a book. I could finally set down on paper all the things I'd been struggling to express. And then I remembered that I'd broken in. It was not my place, not my deck to sit on and drink coffee and daydream about a book.

I spent the day in and around the hut, mostly sitting outside looking at the water, waiting for Anton to walk up the path from the road. I ate most of the food I bought at the shop. When night fell I listened for sounds outside in the darkness. In the bothy, the shadows were unquiet, full of slithering creatures. From the darkest corner my adversary kept up a stream of chatter, raising up dust in my mind, a cloud of debate. I thought solitude would solve my problems, did I? Well, solitude was corrupting, he should know, he'd spent enough time alone. Too long in the wild and men lost their humanity, their ability to be around other people. They began to slobber and howl and walk on all fours. You envy my clarity of purpose, I told him, casting my voice into the darkness. You hate and envy all that is good.

The next day things were treacherous again. The island across the sound shifted on its haunches, the undulating bracken was sown with eyes. A fine blanket of gray cloud covered the sky and I was no more than a thin skin over a hollow, a drum, a cave, my head aching, a metallic taste in my mouth.

Outside was no good, but neither was inside; I lay down on the bed but the room began to spin, and I realized I hadn't eaten, so very slowly I climbed back down from the platform, feeling like an old man. I laced up my boots, an operation that seemed to take hours.

I trudged out, sick and light-headed, my body complaining with every step, then moving a little faster as my legs gained strength. I followed the road up over the moor to the other side of the island, and down through the woods to the little shop at the quayside, where I bought provisions and looked for paper and pens. In the absence of anything better I had to settle for souvenir pencils and spiral-bound children's notebooks with rough paper and pictures of ponies and dolphins on the covers. I made no conversation with the woman who sold them to me, and walked slowly back to the bothy. On the road above the bay, I saw a man leaning over a wall, watching me approach. I nodded at him and he nodded back and as I passed by I could feel the full heat of his scrutiny, a physical sensation like a fire burning in the small of my back. He couldn't place me. He was wondering where I was going, which of his neighbors I was staying with. I turned off the road and followed a muddy path down to the beach, where I walked back and forth touristically for the benefit of anyone watching through binoculars. When I was bored of picking up seashells I took a route back to the bothy that kept me out of sight of the houses, plunging into the bracken again so I didn't have to approach from the road.

I watched the bothy for ten minutes or so, to check no one had gone inside while I was away. When I was satisfied, I went back in, took off my boots and half-collapsed on the floor. I was feeling sick and my hands were shaking, and it took me some time to get a fire going in the stove. I ate and drank water, then sat down at the desk. I felt incredibly weak, but also clear, transparent to myself. The only way out was through. I would let Anton out through myself, let him speak through me. I would follow where he led, and face whatever I found there. I arranged the kitschy little notebooks in a pile, lined up the pencils, and began to write.

I no longer have the pages. I left them on the island. Even if I'd kept them, I doubt I'd want to look at them now. I have no interest in reading my own writing as a symptom, or using it as material for some assessment or diagnosis. My project was an Apocalypse, a revelation of last things, an ancient genre that seemed right for a man who'd crawled away to a desert place to meditate.

I wrote about a paradox, how the earth is in flames but we still find it cold and difficult to touch. How we are not at home. How despite—or perhaps because of—our distance, our inability to experience ourselves as nature, we are in crisis. This "we," of course, was really just an "I," a universalization of my own panic, but I knew I was not alone in my thoughts, even if the conclusions I came to might be unacceptable, even unintelligible to others. We face, I wrote, a risk that is immeasurable, in the sense that it's impossible to quantify. An externality that sooner or later will blot out the sun. I wrote about plagues and melting glaciers and drowned cities and millions of people on the move, a future in which any claim of allegiance to universal human values would be swept away by a cruel tribalism. I wrote about a system that would eventually find itself able to dispense with public politics altogether and put in its place the art of the deal: a black box, impossible to oversee, visible only to the counterparties. There would be no checks and balances, no right of appeal against the decisions of the deal-makers, no "rights" whatsoever, just the raw exercise of power.

I wrote about how our senses will begin to fail us. As the old world of words gives way to the world of code and the only measurable output of the Anthropocene earth is dust and radiant heat, every technical advance will make our human intuitions less reliable. Machine vision is not human vision. Nonhuman agents will have interests and priorities that may not align with ours. With metrication has come a creeping loss of aura, the end of the illusion of exceptionality which is the remnant of the religious belief that we stand partly outside or above the world, that we are endowed with a special essence and deserve recognition or protection because of it. We will carry on trying to make a case for ourselves, for our own specialness, but we will find that arrayed against us is an inexorable and inhuman power, manic and all-devouring, a power thirsty for the total annihilation of its object, that object being the earth and everything on it, all that exists.

I wrote about pointlessness, the utter ruin of all my projects, the supercession of all that I was or could ever be. I described the reduction of my most cherished mysteries to simple algorithmic operations, instructions that could be put on a chip, a disenchantment so total that afterwards, after the shift, it would be impossible even to think back to how it was, to imagine what it was to be alive in the old way. My luxurious mental furnishings, my sensibility and intelligence and taste, all would turn to ashes. And the same thing would happen to everyone else on earth. The destruction of culture was only the beginning. Meaning itself would be revealed as an artifact of a period that was slipping away into history. Afterwards, there would only be function.

We are, I wrote, just clever apes, incidental to the larger purposes of the universe, and whether we know it or not, we are in a race against time. Homeostasis is a trap. Anything that isn't growing exponentially is not growing fast enough. Something implacable is arriving from the future and our only hope, our lifeboat, is an intelligence explosion, an escape from earth before it is enclosed. But we should not expect the monkeys to escape, because most likely the lifeboat will be intelligence escaping the monkey bodies, slipping out before they are tortured to death by their capricious new robot masters. After that, for the masses left behind it will be shock work and the meat grinder, for the fortunate accelerated few, a great leap forward into the beyond. When the music stops, as humanity splits, leaving on the one hand those well-capitalized in individuality, rich in self, and on the other those to whom nothing is owed, who can be used and discarded without compunction, what will we remember about the creatures we once were? The augmented selves who can see in the infrared and will never die; the exploited, only dimly aware of a world beyond the packages moving towards them on the belt. How will we, their ancestors, look to them? Like figures in an architectural drawing, conventionalized, schematic, a little hazy. Just there to give scale to the old buildings.

I filled up three notebooks with these thoughts, painstakingly editing and then making a clean copy in a fourth, which I left on the table with a letter directing whoever found it to send it to my editor for publication. I didn't know if I would survive what was coming, and I wanted there to be a record of my predictions, the reasons I had for wanting to destroy Anton and the future that I believed he was bringing about. Then I tried to write a letter to Rei, an almost infinitely painful process that almost brought me to my senses, because it forced me to imagine what it would be like for her to read what I wrote, and to have to explain to Nina why I wasn't ever coming home.

I didn't expect Rei to see me as a savior or a hero. In fact, I fully believed that she would remember me with bitterness. I'd already put her through such a lot of pain, and my death (which as I wrote seemed more likely than any other possible outcome) would only cause her more suffering. I wrote that I was sorry. I wrote that I loved her, and that my plan was a way to "escape into the present, to which I would gladly belong," a phrase of Kleist's. Sitting up late, writing my last letters, he was yet again my unwelcome companion, and various of his formulations ("a spirit sitting peering into an abyss," "I rolled the dice and I must accept that I have lost") found their way onto the page. By the time I finished it was late at night. I slept for a while, at the mercy of the bothy's busy shadows, which teemed with beaks and spikes and snouts and talons and rasping ragged wings.

In the morning, as soon as it was light, I went outside. The last day had come, and I made ready as best I could. I slipped the knife into my day pack, and waited for the golden hour, when Anton would appear. My mind was clear, or so it seemed to me. The red dust of the bustling world had settled. I was a saint, a desert father, serene and detached. I could watch thoughts fall through my consciousness like pebbles in a pool.

When it was time, I followed the path uphill, over a stile and along a fence line. Some way off was a ruined croft, overgrown by trees. When you stood on the high ground above the bay, you could see several of these copses, old hedges and windbreaks grown to enormous size, hiding stone chimneys and crumbling walls. Instead of dropping down to the beach I decided to go the other way, skirting a bog and heading towards a saddle between a piece of high moorland and a crag, one end of the cliff that loomed over the pastures like a great black wave. Scattered with black pellets of sheep dung, the path grew steep and I began to breathe heavily with the effort of climbing. The crest of the hill rose up in front of me, tall grass and wildflowers undulating in the wind. I was approaching a sort of balancing point. Salt air blew across my face into my nostrils, an anticipation of the sea. Behind me was the human world, the giant net of eyes and ears. Ahead there would be no one to watch me from a yard or a farmhouse window, only a zigzag sheep trail leading down towards the sea cliffs. Once I stepped over the ridge, I would be alone.

A few more paces and the ground fell away. There it was, the blue-black sea, clouds like white horses scudding over- head. Something was going to happen, I was sure of it. My heart was hammering in my chest. I held on to my knees and gulped down air.

The Apocalypse is the time when all secrets are revealed. By scrambling down towards the cliffs, I knew I was only post- poning the moment when the bones of the dead would start up from the earth and I would be turned inside out like the victim of a medieval execution, my innards unspooled and put on display for the crowd. Privacy is the exclusive property of the gods. They see us, but we can never see them. We live like spies, always braced for exposure, while they remain a mystery. The sky was a helmet constricting my head; sweat dripped down my face.

The path dropped into a gully choked with waist-high bracken that scratched my chest as I waded through it, my arms outstretched, expecting at any moment to sink into a bog or a hidden stream. The ground, spongy with water draining off the moor, was just about firm enough to take my weight. At last I scrambled out onto a spur of rock wide enough for me to walk on, and I followed it up out to the cliff's edge. I peered over and saw how nauseatingly high up I was. Far below, a black mat of kelp whipped back and forth in the churning white water. The sheer drop tugged at my eye, enticing my body along a line of force that ran up through the top of my head and then arced down into the void, a potential swan dive that would be all too easy to realize. As I picked my way along the cliff path, the sun appeared out of the clouds, striking the sea with a great silent clang.

As I watched the shaft of bronze light hammering the water, I knew why Anton had chosen the island and what he wanted me to see in it—I was convinced that he *had* chosen it, and I was living and moving in a matrix entirely designed by him, following a chain of hints and nudges intended to lead me to that place. *I am the Magus of the North,* he had told me. *I have opened the book of secrets.* There on the cliff path, I understood. The secret was in that view, beautiful and utterly inhuman. The secret was that all our ends and purposes were meaning- less, that the truth of existence lay in a sort of ceaseless imper- sonal violence, merciless and without affect of any kind. This violence was not tragic or heroic or awful or arousing or just or unjust. It simply *was.*

With this, the last obstacle to my apotheosis fell away. *Now, O immortality, you are all mine!* The cliff path took me to the northernmost point of the island, where at the end of a spit of land sat a slab of stone set on two uprights, framing an empty square of sky. Fate, monstrous and empty. An arch or portal. I could feel savagery very near. Violence lay in wait in the waves, the sharp stones, the light. As I walked the last stretch of path towards the stones I lost my footing. As I tried to regain my balance I looked back at my raised right arm, the fingers of the hand dramatically splayed. At that moment I saw what I was, had a name for it: the *butchered butcher,* the one who sends a spray of small stones into the sea and throws up a hand to balance himself, then looks back and sees, as if for the first time, that this hand was formed to hold a knife or a gun or sword or a spear, to execute an ancient masculine will. I saw the arm supporting my bloody hand, the layers of civilized fat flayed away to reveal the primal muscle beneath. Yes, said the *butchered butcher,* this is the meaning of this hand, this pain is what it is to be a man. This is the idea of North.

After a while I stood up again and went on. I waited at the stones for Anton to appear, for the last battle, for the confrontation that would rescue meaning from the terrible mess I'd made of my life. Then I saw movement on the beach, Finally, he had come! At last! Sweat streamed into my eyes. I was dazzled by the bronze light. I wiped my hand across my face and adopted a warrior's stance. When I could focus again I saw three wobbly yellow dots, which resolved into the figures of three police officers in fluorescent jackets, picking their way across the rocks towards me.

HOME

IN A MOVIE, two spies have to pass through a checkpoint. As they get close, one whispers to the other, "act normal!" Inevitably they are caught. It's an absurd order because it makes itself impossible to obey. To act normal is to be unself-conscious, but when you are told to do it, you instantly ask yourself what normal is. You scramble for a standard or a signature; self-consciousness consumes you. You may recover quickly, but for a moment you've been knocked off course.

As I stand here at the kitchen counter and set out food for the party, I try to fill a bowl with olives normally. I try to open a package of crackers normally, to arrange a cheeseboard in the way a normal person should arrange a cheeseboard, without excessive precision or showiness, presenting the cheese according to some ordinary aesthetic standard, with the right level of care, neither too much nor too little, unwrapping the cheeses—a wheel of Brie, a wedge of Manchego, one of those expensive little goat cheeses that come wrapped in a vine leaf—just as a normal host would, someone for whom the meaning of these actions could never be in question. When I handle the more charged objects (sharp knives, fragile glasses) I don't look round to see if Rei is watching me. My aim is to appear neither too casual nor too intent, no more than averagely aware of their potential as hazards or weapons. When I speak, I modulate my voice. I try not to load my words with excess meaning. This is an important evening for Rei and it is vital that I display no undue excitement, that my behavior should have nothing about it to trouble her or anyone else.

"Shall I open the wine?" Casual, flat. More or less correct, but I hesitate, whereas the normal thing would be to go right ahead and do it, to open the wine without seeking permission, or rather to say "shall I open the wine?" with a slightly different tone, not that of a man seeking permission, someone who isn't supposed to drink alcohol with his medication, whose offer to open the wine might be construed as a covert attempt to drink wine, or at least taste it, to mix wine with psychiatric medication, and who is therefore preempting his wife's reaction, saying that although it may appear that he's about to do this potentially dangerous or disruptive thing, there's no cause for alarm. It ought to be an offer, a throwaway moment of negotiation between two partners preparing for the arrival of guests. I'll do this while you do that. Don't worry, I'll handle it.

"No, it's fine. Just sit down."

"OK. I'll go check on Nina."

Rei is facing away from me, slicing a baguette. Her shoulders visibly stiffen, and this almost-imperceptible reaction makes me feel bleak and angry. What does she expect from me? How long can it go on? I master this flash of temper almost at once. I have no right to it. She is absolutely justified, and though I am not and never have been any danger to Nina, she has no way of knowing that. I am officially someone with a broken mind, someone whose mood and behavior is being pharmacologically regulated. I have acted in ways that were frightening and unpredictable. I have concealed the true state of my soul. But still I'm disappointed. Recently she'd seemed more relaxed. I've been out with Nina to the playground a few times, picked her up from preschool. Each time I've found Rei waiting impatiently for us to get back, pretending to do this or that, cleaning or tidying or scrolling through messages on her phone. Still, she managed it, she put herself through the stress. She has been trying very hard to trust me. This flinch, this little hunch of her shoulders, is a tell, an indication that she's concealing the true pitch of her anxiety. But she doesn't say anything, so I walk down the hallway and crack open the door to our daughter's room.

Nina is sleeping at an angle, her feet hanging over the side of her bed. Her hair, which is getting longer all the time, long enough to tie in a ponytail, is spread around her, thick damp strands of it plastered to her cheek. Her pillow has fallen on the floor and so has her toy, a little black cat, its fur grubby and matted. We were given so many stuffed animals when she was born, but this odd thing with its cartoonish eyes and shiny plush was the one that she chose, the friend that has become indispensable to her. I pick it up off the rug and put it by her head. Her mouth is open a little, and as I watch, she wrinkles her nose, sniffing in her sleep. There's a shadow in the doorway and I turn round to see Rei. Don't wake her up, she whispers. Deliberately, very slightly emphasizing my movements so that she can see the care that I'm taking, I step out and close the door.

"She's fine. I was just putting Furrycat back on the bed."

Sometimes, when she's tired or worried, Rei sets her face in a tragic mask, like something from a Noh drama. I've seen it a lot in the last few months. My wife is beautiful, even when she's hiding behind her mask face, and now that she's made herself so fundamentally inaccessible, now that I've lost the rights I used to have—to coax or cajole her into telling me what's on her mind, to make a stupid joke and receive a smile—that beauty has become painful to me, a sign or index of what I have thrown away. Because I have to say something, and because I can't bear to see that mask anymore, I ask what else needs to be done before the party. Nothing, she says. Just relax. Again, I have to tamp down my urge to push back, to say I *am* relaxed, which of course would blow it all. The injunction to relax is another one of those impossible demands.

Though I don't really need to, I go to the bathroom and sit down on the toilet, just to have a moment offstage, wishing I could smoke a joint, have a drink, take a Xanax, anything to get me through the next few hours. Everyone will be very nice, I'm sure, but they'll all be looking at me sideways. Every move I make will be scrutinized. Because I don't want to stay in there too long *(act normal)* I splash some water on my face, flush the toilet, go into the kitchen and pour myself a glass of sparkling water.

I stand at the counter and watch the tiny bubbles rising up in my glass. I am freshly shaved, wearing my most normal clothes, chinos and a dress shirt, a spy in the house of the sane. I'm feeling OK. Not too dizzy, my mouth not too dry. I've put on weight because of the medication, but not too much. A normal amount of weight.

Everything about the apartment is the same, but everything is different. I feel like Odysseus. I have been gone twenty years and in my absence other men have made themselves at home. Rei is perched on an ottoman, the TV remote in her hand. She's wearing a long dress and a piece of jewelry I don't recognize, a silver necklace with a heavy geometrical pendant made from some kind of dull blue stone. It's natural that she should have dressed up—we're entertaining, after all—but the primitive part of my brain suspects that she didn't dress for me. Since my return, she's been spending a lot of time on the phone with her friend Godwin. She's known him for years, since before we were together. I've no idea if they were ever involved. I suspect they probably were, once upon a time, but it never bothered me before. I like Godwin. He's smart and funny, and between the two of us there's never been any kind of atmosphere. He's never attempted to claim Rei in any way, to suggest that there's something he shares with her that is closed or exclusive. But recently he split up with his wife, and Rei has been the one to whom he's turned, the one who offers him a shoulder to cry on, who goes out for dinner with him and helps him dissect what went wrong.

On nights when Rei goes out with Godwin (I am, I suppose, making it sound more frequent than I should—it's really only been a question of three or four dinners in as many months) she doesn't leave me alone with Nina. Our sitter is asked to stay late, despite my insistence that it's unnecessary, that there's no reason for us to spend the extra money. But as it's Rei's money (since I paid back the Deuter foundation's stipend, my bank balance has been more or less zero) and since she always frames it as my chance to go out on my own, to "see a friend," it's hard for me to refuse. So Paulette sits and reads her magazines in the living room, and since I don't really have a friend to go and see, and the stimulation of the cinema is out of the question, and I ought not to be sitting alone in a bar, even with a book and a non-alcoholic drink, I stay in the bedroom and pretend I need an early night. Inevitably I lie awake in the dark, listening for the sound of the front door, trying to intuit from the sounds Rei makes as she comes in, the tone of her conversation with Paulette, if she's just been grinding against Godwin on the couch in the serviced apartment he's been renting since he moved out of the family home. When she comes into the bedroom, I make my breathing regular and pretend to be asleep.

It's not just Godwin. There's another man, someone she knows through work, a diplomat who's part of the French mission to the UN. I've met him a couple of times. He was apparently helpful during the weeks of my disappearance. He is a peacock, the type of guy who wears blue suede loafers and undoes too many buttons on his shirt. When we were introduced, he looked at me with frank disbelief, as if to say, *this* is who you were trying to get back? I have no doubt that I inspire contempt in him, and he seems like a man who wouldn't take no for an answer, a man for whom the fact of Rei's marriage would be no more than a speed bump on the road to seduction.

In truth I have no evidence that this diplomatic charmer has overstepped any bounds at all, but my dislike of him is so instinctive that I find it hard not to see him in the worst possible light. I torture myself with him, as I do with Godwin and various other men, in fact more or less anyone present-able who comes into our orbit, because it seems obvious to me that I'm no longer good enough for Rei, that she could be with someone better than me in almost every respect, and the only reason we're still together is that she hasn't worked this out. Would I blame her if she slept with someone else? She deserves to be happy, to have pleasure, to be free of this awful stress. What do I have to offer her? I haven't been unfaithful, that's one thing, but nevertheless I've strayed. I've been far away. And I have let her down. No woman can forget that, even if she forgives. It will always be there at the back of her mind. I am unreliable. She can no longer be sure that I'll catch her if she falls.

I should, I suppose, count my blessings. Things could be worse. When I try to reconstruct the chain of events that brought me back home from the island, here to the kitchen counter and my glass of sparkling water, I see so many mo-ments when I could have been lost, figuratively or literally, and all that prevented it was the determination of our friends. Mostly it was Rei. She saved me, and of course that makes me ashamed. I shouldn't need to be saved. And I ought to be able to put my hand on my heart and say I could do the same, that if she were lost I'd have the grit and tenacity to find her and pull her back to me. I know I'd want to do that. I know I'd try. But would I be strong enough? That question hangs over my head like the blade of a guillotine.

THE POLICE OFFICERS I saw on the island beach approached me and asked me to identify myself. When I refused, they arrested me for breaking into the bothy. They weren't armed and I thought about running, but there was really nowhere to go. Even if I'd made it back up the hill and been able to lose myself in the bracken, my way would have been blocked by the cliff. Perhaps I could have followed the sea path and hidden in some cave or cleft, but I would have been trapped, and without food or water I'd have had to give myself up before too long. So I surrendered, and was put in the back of a car, watched from his doorstep by the farmer who'd seen me the previous day and was, I presumed, the one who'd reported me.

The police had come all the way from the mainland to make the arrest, and I was taken back there on a boat and held overnight at a police station in a little town several miles from the coast. They asked me some questions, but I kept my mouth shut, and since I had no means of identification (I must have left my wallet and passport somewhere, though I don't recall throwing them away) they took my belt and shoelaces and left me in a cell to sleep as best I could, stretched out on a narrow bench under a scratchy blanket. I remember that the light was left on all night, and every few minutes someone opened the spyhole and banged on the metal door until I moved or made a sign. The next morning I was fingerprinted and a haggard-looking psychiatrist was sent in to make an assessment. He tried his best, which didn't count for much. As he asked his questions, I looked deliberately up into the corners of the room. He was a youngish man with a ginger beard and a shapeless tweed jacket so old and greasy that the collar had a dull shine. He stank of cigarette smoke, and as he drummed his fingers on the table in frustration, I saw that the nails were stained yellow with nicotine. A twenty-a-day man. Maybe more.

A female police officer, who spoke with an accent that made

her only intermittently comprehensible to me, explained that the owner of the bothy had declined to press charges. Was that Anton Bridgeman, I asked. Gary Bridgeman, maybe? It was the first time I'd spoken in her presence, and it startled her. She said she wasn't able to give me that information, and since I'd done no damage, I'd have been free to go had I been able to prove my identity or in some other way account for my presence on the island. This not being the case, and because I seemed to be distressed, for my own care and protection it had been decided to remove me to a place of safety as designated by something or other, some numbered act or statute. I was frightened, though that word doesn't convey the depth of what I was feeling, the radical terror of a world where nothing, nothing whatsoever, was certain. The conversation was taking place in a shabby little interview room that smelled of mildew and some kind of pine-scented cleaning product. I suspected that Anton was about to walk in and reveal that the police and emergency service personnel were all crisis actors. My worst fear was that his need to prove a point would go further, that in order to demonstrate his power he would put me through some kind of ordeal or torment like that of the victims on *Blue Lives*. I kept watching for clues, signs that the policewoman was not a real policewoman, or that she was in communication with someone through an earpiece. When two other officers arrived to escort me (to where, I had no idea) I panicked, and had to be physically restrained. My memory of what followed is patchy. I think the haggard psychiatrist was called to administer a sedative. I know I spent the next two weeks on a locked ward in a hospital in Glasgow, a Victorian building of reddish-black stone that reinforced my sense that I was participating in a performance, its echoing corridors and pervasive smell of boiled cabbage too precisely what would be expected of an "asylum," an old-fashioned institution that for the most part no longer existed.

During that time I was put on a regime of medication that left me sluggish and nauseous. My expectation of Anton's arrival gradually ebbed, until I was no longer certain he was even involved in my predicament. The experience of being in the hospital was formless and boring. It had none of Anton's visual or narrative style. Though other patients occasionally shouted or caused a disturbance, these events were few and far between. Mostly people sat in a common room and watched a TV tuned to some channel that ran endless cooking and home improvement shows. I slept in a room with three other men, and though I observed them closely, none of them said or did anything remarkable. Like a member of a millenarian cult after the promised doomsday has come and gone, I began to edit my recollections, persuading myself that I'd never thought Anton was directing my actions, that I'd gone to the island in search of enlightenment or peace or revelation or some other reputable spiritual experience, and what had happened to me, what was still happening to me in the hospital, was part of a process of learning or "growth," something I'd initiated or vol-unteered to do. I'd still not spoken more than a few words to my doctors, or given them any details of my identity, but my physical description must have made its way onto some kind of database, because one afternoon I was staring blankly out of the common room window, watching pigeons fight over a sandwich wrapper near the hospital's front entrance, when a voice behind me said hello and I looked up to find my older brother, who I hadn't spoken to for over a year, standing in the doorway wearing a purple Lakers cap and looking just as out of place as he did anywhere that wasn't a sports bar in a second-tier American city.

It turned out that when I didn't arrive in New York on my scheduled flight, Rei went into panic mode. Believing (rightly) that something bad was happening to me, she used her legal connections to have my description circulated to law enforcement in Germany and elsewhere in Europe. The police were not particularly responsive, taking the view that I was an adult man and probably had my reasons for breaking off contact. She was asked, I heard later, whether I was having an affair, or perhaps had a second family somewhere. Frustrated, she hired an investigator, who pulled my credit card records and ascertained that I had gone to the UK. By painstakingly calling hospitals and police authorities, they discovered that someone fitting my description was a patient in a Glasgow mental hospital. A cell phone picture taken by one of my nurses confirmed it and because Rei was in the middle of a case, my brother took time off work and flew from Chicago to bring me home.

I don't have many clear memories of my return to New York. I was heavily sedated. I remember sitting in a window seat on the plane looking down at endless fields of white cloud, as my brother watched Marvel movies and worked on his laptop. He didn't try and make conversation, which was a relief. When I needed to go to the bathroom, he went with me and stood outside the door. I was pushed through JFK in a wheelchair, unable (or not trusted) to walk by myself. Was Rei waiting at arrivals? I can't be sure. I know I saw her later, after my brother had said goodbye with all the emotion of someone going out to get groceries and I'd been admitted to a private mental health facility on the Upper East Side, paid for by Rei's good insurance.

We sat in a beige room beneath a reproduction of an Abstract Expressionist painting by Franz Kline, all jagged black lines on a patchy white ground. I remember thinking that the painting was an edgy choice for a place that would conventionally display something brighter, a landscape or Van Gogh sunflowers. I concentrated on thinking about the painting because Rei was crying, actually holding her head in her hands and sobbing, sitting across from me in an armchair and shaking with the force of her tears. Her pain was too hard to process, the pain I was putting her through, so I thought about art as a form of avoidance, and at that moment I intuited or realized something terrible—that in my chest, instead of a heart, there was some kind of alien device, something inorganic that was emitting a regular pulse, ticking away and governing my emotions, proof that I would never be able to connect to this woman, the woman I loved, or had loved back when I was human, before my heart had been removed and this thing planted in my chest, and I stood up and made some attempt to get rid of it, to pluck it out, and whatever I did must have been violent or alarming because other people came into the room and Rei left and I didn't see her again for several days.

The discovery that I had an electronic heart was terrifying. I'd been the victim of a monstrous crime; without my knowledge one of my vital organs had been stolen. When I was lucid enough to think at all, I tried to work out when the substitution had taken place. Why was I unable to remember such a traumatic event? Luckily the feeling came and went, and after a few days it began to fade, until once again I consistently experienced the organ as mine. Other assaults on my bodily integrity were more insidious. As a patient in a mental health facility it was objectively true that I was under surveillance, but I developed an exaggerated sense of its intensity. I believed that my captors had implanted sensors under my skin, so tiny that although I examined myself thoroughly, running my fingertips over each scratch and blemish, I couldn't detect them. These microscopic devices were using the radio spectrum to transmit information about everything from the airflow through my lungs to the chemical compounds in my blood. The people watching me were analyzing this data and using it to predict and control my behavior. I thought of Monika, and the vast resources that the East German state had used against her. I thought about the leaps in technology since the GDR's collapse. I was entangled in a system of oppression so total that things I could not voluntarily control—the conductance of my skin, the rate of secretion of hormones in my brain—were relentlessly betraying me. Numb with unhappiness, I spent long hours staring at my hands, the pattern of pores, the fine black hair on the knuckles, the raised veins branching out like indecipherable runes.

I was prescribed antipsychotics and a mood-stabilizer, designed to lift my depression without inducing manic episodes. The treatment worked, more or less. My suspicions began to subside. My relationship with my body became manageable, and though I couldn't have said I "owned" it, or identified with it in an uncomplicated way, it was at least bearable to live inside it, and the pressure brought to bear on me by external influences was curbed or moderated, which allowed me a level of dignity, the feeling that although I wasn't autonomous, I could carry on existing in the world.

Most of this struggle was internal, and I knew better than to discuss it with the various doctors and therapists at the clinic. When I was asked how I felt, I was judicious in the way I answered, neither exaggerating my anxiety nor trying to persuade them that I felt fine. The failure to acknowledge one's illness is the primal sin of the psychiatric patient, the quickest way to intensify the regime of control. I would say things like "better today, I think," hoping to give them a sense of achievement, never questioning their authority, their right to make judgments about what was reasonable or proportionate for me to feel or believe. And I did get better. The medication, the soothing environment, the relative lack of stress—all of it helped to restore a sense of control. My actual world-picture was another matter. I didn't talk about the inhuman future that Anton was trying to realize, or about the sense I'd had, before I ever encountered him, that we were all slipping towards disaster. I understood that my reaction had been faulty, that in the face of terror I had failed, broken down. But nothing about my treatment touched on these questions. My doctors were fundamentally servants of the status quo. Their work was predicated on the assumption that the world is bearable, and anyone who finds it otherwise should be coaxed or medicated into acceptance. *But what if it isn't?* What if the reasonable reaction is endless horrified screaming?

After a month of in-patient treatment I could simulate normality with a high degree of precision and since Rei's insurance wouldn't go on footing the bill, a pragmatic judgment was made that I was well enough to go home.

On the day of my release, Rei didn't feel she could face me on her own, so she enlisted an old friend of mine to come with her to pick me up from the clinic. Femi was one of the people that she liked best from what we semi-ironically termed "my former life." Before we got together I'd done a lot of depthless druggy socializing at gallery openings and book launches.

When I became a father, I preferred to spend what little personal time I had on my work, and most of my acquaintances from the art scene naturally fell away. Femi's life had taken a similar path to mine. He lived in our neighborhood. His partner, Zoe, had become friends with Rei and the two of them had been pregnant at around the same time. Femi and I often spent bleary mornings piloting buggies round the park, clutching coffees and swapping rueful stories about sleep-deprivation and work. He was a screenwriter, the kind who seems to make a good living without ever having anything produced, and he had a freelance schedule that allowed him to come into Manhattan during the day. When he and Rei arrived at the clinic, I was waiting in the reception area. He looked around nervously, and I wondered what he'd been expecting to find there, instead of the muted rugs and Danish Modern chairs. He insisted on taking my bag and launched into some story about Nina and his daughter that lasted until we were in a car, sitting in traffic on Canal Street, waiting to get onto the Manhattan Bridge.

Rei held my hand, scrolling through her email without speaking. Femi had obviously decided to blow through the whole question of my breakdown, treating me as if we were just catching up after some ordinary hiatus, a vacation or a work trip. Beyond a perfunctory "how you doing?" he didn't ask me any probing questions, and though he was typically gracious and charming, I realized that he was pouring out words to fill every silence. One minute he was catching me up on gossip about mutual acquaintances, the next insisting I had to try some kind of grain bowl at a new neighborhood café. Everything's a bowl now, man, he said. Have you noticed? I was grateful that he was being cheerful, and a little sorry that he seemed so ill at ease. I looked out of the window as we sped across the river, and for a fleeting moment, I thought that the view of the Dumbo waterfront seemed blocky, simplified, like an image that hadn't been sampled at a high enough rate. I told myself to ignore it, that it was just a side effect of my medication, perhaps my eyes weren't focusing properly, and when I blinked and looked again I couldn't reproduce the effect. Rei asked if I was OK. I was jerking my head around. I said I was fine, just a sore neck. Maybe you ought to book a massage, Femi suggested.

We got in to find Paulette in the living room with Nina, who was wearing a dress and had her hair up in bunches, looking very grown up, no longer a toddler but a proper little girl. I experienced a rush of emotion and held out my arms to her. Oh my darling, I said. How I've missed you. But she wouldn't come to me, hiding behind Paulette's legs. I didn't force the issue, just sat on the sofa and watched Paulette make tea. She seemed as nervous as Rei and Femi, clattering around with mugs and kettle as if it were the first time she'd handled them. She said politely that she hoped I was feeling better. I said that I did, and I was sorry I'd made extra work for her. She shook her head vigorously. No trouble, no trouble. I should just relax, she said, a refrain that was already wearing thin for me—I'll know I'm trusted again when people are happy to hype me up, when they want me to experience strong emotions.

The apartment seemed much the same. Nina's toys were scattered around, books and magazines piled on every surface. Rei had, perhaps inevitably, spread out slightly while I'd been away. A pair of her shoes were discarded under the sofa. Several folders of legal documents were wedged on the kitchen counter between the toaster and the fruit bowl. As ever, the

windows were filthy. The landlord never responded to our re-
quests to have them cleaned, and we hadn't got round to organizing it ourselves. The late summer light filtered in, a dirty
yellow, outlining a trapezoid on the dusty Afghan rug. Nina
was using this shape as a sort of abstract table as she hosted a
tea party for her dolls, slicing imaginary cake and telling off
her guests for snatching before it was their turn. She paid no
attention to me, which was good, since I was finding her little
game almost unbearably moving.

Rei disappeared to take a call. Paulette and Femi were chatting about some TV show. Caught up in Nina's game, I paid
no attention until their conversation flagged. Glancing over,
I found that they were watching me watch my daughter, the
same uncertain smile playing over both their faces. I tried to
work out how I must appear, what signals I was giving off, a calculation of impossible complexity. I felt obscurely outraged—
this was my daughter, I was just watching her playing—and I
wanted to challenge them, to ask what gave them the right to
monitor my interaction with my own child. Instead I mumbled
something about needing a shower, as an excuse to leave the
room.

I went into our bedroom and changed my clothes, rediscov-
ering the row of shirts in the closet, the contents of my dresser
drawers. The bed had been made, but Rei's smell was in the
air, and I experienced another surge of emotion, a mix of relief
and sorrow and unfocused yearning. I moved a pile of laundry off a chair and sat for a while, looking down on the yards
and gardens behind our building. Our house-proud neighbor
was pottering about with a rake and a garbage bag, wearing
a big straw hat. On the other side, the musicians had painted
a wobbly rainbow on their back fence. We had no access to

those gardens. Our apartment was on the second floor, and if we wanted to be outside, we had to go to the playground or the park. I tried to do as I'd been told, to relax, to feel at home, looking down on my rented view. I found I didn't feel much beyond a sort of generalized familiarity. I realized that I could hear Rei's voice, talking to Nina in the kitchen, and went out to find that both Femi and Paulette had gone. As Nina worked on a coloring page, I looked at my wife and she looked at me, the two of us as still and stylized as a couple in a medieval painting. She'd come from the office, so she was dressed in a suit, her hair tied back in a ponytail, little pearl studs in her ears, a woman at home in the world, comfortable with worldly ways, with convention and compromise and negotiation. It occurred to me that both the suit and her hair had a bluish tint, while the light falling on the side of her face was orange, and something about that worried me, the contrast too perfect, too *designed*. Opposite sides of the color wheel. Are you back, she said. I nodded. She reached out and touched my arm. Is it really you?

Was I back? Was it really me? I held her, smelling her familiar smell, barely daring to breathe.

It was only later, after Nina had gone to bed, that we managed to talk. We sat together in the kitchen, over the remains of a pasta dinner. Rei asked me for the third or fourth time how I was doing and immediately apologized, saying she knew it was an irritating question. I tried to take her hand across the table, awkwardly navigating the bowls and water glasses. She allowed her hand to be held, but it felt artificial, as if we were on an early date. After a minute or so, she withdrew it and started playing with her fork.

"Tell me honestly, are you angry with me for having you put in a psych ward?"

"No. God no."

"I know how much you hate—authority and so on. But I wasn't sure what else to do. You were in danger."

"I understand."

"Do you hate me?"

"No. Of course I don't."

"I just want you to be well again."

"I'm going to be fine. I can feel it."

There was something else she wanted to ask. I always know when Rei has a question, even when she's trying to hide it. Her emotions are never very far from the surface, even if they're almost always expressed in pauses and hesitations.

"Talk to me."

"I'm not going to ask you—I mean, I know you'll tell me eventually, when you're ready. About what happened to you in Berlin. But . . ." She trailed away. "Oh God this is hard."

"Go on."

"I don't want to be scared of you."

"You don't have to be."

"I don't want to be. I really don't."

"I know."

"Can you do me a favor. Can you look at me?"

I'd been feigning interest in the table. I met her gaze as steadily as I could.

"Are you a danger to Nina and me?"

"No. I promise."

"You won't hurt her."

"Never, I swear it."

She nodded and got up from the table. For a while she busied herself in the kitchen, wiping the counter, putting things back in the fridge. I sat, frozen in place. For her to have to ask that. For me to have to answer. It was as if a hole had opened up inside me, a great pit of misery that had sucked in all my substance. I wanted to react, to have some kind of feeling beyond raw shock. At the edges of my vision, the world seemed approximate, pixelated. Rei didn't make eye contact when she spoke.

"I've made you up a bed in the spare room."

"OK."

"I'm sorry. I'm having trouble sleeping. I need—I just need to sleep."

There wasn't really anything else to be said. We both got ready for bed, Rei waiting until I'd used the bathroom before she started her own routine. I shut the door of the spare room, a grand name for a narrow space just big enough for a daybed and a desk cluttered with my old papers. Since giving up my office, my usual habit had been to work in libraries and cafés, but after Nina's birth I'd wanted to be close to home, and the money spent on coffee and pastries was no longer justifiable, so this had become my lair. It wasn't pleasant to be shut in there with the detritus of my failed book project, the Post-its on the wall, the various journals and anthologies I'd been consulting before I went away. It was hard to think back to the person who wanted to write about lyric poetry. The very idea seemed like a provocation, a sick joke. I peeled off the Post-its, tidied the books and papers into piles and stacked them on the floor, carrying on until the surface of the desk was clear. It was a version of the routine I always fell into when I was starting work after a break. Tidying my desk put me in the right frame of mind to write, though in this case I was preparing to erase or forget my writing, or at least that particular period of it, to consign some part of my writing life to the past. I was boxing up the train of thought that had led to Berlin, to the lake and the Conference House, to Paris, the island. When I'd finished, I switched off the desk light and lay down in bed.

I was still awake after midnight. The apartment was silent. I was sure Rei was asleep, so I gave in to temptation and went to look in on Nina. All afternoon she'd more or less ignored me, keeping close to her mom, not allowing me to help her with her dinner or her bath or getting into her pajamas. When I tried to sit with her as she watched a TV show, she told me to leave. I want to do it on my own, she said. Of course she hadn't wanted me to read her a story either, though I was desperate to snuggle up with her, to turn the pages and answer her questions and do the best voices for the characters I possibly could. I'd tried hard to persuade her, perhaps too hard, because Rei shot me a look. It was probably easier, she said, if she did it.

I padded barefoot down the corridor and cracked open her door. It was hard to see in the dark, and I stepped carefully inside. Her bed was empty. I experienced a moment of panic. She'd vanished. Someone had taken her. Trying to control my alarm I opened the door to our room. Yes, Nina was in bed with Rei, sprawled facedown, her arms out by her sides. I grinned with relief, but Rei must have heard the creak of the door, because she gasped and sat up in bed. I heard her fumbling with the lamp. Suddenly we were face-to-face. An orange cone of light, a dark background, blue-gray, paler in the places where the light from outside crept round the curtains.

"What the hell? What are you doing?"

"I'm sorry. I just—go back to sleep. I was worried. I didn't know where Nina was."

"You can't—you can't just come in here like this. You can't."

"I'm sorry. I'm so sorry. I didn't mean to wake you up."

I closed the door.

The next day at breakfast, she cried.

"I'm sorry. I'm just not ready. I'm not sure if I can do this."

Nina patted her hand. "There, there, mommy. It's OK."

Wracked with remorse, I promised I'd stay in my room. And if it became too stressful to have me in the house, I'd find somewhere else to sleep. I could call Femi. As I made the offer, I realized that he also had a child at home, so it wouldn't work. Rei shook her head. We'll be fine, she said. I wasn't sure if that "we" included me. She dabbed at her eyes and looked at the time on her phone.

"What will you do today?"

"I don't know. I might go to The Good Bean. Femi said they have a new menu."

"That's a nice idea. Go for a walk, get some air. I won't be late tonight, but call me if you need anything. Just relax."

Soon afterwards, Paulette arrived. She said hello to me and immediately started dressing Nina for the park. She clearly didn't want to stay in the apartment with me for a minute longer than necessary. Rei came out in her work clothes and kissed me goodbye, her mouth dry against my cheek. She was wearing an unfamiliar perfume, and it tugged at something in my brain, some memory, so I held on to her for a moment, longer than was appropriate, trying to work out what it was, until she unpeeled herself from my embrace and began to gather her things. Nina and Paulette followed her out. The door clicked shut and for the first time since the island, I was alone, unobserved, free to do what I wanted. I had no idea how to deal with this freedom, and above all I wanted to be normal, to play some useful role, so I occupied myself by doing housework. I decided I'd make things as nice as possible for Rei when she came back home. When I'd done all I could, scrubbing the bathroom tiles with a toothbrush, chipping away with an old knife at the stubborn carbonized patches in the oven, I went to The Good Bean and ordered the triple-sprouted grain bowl, which I ate as slowly as I could, mindfully chewing each virtuous organic mouthful and watching the twenty-somethings at the tables around me working on their laptops.

Over the next two or three weeks we made small advances. I kept the apartment spotless and cooked elaborate meals. A minor side effect of my medication was that I could barely taste food, but I was mainly interested in pleasing Rei, and took a maternal satisfaction whenever she cleaned her plate. Gradually Nina got used to my presence, incrementally letting her guard down. I was allowed to do small tasks for her; I helped her put on her shoes; I cut her toast into soldiers, buttered it to the edges in the approved manner and arranged it in a pattern on the plate. Good daddy. One evening she climbed onto my lap as I was reading a book, and to my alarm, tears began to run down my face. The reaction was instantaneous, like flipping a switch. I had to fumble in my pocket for a handkerchief.

Each night, Rei waited until I had finished in the bathroom, before taking her shower and brushing her teeth. I would go into my own room and close the door. Then I'd hear her slippered feet in the corridor outside. I slept badly, another side effect of my medication, but I never left the room. Since I found it hard to concentrate on reading, and I didn't want to make Rei nervous by wandering around the apartment, I spent my insomniac hours in an activity that I would have sneered at just a few months previously, filling in elaborate mandala patterns in one of those "adult" coloring books that are marketed as tools for stress relief. It was a pointless task (in general I've never liked doing anything "just to pass the time") and it made me feel like a prisoner whiling away his sentence doing weaving or scrimshaw, but I persisted. I was determined to get well, to be normal. Whatever it took to come back home.

Every so often, Rei and I tried to talk, with mixed results. I've always found it hard to speak on cue about my emotions. I am an articulate person, but only about things that don't touch me. As soon as someone asks what I feel, I get confused. I don't have the immediate access to my feelings that seems, to my eternal amazement, to be the birthright of most human beings. What question could be more profound than *how are you*? It feels lazy to say just any old thing, so I look inside myself and invariably this is a terrible idea. Searching for feelings is like being the lookout on a ship, shining a lantern into thick fog. Objects that appear close at hand recede into the murk, or reveal themselves as chimeras. Somewhere off the port bow are icebergs. At any rate, it takes me a great deal of time to formulate a response, and to the questioner it must seem as if I've been struck dumb. The worst version of this is when Rei asks me to articulate how I feel about her. I love you, I say, which is true, and ought surely to be enough. But she's a lawyer, and she invariably follows it up with some version of the question *why do you love me?* and I feel like she's taking a deposition; her tone suggests that we are conducting a grave and serious investigation, and suddenly it seems extremely urgent to tell the truth. Of course that's perfectly reasonable—anything less, anything pat or cliché would be a betrayal, I've made vows, after all, before God or at least an official licensed by the city of New York—but my very lack of access to the answer, not having it immediately on hand, gives rise to the suspicion that *I don't know why I love her,* or worse, lends the answer (when it belatedly comes) a suggestion of insincerity. Nothing I say is good enough. Something about my tone invariably scans as arch or qualified or mediated, even actively sarcastic. At the best of times, Rei finds me an unsatisfactory bestower of compliments, though I am a man in love, a man all in, his emotional chips stacked on a single number. This was a problem before my breakdown, and since I came home, the stakes have been infinitely higher.

What I told Rei about Berlin was, admittedly, only a fragment of the truth. She'd heard from the administrators at the Deuter Center that I'd been difficult and uncooperative. I'd had an abrasive relationship with some of the other fellows, and I'd made bizarre and unsubstantiated allegations about breaches of privacy. The final straw had been an encounter with the police, after I had tried, inexplicably, to gain access to a secure facility for refugees. I told her about how I'd seen the father and daughter, how they seemed to crystallize everything I'd been thinking about, all the great problems of the world, how in a confused way I'd wanted to do something for them, but in the moment it had been misunderstood. Rei told me that Dr. Weber had implied that I was trying to get access to the daughter. They suspected me of involvement in human trafficking. She hadn't believed it, she said. Not for a moment.

It was particularly hard to talk about Anton, because nothing about that situation was any clearer to me than before. For obvious reasons, I hadn't watched any more of *Blue Lives,* and since I was avoiding the internet, I had no idea what he'd been doing since I saw him in Paris. I suspected that he'd be involved in some way in the growing turmoil of the American election campaign, but I knew that if I went looking for information, I'd be dragged back into all the other questions, everything that, for the sake of my mental health, I needed to keep at a distance. I spoke to Rei about the island in the most general terms. I said I'd been convinced that I needed to confront something, some metaphysical danger, and that it had been tied up with the idea of North. I said I'd seen pictures of the cliffs, and it had seemed to me that if I went there, I'd achieve some kind of resolution. Rei asked me what I meant by "the idea of North." It was an odd phrase. I said, truthfully, that it had made more sense at the time. Whiteness. A kind of white mysticism. I was afraid that if I said more it would spook her, that the extremity of my experiences would lead her to conclude that I was beyond hope of redemption and she would be better off severing ties, taking Nina elsewhere and making a life which didn't include me and my scarred brain.

Rei tried her best to be reasonable, to give me the benefit of the doubt, but she found it hard. One evening, after a long day at work and a particularly fractious bath-and-bedtime, I said something about existential risk and she lost her temper. I always had been selfish, she told me. It was always *my* sensitivity, *my* woundedness. I acted like I was so special, the only sensitive person in the world. In truth, I didn't actually think twice about the people close to me. My pain was grand and romantic, but she was the one who was left to clean up my mess. And what about Nina? What effect would all this have on her? Even now I was clinging to some story about the world ending. The harsh reality was that I hadn't been able to handle everyday life so I ran away. That was all. I had run away and left my family.

It was a terrible conversation. She asked me outright if I'd been planning to kill myself. That's the only thing she had really heard in all my convoluted explanations. I'd disappeared to an island and I'd been going to kill myself rather than stay with her and Nina. As far as she was concerned, all the rest was just noise.

Of course, even when we talked and didn't reach this pitch of confrontation, Rei could tell that I was hiding things. There were secrets that I wasn't ready to share. Hannah Arendt says something about how a life spent in public becomes shallow, how it loses the quality of rising into sight from some unseen darkness or depth. Privacy is not an unreasonable expectation, but my privacy was a threat to Rei. What was I hiding in my black box? What violence, what delusions? So she picked away at it, trying in her lawyerly fashion to breach my defenses, to do what she felt she had to do to protect herself and her daughter. I understood. There were times when she wore me down so much that if I could have turned myself inside out to reassure her, I would have. I would have shown her everything, all the ugliness, if I'd only had a clue how to go about it. I did want to show myself to Rei, to her above all people.

I believe everyone has a place, a mental laboratory where we experiment with thoughts that are too strange or fragile to expose. I believe that we need to preserve it, in order to feel human. It is shrinking, its scope reduced by technologies of prediction and control, by social media's sinister injunction to *share*. The paranoid belief that took hold of me in the clinic—that chips under my skin were sending data to my enemies—while literally untrue, was an exaggerated form of this recognition. It was the place where I retreated in those late night hours I spent coloring in mandalas with orange and teal, the contrasting shades that I had begun to notice all around me, a current trend in Hollywood film grading that I saw everywhere in a visual environment that ought to have felt unmediated, ought to have felt *real*.

Since I needed an activity, I decided to repaint the living room. It was time-consuming and disruptive, a perfect channel for my nervous energy. I did everything meticulously, moving the furniture into the center of the room and covering it with plastic, masking the woodwork, washing the walls, filling and sanding cracks, trying to create the smoothest surface possible. I consulted Rei about colors. Nina offered her impractical opinions (purple daddy, paint it purple) and the three of us made a happy Saturday outing to the hardware store, choosing the paint and watching the guy mix it in one of those loud mechanical oscillators. When the room was done, it looked good, fresh and hopeful, the subtle greenish-gray tint a huge improvement on the dirty magnolia that had been there before.

Rei was pleased, even when I started on the woodwork, sanding down the layers of old lead paint and creating a lot of toxic dust. After a week or so, the doors and baseboards looked good enough that it seemed a shame not to polish the old brass handles, which I did, replacing the ones on the bathroom with vintage ceramic knobs that I hunted down on the internet. Nina asked if I could do her bedroom, which was certainly grubby, the walls smeared and pocked with stickers. Rei found an old poster of a tiger on an auction site and had it framed. She couldn't understand my objection to Nina's desire for orange, and I didn't want to push back too hard, but I bartered them down to a single wall behind her bed, soaking the roller and layering on coat after coat until the color was rich and saturated. As I worked, I began to feel that I was useful, and there might be a road back for me, a means of redemption. In this way, by the time I'd been home for two months, a kind of normality emerged, a routine that suited all three of us. Rei and I began to talk about the future, about maybe taking a vacation, about whether we would put Nina in preschool full-time the following year.

One night, as I was leaving the bathroom, where I'd been brushing my teeth and running my fingers over the dirty grout, wondering about the feasibility of retiling, Rei appeared at the door to our bedroom and beckoned me inside. Sleep in here tonight, she said.

As a sexual reunion, it was tender but melancholy. Rei's body was unfamiliar to me, but so was my own. Another side effect of my medication was the near-total destruction of my libido; though touching her felt like a minor miracle, a privilege that I hadn't expected to earn, I found it impossible to get an erection. It was as if my desire existed at the center of a labyrinth, a conundrum or puzzle that I had to solve before I could complete the circuit. She tried to get me hard with her hands and mouth. I stroked her hair, furrowed my brow, ran my hands over her neck and face and breasts, trying to find the combination that would pick the unpickable lock. Unable to perform, I went down on her, something that almost always turned me on. I wanted to serve her, to give her an orgasm, but she seemed uncomfortable and soon she pulled me back up again. Let's just hold each other, she said. So we did, lying under the covers, our bodies molded together, big spoon and little spoon. Gradually her breathing became deeper and more regular and I realized that she'd fallen asleep. I stroked her shoulder and felt a vast gulf between us, formed out of all the days when we had not been together, the days of my absence and the days before I knew her, when she had said and done things I would never find out about. I could touch her, brush my fingers over her skin, but it was like touching the surface of some mysterious ancient stone. Inside, Rei stretched away to infinity, a galaxy of unseen stars.

I never went back to the spare room. Once again we became a couple that shared a bed. Many other small intimacies returned. Sounds and smells. We watched each other dress. We blearily cuddled Nina when she woke us up too early in the morning. But still there was a gap, a boundary defined partly by sex, which remained impossible, and partly by something else, a mutual reticence: Rei's wariness of me, my suspicion that she was masking her true feelings, that while I'd been away she'd discovered some new part of herself about which I knew nothing. Often, as I've said, I decided that there was a man, someone who was making her feel the things I couldn't. But it wasn't as simple as that, as easily pinpointed. I began to wonder if the loss was permanent, whether we'd be better off going our separate ways.

I had therapy this afternoon. The therapist is in her sixties. She wears long heavy skirts and Indian silver jewelry and cuts her iron-gray hair into a severe bob. In affect, she is not kindly, or particularly warm. She certainly doesn't twinkle or attempt to look sympathetic, which is a relief to me. She receives or rather absorbs my confessions with every appearance of neutrality. She's not the sort of therapist who makes you lie on a couch or face away, and this is another thing I like about her. We sit opposite each other and dispute. Sometimes, when she is concentrating, she twists her legs around in a sort of knot, a girlish gesture that I find reassuring, implying as it does a level of physical tension; it gives me the sense that something is at stake in the stories I tell her. I speak and she nods occasionally, balancing a worn leather portfolio on her knees. Occasionally she makes a note.

How do you camouflage despair? If I tell the truth, I suspect that I'll set myself on the yellow brick road back to the clinic. But if I don't tell the truth to her, someone who is paid to listen, then what hope do I have of finding a way through the *selva oscura*? Why do you think you find it so hard to speak plainly, the therapist often asks. She tells me not to make allusions, to try to talk directly about myself, without filtering what I say through references to books or films or art. She says she doesn't care about my references. I say I don't know how to speak any other way, it is how I understand myself. These references are my work, what I do. She says it's deflection, a form of resistance. I can run down the clock by talking about Kleist or Chinese scholar's rocks, but I won't get any better. I am trying, she says, to present myself as the expert, instead of the patient. It is a thing a lot of her male clients do. I say I don't think of myself as an expert in anything. I never set out to be any kind of authority. I just wanted to be left alone. At some point during every appointment she will remind me that getting well means accepting certain things about what has happened. It means understanding that my picture of the world is distorted. I find this hard to hear, and not just because I'm bored of listening to her say it. It is shameful to be a broken mechanism, to have to sit obediently while someone else goes about putting you right.

Above all, she says, I have to rid myself of my obsession

with Anton. She habitually uses this formulation. *My obsession*. When I asked her to define obsession, she told me she wasn't interested in playing semantic games. I said I was trying to avoid thinking about him. She shook her head. That just meant I was trying to avoid talking about him. Two different things. She was correct, of course. I didn't want to talk about Anton. I understood that I'd overestimated his power, and his interest in me. My belief that he and I had been engaged in some kind of duel was delusional. He hadn't induced or encouraged me to go to the island. At the same time there were elements that I hadn't invented. The dinner in the Turkish café. The quotes and phrases in *Blue Lives*. The Starhemberg content. This afternoon the therapist asked, yet again, what had attracted me to him. I protested that attraction had nothing to do with it, quite the opposite. Those two poles are never just poles, she said. Irritated, I asked if she was implying that I wanted to sleep with him. If so, she was off the mark. She shrugged. There were other modes of attraction. Did I want to be him, to have his status and influence in the world? I threw up my hands. The money would be nice, I said, sarcastically. She gave me a searching look, another of her tricks. Because I'd been aggressive, she would now say nothing until I'd acknowledged my rudeness and made an effort to answer her question. No, I said eventually, I didn't want to be him. I wanted to oppose him, to stop his nihilistic ideas gaining traction. She made all the obvious points. He was a TV writer, not a politician. Maybe his shows were influential, but he didn't have the power to do the things I believed he could do. Shows? I said. I was only aware of one. She raised an eyebrow, evidently a little pleased with herself. As a matter of fact, she had done a little research into this man, since he had previously been unfamiliar to her. Apparently he was about to launch a new television series. It would be (here her voice pulled on the tonal equivalent of rubber gloves) in the *fantasy* genre. Dragons, that sort of thing. Surely I could see that this was not a field for anyone with serious political ambitions. It would be hard to think of anything more purely escapist. I told her that what she said might once have been true, but the internet had changed things. There were underground currents, new modes of propagation. It wasn't even a question of ideas, not straight-forwardly, but feelings, atmospheres, yearnings, threats. What kind of threats, she wanted to know. Well, I said. A lot of people quibbled about terms, but essentially I was talking about Fascism. She said she thought it was unhelpful to make emo-tive comparisons. Some might even find it offensive, a way of cheapening the past. When it came to extremism, sunlight was the best disinfectant. In her experience, people tended to reject such things when they understood their implications.

I saw that I had no hope of persuading her. She was too old, too insulated by her degrees and her shelves of books. I was being, she told me blandly, rather melodramatic about what was essentially a marginal set of ideas. We weren't living in Weimar Germany. I shouldn't feel bad, though. Many of her patients had been experiencing anxiety because of the presi-dential election campaign. With my susceptibilities, it would be best if I stayed away from politics.

The therapist looked at her watch. We were almost out of time. Before I went, she said, she wanted to try to talk again about the question of suicide. I thought to myself, see, this is what your life has come to. Agenda item: *suicide*. Your wife, said the therapist, was in no doubt that this was your inten-tion. She herself had telephoned the director of the institution in Germany (I started in surprise, this was news to me) and it seemed that at least two members of staff recalled me speaking about it. Her tone annoyed me. She was behaving as if she'd scored some point. I said I hadn't been serious. I'd never leave Rei and Nina. I'd written certain things, but only in connection with my research into Heinrich von Kleist and Henriette Vogel.

As I protested, I remembered the sinister way in which all the elements had fallen into place. The lake, Monika, the porter's guns. Death had been daring me to repeat a pattern, drawing me towards itself. I couldn't deny the darkness that had surrounded me on the island, the line of force arcing down from the cliffs to the roiling water below. Had I wanted to die then? No, but what I *wanted* had felt irrelevant. Death had seemed inevitable, the Minotaur lurking, waiting for me at the center of the maze. How had contemplating suicide made me feel, the therapist asked. Exalted? Elevated? Had I believed that I was doing something noble, perhaps something that would make me famous? I denied all of this. I told her I knew the difference between narrative and real life. She said she wasn't so sure. I struck her as a romantic. My obsession with an apocalyptic future was just another mode of sentimentality. I don't usually tell people to think less, she said, but in your case that might be useful. Try going through the motions. Accept that you might have conventional horizons, that conventional things could make you happy. Stop asking for life to be a poem.

I left the therapist's office in a foul mood. What right did she have to be so patronizing? Her bland self-assurance was the product of privilege. She didn't see what was coming down the pike. I didn't understand how people could be so complacent, not with everything that was going on. It was late afternoon, and I still had to run some errands, after which I had to get home to set things up for Rei's party. The session had been a waste of time.

The office was on the ground floor of a large Chelsea apartment building, a huge vaguely Romanesque pile that spanned a whole block of 23rd Street. Feeling increasingly stressed and angry, I stalked down the corridor past the front desk, where a uniformed doorman was talking to a delivery driver carrying a pile of packages. As I pushed open the door and stepped out onto the street, I was struck by the scene. There was nothing visually unusual about it. The afternoon was clear, warm for November. The delivery truck was parked at the curb. An old woman had paused to let a small dog, some kind of terrier, sniff the railings around the base of a tree. Two well-dressed men sauntered along, holding hands. A middle-aged Latina pushed a white child in a buggy, its moon face plugged by a pacifier. Twin streams of cars headed east and west. The order of the cars (black, black, white, taxi) seemed significant, reminiscent of something, some order or progression that I couldn't place. Then, at a stroke, the artificiality of what I was seeing revealed itself to me. The streetscape wasn't real. The sidewalk, the passers-by, the cars, the clouds in the sky, all were elements in a giant simulation. The sunlight was not sunlight but code, the visual output of staggeringly complex calculations. The tree, the railing, the dog sniffing the railing, all had been modeled and shaded and textured and lit so as to appear maximally life-like. None of it existed prior to my observation; it was a world that began with the position of my head, light rays traced outwards from my retinas, determining what needed to be fully computed, and what could be left as an approximation. Maybe the people around me believed in their own fundamental reality, experienced themselves as existing in a "here" and "now." Maybe they were no more than shadows, projections of the system, NPCs who moved in little circuits, always walking the dog, pushing the buggy, holding hands, their routines triggered by my presence.

The feeling persisted as I crossed the street and made my way down Tenth Avenue, past a church and a restaurant with tables on the sidewalk, occupied with patrons doing the things that people at restaurant tables do, laughing and talking and eating and sipping drinks, loops of behavior that I now saw would be almost trivial to generate. There could be a library of such loops, served in a quasi-random way, behaviors for objects that were just complex enough to give me the illusion of bustle and conviviality. I paused at the bookstore where I often went to browse after therapy, noting the window display of pop science titles, among them my former colleague Edgar's latest, a brick-sized hardcover with a quote from *The Wall Street Journal: Wrongthink: The Authoritarian Left and the New Religion of Social Justice. "A must read. Free speech at its most robust."* I walked on, trying to master a creeping sense of terror. If everything around me was a simulation, logically I was too. Despite my belief that I had physical presence, that I possessed weight and volume, that the sidewalk beneath my feet was hard and resistant to my tread, I was no more material, no more "real" than the books in the window, the generic Chelsea passers-by. Did my physical body exist somewhere else, asleep in some pod or medical bay? Or had I been severed from it, my personality uploaded into whatever this was, this perfect replica of early twenty-first-century Manhattan, complete with stickers plastered on the lampposts and a fetid smell rising up from the drains?

I walked on, forcing myself to continue as if I were a person in the real world, the possessor of a real body, with real errands to perform. I went into a food hall, and bought simulated olives from an Italian deli, tasting a piece of Parmesan cheese offered to me by a simulated cheese vendor, experiencing saltiness and umami, marveling at the technology that could simulate ions traveling through simulated channels into taste receptor cells, triggering simulated axons to carry information to whatever array or connectome represented my brain. I bought my snacks and headed to the subway. Standing on the platform, I considered the existential horror of my situation. Since this was no more real than a computer game, what would happen if I exited it by stepping out in front of a train or jumping down and touching the third rail? Would I reboot and find myself back at some previous moment, at the start of some section or level in my life? Would I wake up in my bed, as I had that morning? Or would I perhaps begin again as a child, maybe even at the moment of my birth? It was possible that I'd simply wink out of existence, wiped from the database to make way for some other personality construct. Would that matter in any profound way? Would my death even be *my* death? If I were a simulation, what was there to say that I wasn't one of many copies, that there weren't three or four or a dozen versions of me running in parallel in different worlds? And if there were no longer an original, if that material body had been destroyed or mislaid, or perhaps had never existed in the first place, who was to say that I was the primary version, the most authentic or the best or most advanced protagonist? Maybe I was a spare, a substitute puttering around in some holding tank while other copies forged ahead, fulfilling their destinies. Maybe my creator—some alien manipulator or sadistic posthuman teen—was getting bored of me. At any minute I could be suspended, powered down. Above all, what possible stakes could there be in such a life? If 14th Street station was being generated on the fly as I walked down to the platform, how could anything I did or thought have any consequence at all?

Ordinarily I found a packed rush-hour C train thoroughly alienating, but as I got on, my anxiety ebbed slightly. Something about the airless capsule full of jostling commuters brought me closer to myself. I held on to a metal pole, greasy from the palms of thousands of hands, and attempted to keep my balance as I was flung around, watching the man next to me look at Instagram on his phone. It wasn't just that the simulation had surpassed some threshold of complexity, or possessed some artistic brilliance in its execution (the perfectly rendered smell of McDonald's fries, the sheen of sweat on the face of the young woman carrying manuscripts in a grubby NPR tote bag) but that the very proximity of so many animal bodies made it impossible, or perhaps just pointless, to think of the world as unreal. This was what I had, where I was. I ought to make the best of it. I squeezed out of the car at my station, and as I climbed up to the surface, my pace reduced to a trudge by the rush-hour crowd squeezing into the narrow stairway, the combination of enforced uniformity and unpleasing surroundings made me flash, as I often did when climbing a set of subway stairs in a crowd, on the aesthetics of totalitarianism, all the films and rock videos that use some version of the "Orwellian" trope of shaven-headed men in workwear walking in unison until the flamboyant lead singer breaks free of the crowd, flaunting his individuality, catching the eye of the pretty girl. I emerged onto Fulton Street and, as I crossed, was almost knocked down by a delivery driver on an electric bike, traveling the wrong way at speed. The cliché would be that "I almost jumped out of my skin," but the shock, perhaps the sudden release of adrenaline, had the effect of jumping me *back into* my skin, resetting my relationship with my body so that by the time I reached home I was calm and relatively centered, able to begin making crostini and chopping vegetables for a salad, as if my commute had been completely normal.

Crostini. Salads. Cheeseboard. Beer and wine chilling in the refrigerator. We are ready. Here I am, at the kitchen counter, watching tiny strings of bubbles rise up in my glass. I've got this. On the couch, my distracted wife flips between channels on the TV and checks social media feeds on her phone, caught up in an excitement that I do not share. It is Tuesday, November 8, 2016. Election night. *Historic,* says the TV. *A historic choice.* The therapist advised me to insulate myself from politics, but the warning wasn't really necessary. For months, I have been trying, as far as possible, to avoid thinking about this election. Not that I'm indifferent to the result. Far from it. Though I have tried, with some success, to remain ignorant of the specifics, to avoid the daily cut and thrust of comment and debate, everyone around me is obsessed. Even if I could ignore the conversations, the headlines on the newspapers at the bodega, I could hardly fail to notice the tension in the air, a general anxiety that has nothing to do with my mental state.

Still, I want tonight to be a success. Nina and I have decorated the living room with streamers and balloons. There are hats and whistles, a festival of patriotic red, white and blue. Rei said it wasn't necessary, but I can tell she's pleased. She would have liked to go to the big Democratic Party gathering at the Javits Center, to celebrate Hillary Clinton's win. A lot of people she knows are there, and she was invited, but it wasn't something that I'd be "safe" at, too much excitement, too much stimulation, and though I told her I'd be perfectly happy if she went without me, she said she'd rather be with her family. This, as the TV says a second time in as many minutes, is a historic night, and she wants to be with her daughter, or at least in the house where her daughter is sleeping, to wake up with her daughter tomorrow morning into a world where the most powerful person on the planet is a woman. I agree with her, it's long overdue, and it doesn't seem useful to voice my reservations about Clinton, to make the kind of remark I might have made last year or the year before, to use the words *baggage* or *neoliberal*, or say, as I did once at a dinner party, that "she's just the mask that established power is wearing right now," because it's obvious that her opponent is worse in almost every conceivable way, malevolent, vicious and unstable. He is a gate, a portal through which all manner of monsters could step into our living room. The status quo, bad as it is, looks better than the alternative. Rei and I have always differed on the subject of electoral politics. She says I use cynicism as an excuse to do nothing. I say—well, it doesn't matter what I say, or used to say. Now, I say nothing. Now I just want to help her in whatever way I can.

Instead of attending the party at the Javits Center, we settled on the idea of inviting a few friends over to savor the results of her hard work. Rei has worked very hard indeed for Clinton, organizing fundraising events—talks, dinners, even a comedy night (not usually her kind of thing) attended by the vice chair of the campaign, a glamorous Pakistani-American woman who attempted to look as if she were having fun, despite the cruel headlines in that day's tabloids about her unfaithful congressman husband. I attended none of these. My role in the Clinton campaign has been mostly childcare-related, pushing Nina on the swings while Rei and her friends stood at the entrance to the park, registering voters. We have a sign in our window, and another one in the corner of the room, attached to a wooden pole, as if we're about to go on a march. On Rei's laptop, obscuring the glowing Apple logo, are stickers saying *Nasty Woman* and *I'm With Her.* If her candidate wins tonight, as everyone expects, it will be because of tens of thousands of women like Rei, practical and determined, not too proud to spend afternoons sending email blasts or hovering about the farmer's market with a clipboard.

The doorbell rings, and Rei springs up to answer it. By the time we've poured drinks for the first arrivals, a couple who live on the block (Liz is in advertising, Carla works for an environmental nonprofit), in walk Femi and Zoe, carrying two bottles of champagne. Together we make chitchat. The atmosphere is optimistic and upbeat. I busy myself fetching and carrying, pouring drinks and offering snacks so that Rei has time to talk. Most of our guests have been following the minutiae of the election, and there's a lot of discussion of swing states and battlegrounds and exit polls, all the usual arcana. Everyone is very nice to me, very natural and relaxed. They all ask, how are you, with the slight emphasis on the verb. How *are* you? Meaning: are you still insane? Godwin arrives, and as Rei is kissing him hello, she shoots me a quick glance, as if she's trying to gauge what I think of their intimacy. He's brought a new girlfriend with him, someone neither of us know. Like him, Xu is a photographer. She looks to be in her late twenties, which is to say about two decades younger, and she's startlingly beautiful. I catch Rei watching her, but I don't detect jealousy, more a wry amusement. Godwin is bouncing back nicely from his divorce. *Well,* says the TV, *my best guess is five points.*

We settle in. One or two people gamely put on the hats. When the first results are called, Rei is busy discussing the 2000 Florida recount with her friend Sunita, whose brother is a reporter for one of the cable networks. This means that she's getting text messages about various inside-track stuff, and whenever she reads one of them out, there's a little lull in conversation as everyone leans forward to hear what it says. Trump takes Indiana and Kentucky. Vermont goes for Clinton. Can you imagine, says someone, after all this it'll finally be over. There's a murmur of agreement. Doesn't it feel like the campaign has gone on forever?

I find a lot of excuses to leave the room. I peer in at Nina, sprawled on her bed. I check there's enough toilet paper in the bathroom, that the scented candle on the shelf above the toilet is still burning. Though I'm not drinking, I make it my mission to ensure that everyone's glasses are topped up at all times. The volume of conversation rises. Jokes are made and received with raucous laughter. More Eastern states are called, the races going as expected. Alabama and West Virginia for Trump. Delaware and Connecticut for Clinton. Florida is too close to call.

You know, says Godwin, his wife used to date a guy I know from downtown. He swears the rumors about her are totally true. On TV, the panel of experts is discussing the contest like a horse race, remaining studiously neutral, examining fancy digital charts. Well, says someone else, whatever happens, he's probably going to contest the result. He's not the type to be a good loser. There's a big cheer as Clinton wins New York state by twenty-nine points. That's what I'm talking about, says Liz. I'd be happier if that was Florida, points out her wife. Sunita's husband, who I haven't met before, asks me what I do. I joke that I create antiviral content. I'm not just unpopular, I say. I'm actively antipopular. Rei gives me a sharp look. I am displaying an excess of personality. *Those are some big Trump numbers in Texas,* says the TV. *No surprise there.*

There's a lull. People have drunk quite a lot, and there's nothing definitive on the TV, no real news. They make conversation about personal things, jobs, an art exhibit that's on in Chelsea. I'm looking forward to that new show, says someone. *Spear of Destiny.* It's the same guy who did *Blue Lives.* I can't get into that stuff, says someone else. All the pointy ears and stupid wizard names. We're all suddenly remembering how late we'll have to stay up before it's time for the real action. It's a Tuesday. People have jobs, sitters to pay. Sunita gets another bulletin from her brother. He's hearing that the Clinton campaign is disappointed by some of the numbers. *As Ohio goes, so goes the country,* says the TV. *Voters here have correctly picked every president of these United States since 1964.*

At 10:30, Ohio is called for Trump and for the first time our friends seem nervous. We say things to reassure each other, make lists of states that have yet to be called. You have anything stronger than this, asks Godwin, looking sourly at a half-empty glass of rosé. I bring him a bottle of Scotch, a bowl of ice. He pats my shoulder. It's good to see you, he says. It really is. *The math is hard,* says the TV. *Irrespective of who wins, this will be a historic night.*

Femi and Zoe get up to leave. I've got kind of a headache, says Zoe, by way of an excuse. She and Rei embrace. I go to get their coats from our bedroom. It's cool and dark and I have a strong desire to stay in there, to burrow into the pile of coats and make a nest, or better still, to go right through like a child in a story, to disappear into the land of Narnia, where it's easy to tell right from wrong, and if you're brave and noble you will prevail. From the other room, I hear the TV. *If you can get the Latino vote on your side,* it says. *If you can get the black vote, the minorities.*

Femi and Zoe go home. So do our neighbors, the environmentalist and the copywriter. I don't have a good feeling about this, says Sunita. Godwin is drinking steadily, staring at the TV as if he can alter it by force of will. Xu is in the corridor making a phone call. Her voice sounds shaky. Just after eleven, North Carolina is called for the Republicans. *Trump's path to the White House has suddenly become a lot clearer,* says the TV. I look around at the faces of people who are beginning to face the possibility that the picture of the world they had a few hours ago, a picture based on their occupation of something called the *center ground,* may not be accurate. I take no pleasure in this. It's not like I'm jumping up and down saying, I told you so. But I find that I'm not surprised, that it feels like a continuation of all the other things that have happened to me this year, as if the thoughts I've been trying to avoid are clothing themselves in flesh. On TV, a guest is asked about Clinton's weaknesses. *She's just not likable,* he says. *She has so much baggage.*

I go back into the bedroom and push the coats to one side and lie down on our bed. Outside I can hear sirens sweeping down the street. Something's on fire. Someone's hurt. Someone's been shot. Outside in the city, bad things are happening. Amazing to say, but apart from a few sessions trying vainly to clear my email inbox and dealing with my bank, I haven't been on the internet since I was in Paris. Now I open my laptop and go on one of the far-right message boards where I used to look for Starhemberg posts. It's a frenzy of memes and exultation, pictures of Trump with laser eyes, wrestlers and robots and Pokémon and superheroes and sarcastic cartoon frogs emitting rays and force fields, representations of energy, usually captioned with some version of the phrase *GOD EMPEROR TAKE MY POWER!* Some of the users are playing a game, or something that's not quite a game, making predictions that will "come true" if the nine-digit post numbers end with double or triple digits. IF DUBS TRUMP WINS WITH 88%. Lots of Nazi references, the fourteen words, racist caricatures, animations of Trump cut with Gundam and anime racing sequences, mostly set to a Eurobeat song with the lyrics "Gas gas gas." Many of the posters appear to believe semi-sincerely that they are bringing a Trump presidency into being with "meme magic," the occult power of their content leaking out into the offline world. In the middle of all the anons, I see what I was expecting. A little animation of a spear, rising up in front of an icy landscape. *A new power rises in the North.* The post is signed *Ernst Heim Berg.*

I close the laptop. From the living room, the TV says *he used to call his opponents in the primaries by a number of names, and that seems to have resonated with a lot of folks.* As I go back in, Rei looks round at me, and I see tears in her eyes. She is so beautiful. I would do anything for her. I go over and stand behind the armchair where she's sitting, fretfully twisting a paper napkin. She reaches back and takes my hand. I want to say something conventionally comforting, something like "it'll be fine" or "trust me," but I can't, because I don't want to lie, so I hold her hand, the feeling growing that somehow I bear responsibility for this, that I am the channel, the medium through which this toxic waste is flowing.

It's not that I'm important or special, just that up until now there have been two tracks or timelines: the one that Rei and this little group of our friends live on, in which the future is predictable, an extrapolation from the past, a steady progression in which we are gradually turning into our own mothers and fathers, men and women who make plans and save for retirement, who go to our kids' schools and participate in parent-teacher conferences, our adult bodies too big for the child-size furniture. Then there's the second track, the occult track on which all this normality is a paper screen over something bloody and atavistic that is rising up out of history to meet us. I am the ragged membrane, the porous barrier between the two. Somehow, through me, through my negligence, the second track has contaminated the first. My madness, the madness for which I've been medicated and therapized and involuntarily detained, is about to become everyone's madness. The proof of my sanity, my fitness to exist in the ordinary timeline of parent-teacher conferences and 401(k)s, was an acceptance that the two streams must never cross, that it was my job to keep them separate. I have not done that. Now all our throats are bared to the knife.

At 11:30 Trump wins Florida and our party turns into the Masque of the Red Death. This can't be happening, says Sunita. This is a fucking nightmare. *And one by one dropped the revelers in the blood-bedewed halls of their revel, and died each in the despairing posture of his fall.* We look around at each other, most of us more or less drunk, our stomachs bloated by salty party food. This is not a good place, not now. It is not helpful for us to be together. One by one, each couple calls a car. Everyone wants to be at home, in their own space, near their children. They want to process this event by crawling into bed and poring over the internet and trying to work out what a Trump presidency means for people like us, the unreal Americans, the ones who the new president and his supporters hate most of all. *And the life of the ebony clock went out with that of the last of the gay. And the flames of the tripods expired. And Darkness and Decay and the Red Death held illimitable dominion over all.*

Finally Rei and I are left alone in the wreckage. We move around like a pair of zombies, clearing up plates and glasses. As I rinse them and fill the dishwasher, Trump takes Utah, then Iowa. The TV is showing images from the Clinton campaign party in New York, the camera focused on women, on the worried faces of women, women holding their hands over their mouths, touching their fingertips to their foreheads. There are a few halfhearted chants of Hi-la-ry, snatches of uplifting pop songs from the convention center sound system. "Don't Stop Believin'." "Ain't No Mountain High Enough." Already, the shitposters on the message boards are grabbing images of crying Democrats. *We drink your salty tears.*

Rei and I haven't said a word to each other. There is nothing to say. We work in concert, methodically clearing up the debris, putting the waste into bags, removing all trace of this evening, of our hopes for this evening, the timeline that we hoped we were on. Together, we go in and check on Nina. We spend a long time looking at her, her little chest rising and falling, the tangle of hair obscuring her face.

At 1:30 a.m. Trump takes Pennsylvania, making his lead virtually unassailable. He is now at 264 electoral votes and ahead in Wisconsin, Michigan and Arizona, any of which will make him president. We lie in bed looking at our phones. There is a strange shift between us, as if the balance has altered, that in some way I have become the realist and she the utopian. Talk to me, says Rei. Tell me something.

"Like what?"

"Something true."

"I love you."

She stiffens, then relaxes, molding herself into my embrace. I ask her, "Do you believe me?"

"I have to believe you. You're who I have."

At 2:30 a.m. we are still awake, our phones two glowing rectangles in the darkened room. Trump takes Wisconsin, the ten electoral votes putting him over the 270 threshold. A few minutes later, Clinton calls him to concede. Somewhere on the internet I find a stream of a victory party, a group of raucous men on a stage wearing red MAGA hats. Polo shirts, beards, tattooed sleeves, open bottles of champagne. They are chanting and singing, pushing each other around as if they're in a mosh pit. At the back, a phone pressed to his ear, smiling as he watches the jostling and singing, is Anton.

Maybe I am one of the last people in history who will feel the things I do. Maybe everything I hoped about the world, and hoped to bring about in it, is doomed to fail. Instead of learning useful things, I have filled my brain with obsolete philosophies, ideas with no more purchase or veracity than the four humors or spontaneous generation. I could say I regret it all, the useless information, but what would be the point? It's too late now. These are the elements that make me who I am. Even if I am absurd, and instead of reading novels and philosophy books I should have learned to code or short-sell or strip and rebuild an AR-15, I still have the love I feel for Rei and Nina. That love has never wavered, even when I worried that I was no good for them, and ought to stay far away. Though men like Edgar may point out that the constriction I feel in my throat when I see my wife, or the pang of pride I experience when I watch my child mastering some new skill is just the expression of neurochemicals in my brain, though my intuitions about reality are likely false and I may be a disembodied organ floating in a vat or a point in the state space of some cosmic simulation, still you'll have to burn that love out of me before I will relinquish it. What Anton and his capering friends in their red hats call realism—the truth that they think they understand—is just the cynical operation of power.

It is not quite a year since I arrived in Berlin, and once again I'm lying awake in my bed. This time Rei is awake beside me. Two rectangles of light. It's not much, but I can say that the most precious part of me isn't my individuality, my luxurious personhood, but the web of reciprocity in which I live my life. In Anton's world, hospitality is the greatest sin and the essence of human relations is either subjection or domination. A couple of days ago, I saw a teenager walking on our block wearing a hoodie with a picture of a snarling wolf. We Only Love Family, it said. I suppose it was intended to be defiant, an expression of solidarity, us against the world, but to me that "only" just seemed sad, beaten down, a retreat from some wider and more expansive kind of love. *Homme seul est viande à loups,* as the medieval French proverb has it. Alone, we are food for the wolves. That's how they want us. Isolated. Prey. So we must find each other. We must remember that we do not exist alone. Rei rolls over in bed to face me. If it gets bad, she asks, where will we go? Together we say the names of cities.

Together we talk, holding each other, imagining escape routes. Sometime during the night, Nina crawls into the bed and joins us. Outside the wide world is howling and scratching at the window. Tomorrow morning we will have no choice but to let it in.

Acknowledgments

Thanks to

Michael "Pankow" Boehlke, Dagmar Hovestädt and the press office of the Federal Commissioner for the Records of the State Security Service of the former German Democratic Republic, Daniel Kehlmann, Deborah Landau and my colleagues at the Lilian Vernon Creative Writers House, Cathy Mullins, Anne Rubesame, Taryn Simon, John Tasioulas and above all Katie Kitamura, my first and best. This book would not have been written without the support of the American Academy in Berlin, an institution that shares a location with the Deuter Center, but otherwise bears no resemblance to it whatsoever.

A NOTE ABOUT THE AUTHOR

HARI KUNZRU is the author of five previous novels: *White Tears, The Impressionist, Transmission, My Revolutions* and *Gods Without Men*. His work has been translated into twenty-one languages, and his short stories and journalism have appeared in many publications, including *The New York Times, The Guardian* and *The New Yorker*. He is the recipient of fellowships from the Guggenheim Foundation, the New York Public Library and the American Academy in Berlin. He lives in Brooklyn, New York.

A NOTE ON THE TYPE

The text of this book was composed in Apollo, the first typeface ever originated specifically for film composition. Designed by Adrian Frutiger and issued by the Monotype Corporation of London in 1964, Apollo is not only a versatile typeface suitable for many uses but also pleasant to read in all of its sizes.

Composed by North Market Street Graphics, Lancaster, Pennsylvania

Printed and bound by Friesens, Altona, Manitoba

Designed by Anna B. Knighton